The Queen of Kush

Additional stories about the ancient African kingdoms
of Kush and Ethiopia by Melvin Cobb

The Chosen Vessel Series:
#1 Vessel of Honor
#2 Shadow of Redemption
#3 The Prince of Aethiopia
#4 King of Kings

The Queen of Kush

A Tale of Love.
A Tale of Hope.
A Tale of Defiance.

Melvin J. Cobb

*To Mike,
May God bless and,
keep you always!*

abbott press

Interior Image Credit: Vanessa Cobb
Author Photograph Credit: Alexander Cobb

This is a work of fiction. All of the characters, names, incidents, organizations, and dialogue in this novel are either the products of the author's imagination or are used fictitiously.

Abbott Press books may be ordered through booksellers or by contacting:

Abbott Press
1663 Liberty Drive
Bloomington, IN 47403
www.abbottpress.com
Phone: 1 (866) 697-5310

ISBN: 978-1-4582-2224-4 (sc)
ISBN: 978-1-4582-2225-1 (e)

Library of Congress Control Number: 2019902829

Print information available on the last page.

Abbott Press rev. date: 3/29/2019

This book is dedicated to Karen, Mollie, Christine, Loretta, Cynthia, and to every courageous, determined and beautiful black woman I've ever met.

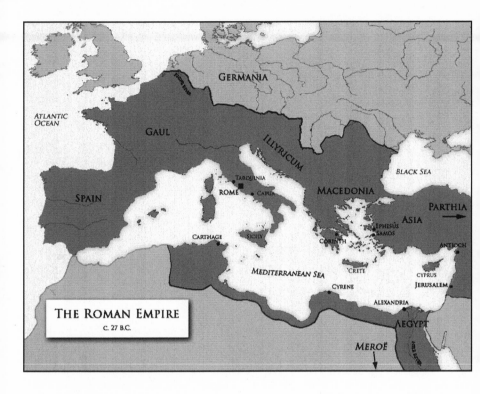

Author's Notes:

Maps – All Kushite and Roman cities mentioned in this book are denoted on the adjacent maps in order to provide the reader with a geographical frame of reference.

Glossary – Authentic Kushite and Roman terms native to the time-period are used throughout this novel. Italicized Meroitic and Latin vocabulary words and their definitions can generally be found in the glossary at the end of the book. Care was given to italicize the words the first time they were used.

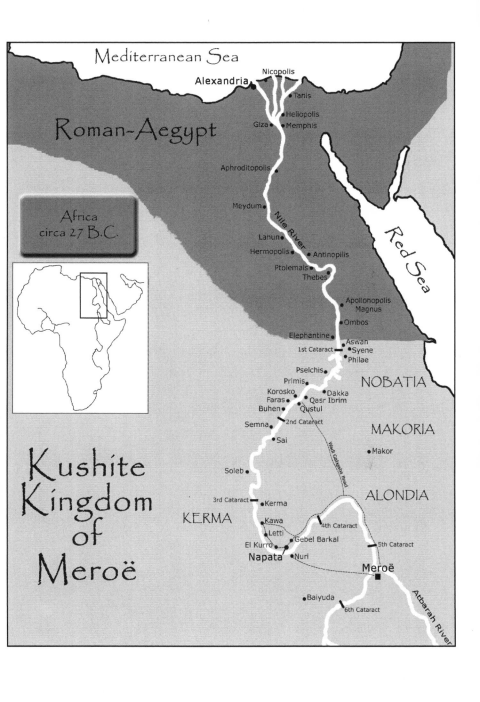

Prologue:

The Prelude to War

In 30 B.C., the legions of Octavian Caesar defeated the forces of Mark Antony and Cleopatra, the last queen of Egypt, ending the 300-year reign of the Ptolemaic dynasty. Victorious, Caesar swiftly laid claim to his prize by declaring all of Egypt—and its vast grain supply—a province of the newly minted Roman Empire. Two legions, the Legio III Cyrenaica and the Legio XXII Deiotariana, were stationed in Egypt to enforce Roman law, secure trade routes, and collect tribute.

Enticed by gold and other natural resources, Rome eventually set its sights on Egypt's southern neighbor, the Kushite Empire of Meroë. After setting up a series of military garrisons along the busy trading routes along the Nile, Rome imposed a tax upon Kush and unilaterally declared the Kushite kingdom a vassal state of the Roman Empire.

In 27 B.C., Octavian (now Augustus) Caesar was confronted with disturbances in the Arabian Peninsula directly across the Red Sea from Egypt. Wishing to address the situation as expeditiously as possible, Caesar dispatched the Cyrenaica and the Deiotariana, under the command of Aelius Gallus, the Roman Prefect of Egypt, to the troubled area.

With the legions departed, the Kushites of Lower Egypt, along with many in the Northern province of Kush, staged a revolt against Rome and stormed the frontier at Aswan. Hoping to win support of the King of Kush, the rebels sacked and pillaged Roman settlements in the area, toppling official monuments, including recently erected statues of Augustus himself.

Convinced that there was a growing threat to Kushite sovereignty, in 27 B.C., King Teriteqas elected to lead an expedition to address the expanding Roman presence....

Chapter 1

27 B.C.
Meroë, Capital City of the Kushite Kingdom

Amanirenas felt nothing other than her husband's fingertips running gently down her bare back. She exhaled slowly and anticipated which part of her body his hand would venture to next. His warm breath caressed her face in a rhythmic fashion that relaxed and provoked her. She silently begged for the moment to last, yet she knew it would not.

She turned and admired him. The dim candles bathed his dark face in a soft golden light that gave him a god-like quality. The sparkle in his deep brown eyes drew her in. Everything about him was strong. His hands, his heart, his resolve, his love for her. Teriteqas was not simply a king, he was her king, and she was his queen.

Soon, he would be gone.

Amanirenas hushed away the thought of his departure and reached up to guide his face closer. As usual, he resisted, a coy grin brushing across his lips. His hand now flowed up her leg, across the curves of her hips and glided between her body and the bed. Her body tensed as he slowly drew her closer, pressing their bodies together until they were one.

She closed her eyes and cursed Meroë. The kingdom was the one mistress she could never completely wrestle from his heart. It had no lips to kiss, no hand to hold, no body to caress, yet it was wickedly seductive, enough to tear him away from her yet again. Her relentless competitor screamed for his attention and always managed to steal it. But not tonight. All creation had to understand that Teriteqas belonged to his queen this night, and not to the formless concubine. She kissed him forcefully, her fingertips pressing against the hard, flat muscles that ran along his back. Tonight, she would squeeze the thought of the mistress from their bedchambers.

Tonight, there would only be the Queen and her king.

𓈖 𓃀

Most of the candles had long gone out. A subtle chill settled in the room as the King and Queen lay nestled in one another's arms. Neither one of them slept, despite the lateness of the hour.

"A year," Amanirenas said bitterly.

"Perhaps longer," Teriteqas responded with a distant tone.

"Longer?" Amanirenas snapped. The thought of the mistress having him for that long maddened her. "You sound unsure now."

"We've talked about this, Renas. It will take at least that long to assess the situation with the Egyptians and address any possible threat to the border...."

"The northern border. Which means it's not necessary for you to go for so long." Amanirenas propped up on an elbow to face him. "This is a dispute Piankhi should handle. As the vizier of the Nobatian province, it falls under his purview."

Teriteqas chuckled at her. "Perhaps. Now that the Roman legions have vacated the region, the Egyptian population in Nobatia may see it as a chance to seize a portion of Lower Egypt. If that is the case, we may find ourselves in a war with the Romans, and I need to be there."

"And I doubt the new *principes* in Rome even cares about Lower Egypt, let alone Kush."

"He thinks he cares a great deal," Teriteqas replied. "He's familiar with the region, and some believe he views Egypt as his personal property. Mshindi said Octavian was there to personally dispatch

2

Antony and Cleopatra several years ago, and he has taken a particular interest in the..."

Amanirenas blurted out a Kushite curse and turned her head.

"Was that for our faithful Kushite general or your undying admiration for the departed Cleopatra?"

"That Egyptian whore vexed me far more than your cousin."

"You can show a little respect for the dead..." Teriteqas chided.

"For what? She prostituted her body for power. That made her a whore. The only good thing is that she was a Macedonian. No true Egyptian woman would have behaved that way—giving herself over to those Roman men. Even having a son by one..."

"But... she was a queen. A very smart and beautiful one..."

"You do know that I can reach the dagger on the nightstand," Amanirenas threatened, playfully yanking a handful of his chest hair. She seethed at the mocking grin that coated her husband's face. Although he denied it, Amanirenas had long suspected the Egyptian queen had once attempted to seduce her husband during one of his trips to Thebes.

"I wouldn't be surprised if she didn't try to lure ... whatever his name is into bed."

"His name is Octavian—although I hear he has taken on the new forename of Augustus." Teriteqas stopped to ponder the reports he had received about this emerging beast called Rome. While familiar with the Ptolemaic dynasty, which for centuries governed Egypt, he cast a wary eye on the great power from the far reaches of the north that now possessed the ancient land. Egypt's new master wasted no time in exploiting the country's vast resources of grain and barley.

"I need more information about them," Teriteqas voiced. For almost a year, every report he received from the Northern Province vizier via the communication runners described the Roman administration as cold and aloof.

"If I'm not mistaken, Piankhi has met with the Roman governor at least twice," Amanirenas stated, closing her eyes.

"Yes, his name is Aelius Gallus. Piankhi described their early relationship as cordial, but things have changed. Ever since they imposed the tax on our caravans..."

"Which we've already declared we are not paying," Amanirenas smirked. The audacity of the foreigners, expecting Kush to pay a form of tribute to their ruler, was amusing to her. To attempt to extort money from a sovereign kingdom was the epitome of arrogance.

"I've never even seen a Roman," Teriteqas reflected, thinking ahead to his upcoming journey to the Egyptian border.

"They're a pale, white race," Amanirenas shrugged, tracing his jawline with a finger.

"Most of them have the white skin, but not all of them do. Some are dark like you and me. Piankhi says that the Roman domain extends far beyond the great sea north of Egypt, and the cities they've built are greater and more complex than any in our land."

"You sound far too concerned about these people," Amanirenas said with a faint sigh.

"Perhaps I should be," Teriteqas said as he studied the fine leopard hide that adorned a nearby chair. "Some empires are judged not by what they can build, but by what they can destroy. These Romans have conquered many lands. And from what I hear, their ... legions ... fight like siafu fire-ants and devour anything in their path."

A soft breeze fluttered into the chamber, causing the candles that were still lit to flicker. For a brief moment, Amanirenas noted an unfamiliar sullen look in her husband's eyes. It was the guise not of a king of an ancient empire, but of an unsure young man courting the affections of a woman who was also being entreated by an older, more astute suitor.

"What is it?" she asked.

"The tone of Piankhi's last message. Even though the legions have gone to Arabia, Roman garrisons have taken residence in the old Egyptian forts at Syene and other locations in Nobatia," he said, envisioning the drama being written by the faceless foreigners threatening to encroach into his kingdom.

"That's why you're taking 3,500 soldiers with you. That, along with the Nobatian regiment of 7,000, should convince them to stay in Egypt. And if not..."

Amanirenas knew little about Northern provinces and even less about the Romans. The city of Meroë was her home, and she rarely ventured away from it, for there was no need to do so. All she needed was there: the nest in which she raised her strapping sons and lovely daughter, along with the esteem of being the kandace. In fact, being the kandace was the only appreciable gift bestowed unto her by the mistress. It was a consolation prize that Amanirenas relished and even flaunted in her twenty-four-year marriage and reign.

Internal skirmishes with tribes and provinces waxed and waned throughout the years, but a conflict with a sovereign kingdom was a nonexistent threat. A prolonged war, however, would give the mistress preeminence in the battle Amanirenas fought for her husband's affections.

"You know my feelings, Teriteqas. If it's land these Romans want, it is better to come to an agreement with them. The gold in that region was mined out generations ago. There would be little harm in ceding them a worthless patch of land...."

"But there would be harm," he retorted gently, not wanting to reignite the debate that had finally abated just a few hours earlier. "It is a matter of honor. A matter of respect..."

"Respect! Must it always come down to respect?"

"Yes, it does. I disrespect the ancestors and all the qerens that have come before me if I do nothing; I devalue the inheritance I leave for our sons if I do nothing. Most importantly, I belittle myself as a man if I do nothing."

"You don't need to fight a war to earn respect. You should find a different way."

A long, silent moment passed, and then Teriteqas kissed her on the cheek. This was far from the way he wanted to spend his last night with his wife.

"I'm sorry, my love," Teriteqas offered. "Mshindi says that the Romans respect strength. If I have to, I intend to demonstrate to their new ruler that intimidating Kush is pointless. They have to understand that we are not the savages they have fought in other regions of their domain. We aren't a collection of fragmented tribes an invader can easily shatter."

"Sometimes we are," Amanirenas responded dryly.

She ignored her husband's sarcastic grunt and looked outside to the starry night sky. Unwilling to surrender more time to an unwinnable battle, she finally relented. Teriteqas was convinced that his presence would solidify the bonds between the northern provinces of Kush and that unity would be a deterrent to further Roman incursions. Nevertheless, she was skeptical that Shabakar, the vizier from Kerma, would actually support Piankhi—given their history of ill will.

"The viziers will stab us in the back before it is all over. They have done it before, and they will do it again," Amanirenas said. "Let the Romans have the Northern provinces if they want them. They can have Kerma as well...."

"So the truth comes out," Teriteqas said with a smile. "You're still angry with Shabakar and Piankhi. They were only acting in their best interest when they supported the rebels in Lower Egypt last year. Remember, I did support their action...."

"Yes, but it was after the fact. They did not ask permission; they used your name to authorize the attacks on those Roman forts. They should have consulted you first."

"I appointed them—so they do speak in my name," Teriteqas chided, stroking her face lightly. "We have to trust their judgment."

"That would be easier to do if I felt their interests were actually aligned with those of the *Amani-aa'ila*. They are supposed to serve you, not the other way around. Perhaps if they had white masters, they would realize how disrespectful they've been to their own people...."

"You don't mean that," Teriteqas said, taking her hand and caressing it. "Yes, they've made mistakes, but they are still *our* people, and this is *our* kingdom. And it needs to be protected."

"Well, at least you're not taking all three of our sons with you."

"You're determined to bring up everything tonight, aren't you?" Teriteqas jeered, friskily poking her in the side.

"Kharapkhael should stay here to continue his tutelage under the grand vizier. He needs the training."

"Yes, but if our eldest son is to succeed me someday, he will also need to be well versed in the language of diplomacy—with words or with the spear. It will be a valuable experience for him. In addition, Kharapkhael's absence will provide more opportunities for Akinid and Jaelen as well."

Amanirenas acquiesced and lay back in bitter silence as she watched the moon creep into view. It seemed the mistress would win again.

Chapter 2

26 B.C.
Napata, Sacred City of Kushite Kingdom of Meroë

Amanirenas had no tears left to shed.

At first, it seemed like a hellish nightmare from which she could not awaken. However, the cruel twist of fate was all too real as she pined away in the tar pit of her grief. The loss of her eldest son Kharapkhael to sickness six months earlier had violently sucked the breath from her lungs and cast a ruthless shadow over her family. However, this was the greatest of all possible losses.

She stood alone next to her husband's body, which was draped by a finely woven red and gold cloak—the same one that had adorned him on their wedding day. He was so uncharacteristically still—even though the fluttering torches that lit the funerary pyramid made the body appear to move in cadence with its quivering motion.

One colorful relief on the wall depicted the king as a youthful man engaged in battle with his enemies, while another showed him as a benevolent ruler towering among his subjects. While both murals were accurate, it was the image on the center wall that Amanirenas most admired, for it portrayed him as a husband and father. She noted how the eyes of the woman and four children gazed longingly up at him, as if he were an enchanted god.

Killed while leading a battle against the Roman garrison in Dakka, the Kushite qeren now lay quietly in his pyramid, his *kha* dwelling peacefully with his son and other ancestors in Henel. She gently stroked the ornate shroud and longed for death. Only in death would she likely hear his deep voice beckoning her to sit with him. Only in death could she hope for his spirit to caress hers as he so delicately did during life. Only in death could she hope to escape the desolate loneliness that captured her every thought. Only in death would she be free from the burning desire to take revenge upon the Romans and balance the scales of justice. She prayed to Apedemack for the strength to execute what love demanded be done.

A set of strong hands gently gripped her shoulders. Knowing it was her son Akinid, she purposefully refused to turn around. The seventeen-year-old's striking resemblance to his father would only drive her further into the recesses of despair.

"All of the preparations have been made," the young man said. "The Council of Ministers will be awaiting your arrival at sundown this evening."

She reached up and grasped one of his hands. "What have you heard?"

"They're with you," Akinid answered slowly.

"No, my son. What have you heard?" She turned just far enough to see him draw a tentative breath.

"Nothing you don't already know. The vizier of Nobatia continues to press the other provinces to support a full-scale war with the Romans. However, Mshindi is still critical of the notion."

"You would think Vizier Piankhi could convince his general to do what he has been trained to do and fight a war," Amanirenas sighed. "Mshindi should be the last one to oppose a full out assault on the Roman strongholds in southern Egypt. They murdered our king—his cousin."

"He wants to fight. But on suitable terms."

"There are no suitable terms with Rome!" the Kandace said, turning to face her son. "They've been probing our borders with their garrisons. Your father understood this, even when I did not."

"Mshindi isn't blind."

Amanirenas rolled her eyes away from him. "Then he's is afraid! All he talks about are the legions of the Romans...."

"And he should be from what I've heard," Akinid retorted. He had spent hours during his childhood listening to the General Mshindi describe the unimaginable maneuvers performed by Roman legions that he witnessed as a soldier in Egypt. "Father only dealt with garrisons made up of a few cohorts. What if we get there and the two legions have returned from Arabia? No Kushite army has ever faced a legion at full strength. Mshindi feels we need to analyze their strategies more before we do so, and I agree with him."

"And we will do so," Amanirenas responded coldly. Although she possessed only a rudimentary understanding of the standard Roman legion, to her everything came down to numbers. No matter how skilled they were, Roman pride still had to yield to the law of mathematics. "Your father had 3,500 men with him. I will have more than 20,000."

She turned back to her husband's body and ran her fingers lightly across his shrouded face. "Please send Jaelen in. He needs to say goodbye to his father."

"Yes, mother," Akinid replied in a hushed voice, reminded how hard his fifteen-year-old brother was taking the loss of their father.

"Akinid, we will avenge him," Amanirenas promised as she placed her hand above Teriteqas's motionless heart, "I swear by Isis, I will avenge him."

Chapter 3

26 B.C.
Napata

The official time of mourning Teriteqas was finished, but Amanirenas could only imagine what life without a grieving heart might feel like. Her very soul yearned for her fallen husband, whose remains now resided in a sealed plush sepulcher for all eternity. She wanted desperately to see, to hear, and to feel him once again—yet such a moment would not come until she, too, strolled the corridor of light into Henel. However, there was much to be done before she could relish that joyous moment.

She took the initial step of providing comfort for her husband's insatiable mistress an hour earlier when she officially accepted the title of Queen-Mother in the temple of Isis. Thousands of Kushite souls descended upon Napata to embrace the newly anointed embodiment of the goddess as she crowned her son Akinid as co-regent.

The coronation of Akinid was a moment Amanirenas anticipated for several years, but never imagined it would occur in the shadow of Teriteqas's death which itself dwelt beneath the specter of war. As the Queen-Mother of Kush, the task of igniting the torch to expunge the encroaching darkness fell to her. Rancor and hate set her heart ablaze with the only fire strong enough to deliver both herself and the mistress from the darkness that consumed her husband.

She entered the antechamber in which her sister Amanishakheto awaited. Together, they would perform a ritual sacrifice unto Isis and the ancestors of the Amani'aa'lai.

Amanishakheto was adorned in the ornate gown worn for the ceremony. At thirty-five, she was five years younger than her sister, yet she always managed to look at least ten years younger than that. It was a trait that Amanirenas silently envied, yet she reveled in the fact that she was still the eldest and therefore the inheritor of the Amani-aa'ila matriarchal divine right to rule.

Nevertheless, Amanirenas's status did little to curtail the intense rivalry that had warped their relationship since childhood. Their father always seemed amused by the enmity, while their mother at times appeared to encourage it, as if she were trying to determine which of them possessed the stronger will. As a result, Amanishakheto's ambition and competitive drive rarely went on hiatus, and the sisters seemingly competed for everything from jewelry to men. For years, Amanirenas felt that she had ultimately won the latter battle, managing to outmaneuver her sister for the heart of Teriteqas—a man whom they had both coveted with a burning desire, with Amanishakheto being left with the consolation prize of Mshindi, Teriteqas's conspicuous cousin. Amanirenas was blissful when her rival sister married the soldier and departed for the kingdom's northern province of Nobatia, where Mshindi served as the pelmes of that region's militia.

However, today's occasion brought Amanishakheto back to Napata and presented yet another opportunity for old wounds to re-open and bleed anew.

"You look beautiful," Amanirenas said, noting her sister had changed and now wore a black and gold gown accentuating her curvy hips.

"You're the Queen-Mother. All eyes will naturally be on you," Amanishakheto responded coolly. She signaled the attending priest to prepare the sacrifice. "I'm certain you're a proud mother today. Akinid will make a fine qeren. I'm only sorry Mshindi could not be here."

Amanirenas breathed slowly, watching the priest dissect the adolescent falcon.

"He loves Akinid and supports him fully," Amanishakheto added as she washed her hands in the ritual basin and picked up the sacred utensils.

"I do not question Mshindi's loyalty or intentions. Someone had to remain in Nobatia to occupy the Romans until we arrive," Amanirenas said, performing the ritual washing as well.

"I only hope you allow him to perform his duties unabated," Amanishakheto said. "He has a strategy to engage the Romans. I advise you let him carry it out."

"As the Queen-Mother, I will have the final say of how and when we engage the enemy."

"Of course, sister," Amanishakheto remarked, subtly rolling her eyes away. "Just remember to focus on the goal at hand."

"And what does that mean?"

"Wars are fought with the head, not the heart. You always did let your emotions cloud your judgment. Even mother agreed with that appraisal."

The priest stretched the dead falcon across the altar, the bird's wing span covering the platform. The sisters placed their blades along the raptor's right and left wings and in unison, sliced off the arms.

Amanishakheto turned toward her sister. "You have a strong stubborn streak in you, Amanirenas. That characteristic has served you well as a kandace. But it was always tempered by Teriteqas. Without him..."

"You're mistaken, sister. I am not the one who was in constant need of a man's attention to bring value to my life. I'm not the one who would do anything to get that attention."

Amanishakheto flashed a wicked smile. "No, but you did need a man to validate your identity and fight your battles. You were so needy you had to steal one."

"Leave us," Amanirenas commanded the priest who promptly exited the chamber.

"We're not finished with the ritual," Amanishakheto commented.

She recognized all too well her sister's fiery gape and braced for the emotional barrage that usually accompanied it.

"I am not going to play this game with you, Amanishakheto. You have had years to get over the fact that Teriteqas spurned you. He did so because you were immature and conceited. The fact that you can't see that now only proves the point."

Amanishakheto attempted to look away, but her sister swiftly slid over and recaptured her dark brown eyes.

"I don't see why you can't be satisfied with the man you have—or is it impossible for you to do so because he, too, preferred me over you? But rest assured, my sister, there's nothing you possess that I want."

The fire prepared for the waiting sacrifice was accentuated by the burning silence that filled the antechamber.

"For the sake of your son, and for the sake of my husband, I pray your stubbornness will be tempered with wisdom," Amanishakheto said evenly. "Our mother used to say that a queen is usually the only one strong enough to talk sense into the king. It is my hope Akinid has the fortitude to withstand your passions and do what is best for Kush and my husband."

"Thank you for your prayers, sister. I assure you, I will do what's best for my son and all who follow him."

Amanishakheto drew back from the older woman and scrutinized her carefully. "Fate is taking you into a man's world, and men respect clarity of speech and intention."

"Your point is taken. And I can handle myself. Is there anything else you wish to say?"

"What are your thoughts on the situation with the Romans? You will have a great deal of influence on Akinid and the Council of Ministers."

"Is it a matter important to you or to Mshindi?" Amanirenas questioned coarsely. "I'm certain you intend to return and report my words to your husband..."

"I remember when you became the kandace," Amanishakheto interjected. "All you dreamt of was having a family and decorating the palace. That is what you did for nearly twenty-five years while

14

Teriteqas made the important decisions regarding the kingdom. Issues of administration were not important to you—only the image you presented to the people. You have to understand that those days are now over."

"You're being contemplative. This doesn't sound like you, Amanishakheto."

"I want to be certain that you have the appropriate perspective on what's best for the kingdom," Amanishakheto voiced, noticing how her sister's face tensed up.

"Proper perspective? Word has gotten to me, sister, that you intend to convince Akinid to give in to the Romans and pay the tribute they demand."

"I'm not the only one who feels that way. Many nobles and viziers agree. Including Piankhi and Mshindi," Amanishakheto responded in a measured tone.

"I do understand the climate of the realm I rule," Amanirenas retorted. "And this is where your naiveté betrays itself. If we pay the tax levied upon us and accept the status of a client-state to Rome, then Kush will lose its sovereignty."

"You don't know that for certain," Amanishakheto pressed. "I know you've neglected to disclose everything the envoys from Egypt told Teriteqas before he died. Particularly about how the overall governing structure of Kush would remain intact if he accepted their terms..."

"Their terms, not ours! He refused to submit to them, and so do I! I refuse to be the queen who loses the Northern provinces. I refuse to be the queen who surrenders a third of my kingdom's wealth to a tribe of white-skinned intruders!"

"That wasn't your position before Teriteqas left."

"It's my position now.... I thought the two of you would support my change of heart in the matter."

"Mshindi and I spent hours talking about this before I made this journey," Amanishakheto stated, boldly drawing closer to her sister. "I listened closely to Mshindi and other soldiers from Egypt as they described how the Romans make war. Now that Teriteqas and

Kharapkhael are dead, I am not convinced that Kush would prevail in a prolonged conflict. I think it would be better to lose a third of the kingdom and pay the Romans than to lose it all and become their slaves. And we both feel that way."

"How easily you would give up that which does not belong to you!" Amanirenas snapped, swiping at the sizeable royal pendant secured to the necklace Amanishakheto wore. "The two of you think like the cowards you are! You believe your lifestyles will not be altered. Do you somehow figure that the Roman prefect in Egypt will allow my Akinid to retain his title and his manhood? To hold on to any inheritance passed on from his father?"

Amanishakheto suddenly caught a glimpse of the sullen soul entombed behind the Queen's heated façade. For a moment, a surge of pity extinguished her burning frustration with her.

"Sister, you're not thinking about your sons or the kingdom. You are thinking about your husband. I knew Teriteqas well and I, too, mourn him, but the future is at stake. We have to be cautious how we deal with Rome...."

"The Romans! They murdered my husband! They did not see a king or emperor in him. They saw a black, flesh-eating barbarian! That is what they think of the Kushite royal line! That's what they think of you and anything that would issue from your womb!" Amanirenas exhaled through clinched teeth and shook her head. "Any person who refuses to bend the knee to their dictates is a threat to them.... And I refuse."

"I love and respect you, Amanirenas, but you're being foolish. If you love your son, who is going to do whatever you say—and if you love Kush, which sees you as the Queen-Mother and will follow you in all things—how is it that you cannot see that both of them can be lost if you take 20,000 soldiers to Egypt and aggravate this giant?"

Amanirenas quietly caressed the intricate carvings on her own royal necklace before turning to her sister and capturing her eyes with a mournful gaze.

"Amanishakheto, I know you love Mshindi, but how hard do you love him? How deeply can you feel him? What would you give for him? Would you kill for him if you had to? I would have killed for my husband.... And now... I have to kill for my husband's memory."

A foreboding shadow fell upon Amanishakheto as she pondered the Queen-Mother's avowal. "Killing for him won't bring him back, and doing so would condemn many other women to your private anguish, including myself. There can be no triumph in that."

Amanirenas slowly started for the door, but then stopped to consider the fact such profound words rarely flowed past Amanishakheto's lips. She was surprised by the only response her tormented soul could offer the younger woman: "Isis has promised me victory."

Chapter 4

25 B.C.
City of Syene

Devestation The eastern wind carried the smoke billowing from the fortification beyond the horizon, testifying to the fact that yet another Roman garrison had fallen to the Kushite spear. Scores of tall black soldiers roamed through the fort, many carrying mementoes from abandoned barracks or dead Roman soldiers.

Flanked by her bodyguard, Amanirenas walked through the streets of the city adjacent to the vanquished military outpost, savoring her third consecutive victory in as many months. Her gold-laced leather torso amour gave way to a knee-high blue and gold dress, causing her to shimmer like a jewel in the midst of the cocoon of towering men in black and red.

Her hair was cut shorter than normal, but still retained a crop of curly black locks, most of which were held at bay by a gold tiara encrusted with colorful gems.

Her face was unsentimental, as she refused to reveal her absolute joy at the devastation wrought by her overwhelming force. Every white body lying splayed and motionless in a pool of blood increased her satisfaction and suckled a thirst she knew would never be quenched permanently.

"This way, my kandace," a soldier bearing the green sash of the Kerman regiment pressed, bowing his head. "They are over here."

Within a few steps, the Queen's party came upon a team of Kushite soldiers guarding six Roman soldiers on their knees, their heads lowered in shame.

Amanirenas studied their uniforms, trying to determine which one held the highest rank. Her eyes settled upon the second from the right, if for no other reason than because his red cloak was still affixed to shoulder clamps on his amour.

"That one," the Queen said with a nod, prompting one of the guards to use the tip of his spear to prod the Roman's head up. As the man looked up, Amanirenas noted the startling contrast of his dark hazel eyes set in his dirty pale face. How such beautiful eyes could be the gateway to such a filthy soul was beyond her. She was certain the gods he served had their reasons for playing such a cruel joke, but she couldn't care less at the moment.

"We believe this is one of the bodyguards of the commanding officer," the soldier who had escorted them there announced.

"And the commander?" Amanirenas demanded impatiently.

"Dead," another Kushite answered as he approached.

"Pelmes Mshindi, I was expecting you later," Amanirenas said.

The Kushite general offered a bow. "My inspection of the fort didn't take as long as I thought it would. I found the body of their praefectus castorum. The man before you is a centurion."

"I see," Amanirenas said, inwardly impressed with Mshindi's knowledge of Roman military structure. She found his familiarity with the enemy extremely helpful, even if she often eschewed his tactical advice. His surgical approach to battle was a poor substitute for her preference of using blunt force and overwhelming numbers to choke the opponent. While she was certain that he silently resented her slights, she did not care, as her only focus was thoroughly dominating the enemy.

"With this sort of progress, we will be able to advance into Elephantine in a week," an imposing bald bodyguard hinted.

"I want to be there a lot sooner than that, Sabrakmani," the

Queen stated. The comment evoked an agitated glare from her chief bodyguard, but he chose to remain silent.

Mshindi, however, had different thoughts. "I recommend that we leave a garrison of our own here in this fort, like we did in Qasr Ibrim. Doing so will..."

"Weaken our forces and leave us with fewer options as we press forward," Amanirenas stated firmly. "I want the flexibility our numbers offer us should we go beyond Elephantine and up to Thebes."

"I can't believe you are still entertaining that thought," Mshindi countered.

"We have the numerical advantage, and they've yet to offer any real resistance."

Mshindi sighed. "My kandace, we've only confronted defensive fortifications. We've yet to encounter a larger fighting force equipped for offense."

"So you've told me, general. I've waited months for Prefect Gallus to counter with one of their specialized armies, and all they've sent out is a handful of centuries. I'm beginning to believe the Romans care less about Egypt than we first thought. Otherwise, they would defend it better."

"Their defensive posture may simply reflect what they think about us," Sabrakmani noted, drawing a cold glare from the Queen. "They may not see Kush as a threat."

"Why else would they set up forts along the Nile and extort tribute from our people?" Mshindi added.

Amanirenas's cold eyes shifted between the two men—both cousins of her late husband. "We will continue to move north until we meet significant resistance from the enemy."

"Yes, my kandace," Mshindi acknowledged, once again forfeiting the fight. "There is one other matter, though. Someone decapitated the statue of Augustus Caesar that stands outside the fort."

"I ordered Akinid to cut off the head and send it to Meroë with the next group of runners," Amanirenas answered pompously. "The head is to be delivered to Jaelen, who will then bury it under the threshold of the entrance to the *dufufa*."

"To tread upon the head of our enemy every time we enter the building," Mshindi noted. "You should make sure the rest of the statue is thrown into the river. The Romans will not take kindly to the desecration of their monuments and temples."

"No more than we appreciate them desecrating our land with their presence," she replied turning to walk away. "Send these Romans to Korosko with the others. And I forbid anyone to hide the evidence of our triumph. The headless statue will stand in place."

Chapter 5

24 B.C.
City of Ombos

Tribune Cassius Marius could hardly stand the revolting taste of defeat lingering in the air like the bitter odor of decaying flesh. His initial inspection of the Roman encampment outside the city of Ombos was both unannounced and informal—precisely how his commanding officer wanted it. Egypt's new governor had predicted that Marius would only be able to assess the garrison's factual status by arriving in an impromptu visit—a move that would reveal the true mettle of Decius Gallus, the garrison commander.

Marius was unimpressed by what he saw. It was plain to see, through the long faces and sluggish body language of the troops, that being driven out of Elephantine by the ravenous Kushites had taken an emotional toll on his fellow Romans. Most of them were already aware that word of their sixth defeat at the hands of an army led by a black warrior queen now circulated throughout Thebes and probably Alexandria. The fact that Prefect Aelius Gallus had been summoned to the fortification at Apollonopolis Magna did not bode well for the garrison's standing command unit, and it appeared that most of the base level foot soldiers knew that something momentous was afoot.

Cold and unsympathetic, Marius threw open the flaps and

entered the command tent, not even bothering to remove his helmet. His hard stare was met by Decius Gallus, who rolled his eyes in spite. "So what news do you bear, Cassius Marius?" Gallus questioned bitterly.

"Nothing you shouldn't already know by now," Marius said flatly. "I've arrived with three cohorts from the *III Legio.* My orders are to prepare for the arrival of Gaius Petronius, the new Praefactus Aegyptus, by order of Augustus Caesar."

Decius turned and grunted. "So, this is it? My father is hardly given a chance to rectify this situation before he is replaced."

"He was given more than enough time," Marius countered. "Caesar gave him a chance to redeem himself after his failure in Arabia, and he responds by allowing some half-naked black woman to emasculate him and drive our soldiers from their own fortifications!"

"They're more sophisticated than you think," Gallus said, rubbing his eyes.

"Sophisticated? I hear many of their soldiers fight with pikes and use raw-hides for shields. This shouldn't even be a skirmish."

"Well, it is!" Gallus shot back with fire in his eyes. "Perhaps you'll feel differently when you see 20,000 Kushite barbarians bearing down on your position."

"And that has been a large part of the problem. Your father gave them too much leeway by maintaining a defensive posture. Prefect Petronius intends to change that."

"Oh? With one legion? 5,000 men will not be very effective against 20,000, even poorly equipped Kushites."

"That is why he is bringing two legions, in addition to 800 cavalrymen," Marius said, folding his arms defiantly. "He has the *Cyrenaica,* as well as the reconstituted *Deiotariana.*"

"The *XXII* is at full strength again?" Decius asked, sitting on his desk. For months, he and other officers recommended that his father send for reinforcements; however, the elder Gallus refused to do so. The inexplicable tactical error finally did him in, and now someone else would have the glory of the kill.

"What kind of man is Petronius?"

"He is very calculating and does not intend to repeat any of your father's mistakes." Marius traced the ivory hilt of his sheathed gladius. "During the next battle with the darkies, we *will* be the aggressors, and they will be facing two legions at full strength."

Chapter 6

22 B.C.
The Battle of Napata

Death approached.

Slowly and methodically, the massive dark specter advanced from the east in the form of the *Legio III Cyrenaica*.

Kandace Amanirenas glared at the beast, her blood simmering with revulsion for the creature that had stolen so much from her. For nearly two years, it had pursued her from Syene, leaving in its wake a debris field of death and smoldering villages in the Northern province. She knew it would come swiftly, and it did—along with its ferocious twin, the *Legio XXII Deiotariana*. Together, they ate away at northern Kushite land as leprosy consumed human flesh.

Now, here they were in Napata. She allowed herself to feel only rancor as the living machine drew closer to the line of Kushite men that stood as a sentinel over the most sacred ground in Kush.

Ever since the Romans had slewn her son Akinid in Dakka, the beasts had ravaged and bludgeoned their way through Kush, and now they were arriving for her. She tightened her grip on the handle of her sheathed sword. If the Romans wanted to dole out retribution for her desecration of their precious temples and statues in Syene and Philae, they would have to march through her version of hell to reach their goal.

The vicious fighting commenced as the steady line of legionaries smashed into the Kushites. Despite a spirited effort, the black defenders wilted like water lilies in the desert heat. A second wave of Romans fluidly changed places with the first—only to give way to a third a few moments later.

Amanirenas seethed at the venomous efficiency of the invaders. Indeed, she had witnessed it several times before, but today was different. Napata, the seat of Kushite religion and culture, was under siege.

She gave herself a moment to admire the moon as it sank into the blue western sky. Even though it was chased from its position by the blazing late morning sun, its crescent form retained a peaceful demeanor, unfazed by the deadly spectacle below.

Amanirenas and her retinue watched stoically from an elevated enclave that protruded from the base of Gebel Barkal. The conflict was far enough away for her to see the entirety of the long Kushite skirmish line as it engaged the legionaries. Upwards of 6,500 Kushite soldiers stood between the invaders and the city that had served as the spiritual center of the Kushite kingdom for well over five centuries. Though just a fraction of the vast force of 20,000 that held the Romans at bay in the north just a year earlier, the group of determined men stood their ground. War cries echoed through the hallowed streets below, chasing out what remained of the city's terrified population.

A half dozen men stood behind her, all of whom were members of her bodyguard—at least what was left of it. She commissioned the other two dozen men to accompany her son Jaelen as he spearheaded the defense of the city. Three of the nine members of her war council road with the prince into battle, while another three were sent south, to the safety of the capital city Meroë.

The other three council members were unaccounted for and had likely fled west or were dead.

Having devised the tactics employed to defend the city, Amanirenas had a good idea where her son was in the midst of the chaotic confrontation. Anxiety mercilessly gripped her as she watched the maniacal Roman line advance and mow down Kushite troops as if they were crops for the harvest. The nearly 5,000 legionaries executed swift and precise maneuvers that caused them to resemble a living sword being driven into the heart of a black leopard.

"No," said a deep rueful voice behind her. It was Sabrakmani, the chief of her bodyguard. "Over there," he said pointing southward toward the Nile. The Queen scanned that direction, expecting to find the standard and flags used to denote the location of the prince. However, what she saw instead made her heart flutter anxiously.

Cohorts from the *Legio XXII Deiotariana* slowly emerged from a wooded region and marched to cut off access to the port that serviced Napata. Hundreds of people fled in the opposite direction as the soldiers heartlessly cut down and trampled anyone in their path.

"They've cut off the first route of escape," Sabrakmani noted, stepping closer to her. "There is probably another pair of cohorts advancing due north of Gebel Barkal."

"We knew this would happen," Amanirenas responded coolly.

"Yes, but not this quickly. If the battle goes poorly, we won't have time to make it from this perch and to the secondary port."

"Then the battle must not go poorly," the Queen replied, finally able to locate the standard demarking where her son's cavalry division rode.

"It already is," Sabrakmani stated flatly.

The Queen took her eyes away from her son's standard and glanced at her chief bodyguard. The bald man was tall and sturdily built, and he possessed a keen military mind. She leaned on him greatly to help evaluate the tactics employed by her war council. Though slightly younger than her husband had been, Sabrakmani possessed the wisdom of a much older man, and his intuition was usually accurate.

"The Romans already have the advantage," he appraised, watching a fifth row of Romans maneuver into the front line.

The Queen clinched her teeth. The advantage he spoke of was the flat terrain, which heavily favored the Roman fighting style. The Kushite cavalry was the only force they possessed that could counter the disciplined Romans in this landscape. If Amanirenas feared anything, it was that the Romans were well aware of the Kushites' current weakness. Her son Akinid was killed while leading a cavalry charge in a similar situation in Dakka.

"Might I remind you of the paqar's orders should they fail..."

"That you may, Sabrakmani," Amanirenas retorted, as the horseman bearing her son's blue and gold Amani-aa'ila standard accelerated toward a maniple of legionaries. Hordes of Kushite ground troops rushed behind them, a cloud of dust swirling in their wake. Her vengeful appetite would be sated today no matter what anyone thought. "But, the paqar is not in command, I am. And ... failure is not an option."

ℱ ℺

Prefect Gaius Petronius sliced his hand through the air to signal his officers to commence the next phase of the assault. The order was quickly relayed through a series of banners, and within moments, another cohort of the *III Legio* started its advance toward the front line, which was a quarter mile away. Soon, the overwhelming bulwark of 480 men would bear down on the enemies' left flank with the sole purpose of collapsing their defense and crumpling their skirmish line like an old garment.

His body, plated with the decorative Roman armor, was drenched with sweat brought on by the late morning sun. It was a condition suffered by all of his countrymen, yet it was preferable to that of the Kushites they battled. A scant number of their opponents donned any sort of protection at all—some even fought in loincloths.

Sweat rolled into Petronius's eyes as he pondered the waning rival. The Kushite armies they had encountered in the north nearly two years earlier had been far better equipped and trained, and they even seemed more motivated than the rabble before him today. From his experience in Gaul, Britannia, and other regions of the Roman dominion, the indigenous people generally fought harder and more relentlessly the closer the battle drew to the heart of their kingdom. Such was not the case here. The dark-skinned enemy seemed fragmented and demoralized.

Now, somewhere in the condemned city before his army was the last paqar and the Kandace—the Prince and the Queen—the primary instigators of this conflict. The Queen once sought peace in Dakka after her son had been injured in battle, only to rescind her petition and launch another attack. While impressed with her determination, Petronius was convinced that the Queen's impudent transgressions and defiant conduct had to be atoned for. For over a year, the *Cyrenaica* and *Deiotariana* had pounded their way southward with the sole purpose of extinguishing the royal line and eliminating any hope the Kushites entertained of maintaining a sovereign kingdom. However, hope could be an audacious foe when given the opportunity.

Indeed, it was the brazen resolve of the Kushites that had drawn Petronius into the conflict to begin with. No one in Rome had given the black barbarians serious thought until they had marched into Lower Egypt with a massive army and shattered garrisons in Syene and Philae. Even that caused more embarrassment than injury to the empire. The loss of standards, religious implements, and several statues of Augustus Caesar—all at the hands of a black woman—were a blow to Roman vanity, and this was enough to make Augustus himself take notice.

Petronius recalled the day the newly minted principes extracted him from a comfortable life of retirement in Capua to salvage Roman pride in Egypt. Augustus did not need to do much convincing, as Petronius was a slave to his own reputation as much as the empire was subservient to its own standing as a world power. As a young man, Petronius had distinguished himself as a first spear centurion in the legendary *XIII Legio,* and on several occasions, he had drawn recognition form from Gaius Julius Caesar himself. However, what daring and brutality won for him under Caesar, cunning and ruthlessness secured for him in service of Augustus. His service as a tribune in the *Legio V Macedonia* in the pivotal campaigns in Actium and in Alexandria against Antony and Cleopatra had solidified his status.

Few were surprised when Augustus had selected Petronius to replace the disgraced Aelius Gallus as prefect of Egypt, whose epic failure in Arabia was upstaged only by his inability to corral the niggling queen and bring her to Roman justice. Thus, Petronius was commissioned with the explicit task to hunt down and exterminate the initiators of the disconcerting and embarrassing engagement.

Through guile, deception, and outright craftiness, the resilient Kandace Amanirenas had managed to evade capture thus far, but for some reason, she had decided to make her stand here, under the shadow of their holy mountain. Nevertheless, there would be no retreat from here, as her next journey would be to Rome, paraded naked through the streets at the head of his triumph.

The pounding of horse hooves drew Petronius' attention. The steed he sat upon remained motionless as several Roman officers approached.

"Prefect, the XXII has successfully cut off the port from the city," a tribune reported, his fair face covered with the red dust of the land.

Petronius gave a faint nod, his hawkish eyes fixed upon the enemy's faltering centerline. While there was a slight chance that the Kushites could puncture his left wing with a concerted push, he doubted that whoever contrived their battle strategies was aware enough to see the weakness.

"Give the signal to advance the center wing," Petronius commanded. "This ends today."

Failure is not an option.

Chapter 7

The Romans were like ants to Batae: When he killed one, two more appeared in his place. Out of all the men in his regiment, he boasted the longest stamina in battle. Yet, today, the fierce reality of that boast led him to the gravest of all scenarios: He was the last member of his regiment left standing.

The Kawa regiment *Shukar* had consisted of 350 men and held the charge of bolstering the centerline. It was an impossible task, and his regiment commander had stated as much. Nevertheless, the army once again dutifully followed the Kandace's flawed plan directly into the Roman long shields and gladius, and right into disaster and inevitable defeat.

Batae's massive stature allowed him to see over past the ever-advancing legionaries and catch occasional glimpses of the carnage left in their wake. What had been the Kushite left flank was now a solid wall of Roman hardware trampling the lesser equipped Nubians. The sight of it sickened Batae and fueled his fury. He fought on and charged an advancing group of Romans, determined to exploit the weakness he found in their strategy.

Unlike his compatriots, he fought with a long spear in the right hand and a short sword in the left. Instead of bearing down either of his weapons on the Romans' shield, he violently attacked the creases in between the men. That the Romans advanced by marching shield to shield made them very formidable; however, Batae found that attacking the edge of the shields threw one of the soldiers off balance and forced them to break ranks. A moment of chaos was all the massive Kushite needed to kill or maim upwards of two or three Romans before they could restore their formation.

Hazy black smoke from the city behind him soon caught his eye. It was an ominous sign that the invaders had breached one or both of their flanks. His temper rose, yet his spirit dropped. Although it was against his fighting style and his very nature, he started to fall back, cleaving yet another Roman as he did so.

There was not a living Kushite soldier in sight—only legionaries. To his surprise, Batae found himself behind the first wave of Roman soldiers, with the second one two dozen or so paces away—yet slowly advancing. He scanned the formation and guessed that it was what the Romans called a century. For a moment, he stood his ground, determined to take on all 80 men single-handedly.

How dare these jackals infect my land? he thought. Then, for a brief moment, he recalled the only other time in his life he had visited Napata. He had been a young boy then, and his father had been forced to transverse the Nile from the north to pay a fine levied against their property. It was a very bitter time. It was...

This isn't my kingdom. It belongs to the paqar and the Kandace, so let their sorry asses defend it! Batae lowered his long spear and ran north, parallel to the advancing century. He headed toward a tree line, hoping to obtain some measure of cover before the Romans completed their advance. He picked up speed, but he was accosted by a familiar voice.

"Batae!" the voice called in a muffled manner. "Batae, help me out of this!"

Batae stopped and quickly glanced around; however, all he could see were dead Romans mingled among a far greater number of Kushite dead.

"Over here!"

Batae followed the voice to a heap of mangled Roman bodies. He pried them apart and found an overjoyed Kushite face staring back at him. Batae instantly had the urge to toss the body back on top of him.

"Pedese," Batae muttered indifferently and turned to leave.

"No, wait, Batae. You have to help me out of this. My leg is jammed..."

"I don't have to do anything but get off this battlefield."

"But we're wearing the same tunic. We're in the same regiment..."

"One you mock and disrespect."

"It was nothing personal," Pedese stammered, ignoring the pain inflicted on his leg as he tried to extract himself. "Let's forget the past. We can help each other now!"

"I doubt it," Batae voiced ruefully as he leaned down and pulled at the amour plating of two dead Roman soldiers that had somehow become locked together. Batae didn't even bother to ask himself how such an unlikely cluster had come into being. The improbable and incomprehensible always seemed to occur around the guileful Pedese.

As soon as the shorter man was free, the two darted toward the trees, narrowly avoiding the century as it continued toward the city.

꿀 ꩜

Tribune Cassius Marius grinned feverishly at the sight of the carnage his cohorts had inflicted. He hated everything about Nubia and reveled in every moment of its torture. While the five other tribunes in the *Legio XXII* loathed their trek into the Kushite heartland, Marius tried to see it as a pleasurable hunting expedition. His sadistic outlook had doubtlessly contributed to his promotion to "full-stripes," granting him seniority over his fellow tribunes from the equestrian class. Thus far, the Kushite uprising had afforded him the opportunity to command men in battle—a rarity for most tribunes.

He goaded his brown horse to traverse the edge of the Nile to get a wider perspective of the damage his troops had inflicted on the port just outside of Napata. Their mission was simple: destroy the port and cut-off any means of escape for the royal family and governing officials.

Surmising that the area was secure, he pondered the option of leaving several hundred men at the port while he took the vast majority of his forces into the city to attack the defending Kushite army from the rear. The maneuver, however, would likely draw the ire of Petronius, and that was something Marius could ill afford. Being a young officer, Marius's career was ahead of him, and developing a reputation of insubordination was not wise, particularly if your commanding officer was a personal friend of the principes.

"Atticus, what do you have for me?" Marius asked the approaching centurion.

"The streets are deserted," the fair-skinned soldier reported. "It looks like the cleverer barbarians fled west."

"Very well, set fire to the rest of the structures. But spare anything that resembles a temple or place of worship."

"We'll do our best, but there are reports that Kushite soldiers have retreated into some of the temples."

Marius sneered at the information. Petronius issued standing orders that temples were not to be desecrated. It was actually a directive from the principes himself, who always opted not to wage war on the religion of the enemy.

"I understand, but if armed soldiers are assembling in a temple, it makes the structure a fortification, not a house of worship. Treat it as such!"

"Yes, tribune!" Atticus enthusiastically responded and then hurried away.

Marius swatted at a swarm of flies that buzzed around his helmeted head. The insects, the heat, and the smell all reinforced a singular contemplation: *I would kill their gods if given the chance!*

Chapter 8

Amanirenas refused to allow the fiery tears to flow from her red eyes as she beheld the complete route of the last of her forces. She rubbed the worn hilt of her husband's dagger, which straddled her hip. The prospect of avenging his death today seemed to fade with the swirling smoke from the city below.

In tormented anguish, she silently watched as Romans marched uncontested into the vicinity of her Napatan home. Her personal dwelling would now join the long list of homes pillaged by the ravenous invaders. The very place where she had raised her children, built a home, and made love to her husband would soon be violated in the cruelest manner.

Sabrakmani approached her and spoke; however, she could not hear him. Her mind was busy processing the death rattle of the ancient Kushite kingdom. That she should preside over the funeral of such a proud kingdom was not her greatest lament; it was that she was doing it at a distance, from the cleft of a mountain. She could no longer see the standard of her son's cavalry unit and fiercely regretted that she had not charged into battle with him at the head of the army.

Across the Nile to the south, she could see scores of pyramids stretching out from the royal cemetery, as if they were reaching to extract her soul from her weary body. Teriteqas' tomb was lost among them, yet she knew precisely where it was. She recalled the day she had lain him to rest—how she had kissed his cold hands, hoping her warm breath would somehow reignite the flame of life in his once fiery eyes. She longed for his touch and craved the heat of his passion.

"Safre confirms that another cohort is approaching from the northern face of Gebel Barkal. It's the rest of the *XXII Legio*," Sabrakmani was reporting. "We have to leave now, before they manage to traverse the mountain and cut off the western passage."

"What about the paqar?" Amanirenas managed to respond through the gambit of contrary emotions.

"There is no word," Sabrakmani replied, stepping in front of her, his great frame impeding her view. "Only that the enemy has advanced into the temple complex and cut off access to the river. But you already know that." He could feel the heat of her hatred through her scornful glare. Her once sparkling brown eyes were now a cauldron of anguish, wrath, and helplessness.

"I need to know about my son."

"We have a contingency for that. However, if we do not start off this mountain now, we may never make it to Meroë to regroup with him."

Sabrakmani reached for her shoulder, a gesture completely out of character for him. Yet, his simple action did more to move Amanirenas than any number of persuasive words. She swiftly turned and started up the short incline that led them to the beaten path leading down the mountain. The descent would take time; however, it would also give them a clear view of the Roman legionaries approaching from the north and how to best avoid them.

As they reached the apex of the incline, Amanirenas glanced back at the burning dream and allowed herself a moment to mourn. She offered an apologetic nod to her ancestors for allowing an enemy to sever a thread that went back several millennia. As a punishment to herself, she refused to take a final look at the pyramids. Her own tomb rested next to her husband's, but in that moment, she embraced the horrific thought that the final queen of Kush might never occupy her grave.

The mistress was dying and would likely expire at the hands of a pale Roman master.

☙❧

Pedese could not recall ever having seen the streets of Napata so still. The avenues usually thrived with conversing people from all corners of the kingdom. But today, the streets were littered with motionless bodies affixed in the grip of death. Had he and Batae not been chased by a dozen or so legionaries, he might have stopped and rifled through the belongings of some of the victims they had fled past.

"Batae, we should at least stop and change our tunics," Pedese called as they hurried down a narrow alleyway. They belonged to one of the few regiments actually adorned with a uniform. Pedese had never really cared for the black tunic or the red sash that bound it at the waist and was eager to shed it once and for all. One thing he would not get rid of was his sword, which he gripped tightly as they ran. It would be his lasting souvenir for the Kandace—a memento by which to remember her failed rule.

He glanced back and noted the Romans that gave chase were no longer behind them. Before he could announce their good fortune, five legionaries rounded the corner before them, their shields protruding like bulwarks.

Instinctively, Batae slid his long spear in between the first two shields and forced them apart. He slammed into the closest soldier and drove him back into the two behind him. Annoyed, Pedese grasped the top of the shield from the other soldier and yanked it away. The audacious move surprised the Roman, who hesitated to thrust his short sword at the stalky black man before him. Pedese used the moment to stab the invader in the neck, forcing a thick shower of blood to gush forth.

Batae violently shoved the two soldiers he was engaged with into an abandoned fruit cart. The heavily armored men tumbled to the ground while Batae sliced freely at their legs.

Pedese considered charging the two remaining soldiers, but he abhorred his odds. He was on the verge of retreating altogether when a Kushite warrior appeared behind them and impaled one of them with a spear. Buoyed by the surprise, Pedese rushed at the remaining Roman as he turned to see his companion fall. Pedese managed to slip his blade between the Roman's plated armor and into his back.

"This way," the Kushite warrior barked. Without hesitation, Batae and Pedese charged after the man.

Batae noted that the man wore the tan and back kilt sported by Kushite cavalrymen from the province of Kerma. "Where is your unit?"

The warrior came to a sudden halt and gestured for his companions to be silent. The hard sound of Roman hobnail footwear clashing again on the stone street slowly drew closer. The three men slipped into a small nearby temple and waited for the column of two dozen legionaries to marshal past.

Pedese peered through an open widow and sighed. "They're gone. We need to get to the river."

"No," the cavalryman replied, wiping the sweat from his eyes. "They've cut off access to the port. Going west is the only option."

"No way!" Pedese exclaimed in a hushed voice. "We need to get across the river and head south."

"You can go wherever you want…"

"Hey," Batae called to the warrior, "what unit were you with?"

The man studied Batae for a moment, noting that the tall, dark-skinned soldier possessed a calm demeanor, despite the horrendous fortunes of the day. "My name is Khai. I was with the 2nd Semna cavalry division."

Batae tried to picture the unit, but then shook his head. The Queen had assembled regiments and divisions from throughout the kingdom to defend Napata. Many of the units had been reconstituted from those decimated by the Romans during the many skirmishes that had led them to the current debacle.

"I've never heard of that division."

"They were assigned to ride with the prince's bodyguard when the battle started," Pedese announced before Khai could utter a word. "I heard it from one of the commanders. I do pay attention to some things," he said to Batae.

"We fought as long as we could, but the Romans had archers and these long spears that I've never seen before." Khai rubbed his eyes briskly as if to brush away a nightmarish vision that refused to leave his sight. "I lost my horse, and then the division was splintered."

Batae grunted coldly. He estimated that the cavalryman was a little older than himself—perhaps early to mid-thirties—yet he possessed the demeanor of an older man or a regimental commander.

"We were in the midst of them—hundreds of them—but I somehow managed to get out. West is the only way to go."

"The prince won't like that," Pedese mused sarcastically.

"The prince is dead," Khai said flatly. "He took two arrows to the chest and one to the head as we made the charge. It knocked him to the ground, and he didn't get up."

"The war council that was with him?" Batae asked.

"All struck down during the hail of arrows. I was bringing up the rear, so I saw it all." Khai surveyed the clearing just outside the temple and nodded. For the first time that day, he was sure of something. "The war is over. You two do what you like. I'm going to head west and go home."

Batae let the man's words settle in and then embraced the forlorn truth that had haunted him since the sun had crept over the eastern horizon that morning. It was a truth that all warriors both lamented and longed for: *The war was over, and it was time to go home.*

Chapter 9

The streets of Napata were quiet, with only the shadow of death slithering through the ashen thoroughfares. Gaius Petronius and two soldiers roved the pathways, inspecting the desolate handiwork of his legions. Some streets were barren, while others were littered with dead Kushites.

The principal fighting had ceased several hours earlier, ending in yet another sound Roman victory. Inevitably, the trio came across the corpse of a fallen Roman legionary; however, Petronius knew the body would not remain there for long. Recovery corps were already at work gathering the Roman dead for the appropriate funerary ceremony scheduled for that evening. Despite the massive number of Kushite losses, Petronius estimated the Roman casualty list to be light—even though any losses would be felt this far into a hostile country.

They stopped in front of what Petronius learned was called a dufufa. All of the Kushite cities they passed through had one at its heart, as it typically served as the central administrative structure. This one however, was far more immense than any of the others his army had come across. Petronius studied the intricate reliefs and colorful murals that adorned the building's façade. Though a large percentage was scorched, he could still make out the image of a curvy woman whose head was bejeweled with a tiara. At her feet were images of far smaller men, all of whom were bound with chains and prostrated in a subservient fashion to the woman.

"Are these captives supposed to be Romans?" asked one of the officers, who was also studying the image.

"Indeed they are," a fellow tribune replied, pointing at the unique Romanesque headdress of the prisoners. "It's still fairly new. They likely painted it to commemorate the Queen's victories early last year."

"Two years ago," Petronius said, stepping closer to the mural. "And they weren't victories, Decius. Victories are earned by armies on the battlefield."

"I'm sorry, my lord, but my father always did disagree with you about that."

Petronius refused to look at the young tribune. The man's resemblance to his father, Aelius Gallus, was uncanny—as was his lack of tact. The young man never passed on an opportunity to defend his father's farcical decisions, which had led to the Kushites gaining the upper hand in the initial days of the conflict. Out of respect to the former prefect, Petronius retained the young tribune as an officer in the *Legio Cyrenaica*, although it was actually more of a political move. He could have easily reassigned him to the garrison in Thebes, but the wisest choice was to keep the audacious young equestrian nearby to monitor his actions.

"Yes, Tribune, I know. Your father believed these people to be worthy opponents," Petronius said as he scraped haphazardly away at the image with the tip of his *pugio*. "But look around. The evidence testifies otherwise. I have never been a part of such an unpretentious campaign. These people were beaten like the tribal barbarians they are. I kept waiting for the conflict your father insisted would come, but it never arrived, and here we are in their most sacred city."

"Granted, it isn't Rome or Alexandria, but these people are far from the disorganized rabble of Gaul...."

"They are also far from the orderly militias of Parthia," Petronius countered. "As much as it may disappoint you, Decius, your father was the prefect of Egypt when this ... army attacked several garrisons, looted basilicas, and carried away Roman citizens as slaves. That he was

41

not aware of what this rogue tribe was capable of is yet another mark against him. That he could not rectify the matter before Augustus learned of it will forever taint his reputation."

"Perhaps so, but it is a matter of honor that I intend to rectify someday," Decius started, before Petronius turned his back and started to walk into the dufufa.

"I will strike an accord with you, Decius. I will not disparage your father's honor if you do not attempt to defend it."

"With respect, Prefect. Perhaps this campaign would have been more of a challenge for you had my father not killed their king before the emperor had you replace him. I imagine that was left out of the official report to Rome."

Petronius stopped and turned to face the young tribune. However, Decius was not deterred.

"I believe it is safe to say that neither Queen Amanirenas nor her sons were as effective leaders as Teriteqas was. And you benefited from that, Prefect."

Petronius thought about the patronizing words as he envisioned the lifeless body of the juvenile prince lying in state back in the Roman camp. The boy was no more than fifteen years old, and from what Petronius understood of the Kushite culture, he had less authority than the Kandace. He assumed that the youth lacked the age and martial experience to contribute anything of substance to the Kushite military effort and epitomized the sad state of the Kushite militia.

Petronius's early encounters with the Kushite armies along the border were often abbreviated because the enemy would attack and then inexplicably retreat. At first, Petronius was circumspect of the tactic and tried to discern its strategic asset. Yet after the third skirmish against the Queen's forces near Qustul, he noted a pattern: The enemy attacked with fewer solders each time, even though they had the advantage of geography. Following his intuition, Petronius surmised that the blunders were occurring not on purpose, but because of lack of coherent governance. In response, he changed his tactics. Ignoring the army, he drove southward and started attacking the towns and villages they came across, dragging away scores of inhabitants to be sold in the Romans' Alexandrian slave markets. The actions proved fruitful, as the Kushite army, which at one point had outnumbered his forces six to one, slowly dissipated. The rabble that defended Napata was a shell of the army that they had faced in Qustul.

"Yes, I took advantage of the king's death," Petronius stated with a gleam in his eye. "The gods offered me a ripe piece of fruit, and I accepted it. I have no doubt that it was an act of mercy. And I believe it is important to recognize when we are being offered the gift of mercy. Much like I am offering it to you right now."

Decius stiffened up as the older man's tone deepened.

"You're a young tribune with a tainted surname. Fortunately, you are a more gifted commander than your father. I appreciate your insistence on defending him; however, your first loyalty should be to Caesar, and since I embody Caesar's authority, it should be to me. Is that clear?"

"Yes, Prefect," Decius delivered flatly.

Petronius glared at the man for a long moment with threatening eyes. "Once we return to camp, summon Tribune Marius from the XXII Legio. Our next objective is to capture the Queen of Kush. I want a live trophy to present to Caesar."

𓆼 𓂀

The harsh sound of metallic screeching filled the air. Nervous sweat rolled across Amanirenas' temples and down her neck. Her golden-laced black kilt was already drenched with sweat from their descent down Gebel Barkal into the surrounding bush. Now, at the behest of Sabrakmani, she waited in stealth for the outcome of an unexpected fight between her dozen bodyguards and an unknown number of Roman legionaries.

Eruptions of death screams droned past the abandoned hut that sheltered the Queen and her servant, Saiesha. Though the young woman wore a courageous visage, her trembling body betrayed her true emotional state.

Amanirenas wrestled against the tenacious grip of anxiety that choked her. The number of unknowns had seemed to compound since the sun had started its trek through the sky that morning. She did not know the condition of her army—whether it was shattered of coherent. She did not know the status of her son—whether he was dead or alive. She did not know what was transpiring in the clearing just a few paces away.

She drew a steady breath and unsheathed her sword.

"My kandace, no!" Saiesha said as her mistress moved to the edge of the hut.

"This day can't end without me killing at least one Roman," Amanirenas spat bitterly. Before conducting her kha to Henel, Osiris would have to pry her hands from a white invader's neck.

Sabrakmani burst around the corner and nearly skewered himself on the Kandace's drawn sword. He sidestepped the blade and swiftly caught her by the arm.

"We must go now," he commanded, towing the Queen into the forest behind the hut.

Amanirenas resisted, but she was no match for his determination. Sabrakmani was the only man alive from whom she would even tolerate such action.

"How many Romans were there?" the Kandace inquired.

"More than enough."

"What about the others?" Saiesha asked, quickening her pace to remain in step with Sabrakmani.

"They are doing what they have sworn to do," he replied stoically, surveying the path ahead of them for threats. "Giving their lives for the Kandace."

No words were spoken as they fled through the forest. Amanirenas sensed that they were heading west, as she was able to get a glimpse of the river on several occasions. They finally stopped when they came to the edge of an immense glade.

It was at that moment that Amanirenas realized that she had run the entire way with her sword in her hand. Breathing heavily, she swiped at a branch of a nearby tree and severed the limb; she let out a torturous scream as hot tears streamed down her face.

"We're all alone," Saiesha stated, on the verge of tears. "Sabrakmani, what do we do?"

The bodyguard seemed unfazed by the loss of his team. Saiesha knew that he was likely drawing from some reservoir of strength that soldiers held in reserve, but it did little to comfort her.

"Where can we go?" the young servant pressed, still trying to catch her breath.

"There is an old temple complex beyond this glade. If we can make it there, we can take cover in the ruins for the next couple of days. It's far enough off the main road that it should be safe."

"Then what?" Saiesha asked.

"We have to get across the river and go to Meroë, but when we can do that depends on the Romans."

"Why?"

"They'll be looting Napata and maybe even Nuri for the next couple of days," he replied dispassionately. "They built their river rafts before the battle, so they will either head north back toward Egypt or south..."

"To Meroë," Saiesha uttered softly. Thoughts of the capital city suffering the same fate as Napata intensified her anguish.

"It will be difficult, but we have to make our way south. I know of a place up ahead where we can get a boat..."

"No," the Queen said curtly. "We can't go. I have to know about my army first."

"Your army? It has been shattered—and given Roman efficiency, they are likely all dead. We have to go to Meroë. At least the battalion there may be able to mount a defense, and the terrain will make it hard for the Romans to maneuver. That's where you should have made your stand."

"I did what I had to do," Amanirenas shot back.

"No, you did what you wanted! You should have abandoned Napata, but you wanted to defend the city Teriteqas is buried in at any cost. It was another tactical blunder."

Amanirenas turned away to sidestep the continuation of an argument that had persisted for nearly two years. As Sabrakmani had predicted so many times, the outcome of their last battle was just as tragic as the action that initiated it.

"You weren't defending a city today; you were defending a broken heart. It went just like every other battle has for the past two years…"

"No! We were defeated because the men didn't fight hard enough!"

"Is that what you saw?" Sabrakmani stepped closer to the Queen and locked eyes with her. "Those men fought for a completely different reason than the one you intended for them."

"Rome took my husband and my son … That's reason enough for them to fight," Amanirenas said wearily, her rage sapping her strength. "Now, I don't even know about the only son I have left."

As had happened so many times before, a wave of pity swept over Sabrakmani as he watched the royal veil shrouding the Queen-Mother in arrogance slowly fade away. Soon, all he saw was what she refused to let anyone else see: a heartbroken woman deprived of her lover and soulmate.

"Teriteqas was my blood, and I loved him," Sabrakmani said, his tone softening. "But the idea that he died for was greater than he was. Amanirenas, you are killing that idea."

"The kingdom," she moaned, turning away, "it always comes back to the kingdom. My family be damned; yet Kush must live!"

"You are the Queen-Mother! The kingdom of Kush is your family!"

"No, Sabrakmani, it is a leech that has sucked my blood for too long! It has stolen everything from me." Amanirenas threw down her sword as a wave of despair crashed against her heart. By the blessings of the gods, she was given Teriteqas's heart—until the mistress stole it away, along with the fruit of their union.

"Perhaps I should let it die," Amanirenas said, staring at the sword.

Sabrakmani picked up the weapon and thrust the blade into the soft soil. "You may have already killed it."

The bitter words slapped the Queen harshly. "What are you saying?"

"It's obvious. Some part of you wanted this to happen all along."

A wicked silence suddenly hushed even the birds in the surrounding trees.

"I wanted revenge, Sabrakmani."

"Yes, but not against the Romans."

"Then against who?" Amanirenas demanded. The massive bodyguard folded his arms defiantly in response. Amanirenas glared at him in frustration. Like the other men in Teriteqas's family, Sabrakmani knew exactly when to go silent. "Answer me! If you think that I ..."

"I think someone is coming," Saiesha interjected nervously.

Sabrakmani quickly confirmed her suspicions and promptly ushered the women behind an enormous fallen tree. Within a few moments, several women bearing bundles of linen briskly emerged from the forest and rushed down a path into the glade. Within a heartbeat, they were gone.

Sabrakmani arose from hiding and then gave a nod to the perplexed women.

"Why should the Queen-Mother have to hide? They weren't even soldiers." Saiesha inquired.

"The Romans aren't the only ones we have to be on the alert for," Sabrakmani replied.

"What?"

Sabrakmani patiently looked at the servant, who was still in her early twenties. The girl's stylish hairdo remained intact, despite their harrowing escape into the jungle. "We have just lost a major battle, and there are plenty of people in the kingdom who resent the Amani-aa'ila for bringing the Romans down on them. Until we make it to Meroë or find a significant number of our soldiers who have survived, we have to be very careful about anyone we come across."

"I don't want to go to Meroë, Sabrakmani," Amanirenas said sternly. They both understood that their previous conversation was not yet complete, but they silently agreed to let it go for the moment. "I'm going north."

Sabrakmani dropped his head and almost laughed, for there was but one rationale answer to her statement. "To Piankhi and Mshindi?"

"They're my only option now. Mshindi has the last true standing army in the kingdom."

"He will likely skewer you on sight—and Amanishakheto will probably help him."

"I am still the kandace..."

"With no army. With no bodyguard. And with no leverage."

"The Romans devastated a quarter of the Nobatian province. I believe Piankhi will want revenge on them for that. And Petronius will have to head back north at some point..."

"You seem to forget the insults and the ultimatum you levied on those men that forced them to withdraw from your expedition last year," Sabrakmani remarked, recalling the impassioned argument in which both Nobatia's vizier and general accused Amanirenas of conducting the conflict as it were a private war.

"I can't let it end like this, Sabrakmani."

"You may not have a choice."

Amanirenas begrudgingly acquiesced to the fact Sabrakmani's cynicism was likely warranted. "I understand the risk, but I am willing to take it. Mshindi is a soldier who understands what it means to obey orders. As for Amanishakheto, she is a member of the Amani-aa'ila and will fall in place. However, if you do not wish to accompany me, I am willing to release you from your obligation."

Sabrakmani smirked and started down the dusty path before them, scoffing at her attempt to entreat his sense of honor. Ironically, it was her one ploy that always worked on him.

"My kandace, I have no reason to fear the wrath of Mshindi or Amanishakheto. I am not the one who drove the army to ruin, nor am I the one who betrayed a trust and stole a lover. But we do not have to get into that right now. We need to get to the ruins by nightfall."

Chapter 10

Batae and Pedese bickered liked an old married couple Khai once knew from the province of Kerma. The two argued over honey wine, lack of pay, and which province possessed the most beautiful women. Pedese, the more boisterous of the two, had solicited his opinion on several occasions, but Khai had managed to evade entanglement in the meaningless debates by intentionally staying several paces ahead of them. If anything, he found the coarse and at times vile banter entertaining and a welcomed relief from the depressing finality of their new reality.

For nearly two days, they had stealthily made their way around the Gebel Barkal district, narrowly evading the Roman patrols who stalked the region like wolves. On several occasions, they had observed helplessly as Roman legionaries marched down the roads with captured Kushite soldiers—some to be executed, others to be sent north to entertain the Roman masses in the arena.

Agreeing that there was safety in numbers, the trio made its way west together. After finally making it to the outskirts of Napata, they were at least another hour from Batae's hometown of El-Kurru. Khai shuddered at the gloomy prospect of continuing with Pedese after Batae's departure. Pedese's hometown of Kawa was much further north, and it could easily take them weeks if they remained on foot. As a result, Khai spent most of his time trying to figure out a way to procure a boat when they got to El-Kurru. He did not hear Pedese until the third time the younger man called his name.

"Khai! Fool, are you deaf?"

"Sadly, I'm not," Khai muttered, keeping his pace.

"Batae here says he would rather keep fighting..."

"That's not what I said, you idiot," Batae grumbled. "I would prefer fighting over my former occupation."

"And what was that?" Khai asked, glancing back.

Pedese cut in gleefully. "This great son of Apedemack bred goats! Can you imagine that?"

"No," Khai responded, rather shocked. After seeing how Batae had dispatched the Romans back in Napata, Khai found it difficult to believe that the massive man had done anything other than fight.

"That's what I thought," Pedese chided. "I look at him and I think surely he is a hunter of lions. But no, he breeds goats!"

"At least it's useful," Khai said. "What did you do before the war?"

"He spent his father's money and chased women," Batae interposed.

"No sir, they chased me!" Pedese exclaimed. "But ... I never ran."

"Is that all you did?" Khai asked, quickly losing interest in the exchange.

"I worked for my father, who is in the employ of a peshte."

"He's not being truthful," Batae said mordantly. "His father is the pelmes-ate of Kawa."

"Is that true?" Khai asked Pedese skeptically.

"Afraid it is," Pedese smirked.

"What's the son of such a high ranking governmental official doing fighting in the infantry? I thought men of such rank were exempt from serving."

Pedese glanced off the path for a moment. "My father has four children, of which I am the eldest. Even though I was exempt, I volunteered to go."

"That has to be a lie," Batae stated, shaking his head.

"No, it's true. My father believed in this senseless war and wanted to send my younger brother. Since the idiot boy could never beat me in a fight, I did not think he had a chance against a man who actually wanted to kill him. Therefore, I convinced our father to send me."

"I'm impressed," Batae said with a smile. "All this time I thought you were a selfish bastard concerned only for yourself."

"Oh, I am. It does not help that my father despises my lifestyle, along with the fact I refused to follow his lead into government. I left that to my brother, Pahor. I think it was a good exchange."

"You said your father believed in the war," Khai said as the path they were following took a sharp turn from the river.

"Of course he does; he's a government official," Batae asserted, not attempting to mask his cynicism. "He'd do anything to keep the system intact that sustains his position and status in this corrupt kingdom. They will support the war, but they will not fight it. They leave that to people like us."

"It works, doesn't it?" Pedese declared defiantly. "The underprivileged always spill their blood so the Amani-aa'ila and the nobles can have their kizra and booza."

"And you're fine with that?" Khai asked.

"If I were, I wouldn't be here," Pedese said. "What about you? You have hardly said anything about yourself. What did you think of this grand conflict with the white-skinned stalkers?"

"I don't think it's over," Khai said.

"What? The Romans kick our asses from Nobatia to Gebel Barkal and then sack the sacred city—which they are burning right now—and you say it's not over? Surely, you thumped your head when you fell from your horse."

"There's still the *Teriahi* regiment in Nobatia."

"You mean the army that abandoned our thoughtless kandace and wisely skipped to the west side of the Nile last year? Those idiots are probably fighting each other as we speak."

Khai stopped midstride and faced Pedese. "I fought side-by-side with many of the men from those regiments in the beginning. You talk a great deal Pedese, but you say very little. I do not understand what motivates you to fight, but I know why the men in those regiments took up arms. I have heard stories of how the Romans treat a conquered kingdom. How they take its food from the field and its gold from the ground. We cannot let that happen here. This is our land; we have to fight for it."

"No," Batae said curtly, "this is not our land! It belongs to the Amani-aa'ila. Always has." He drew his sword and hacked away at stray tendrils littering the path as they started to walk again. "Everything my family produces is taxed and taken by the royal and noble classes. We work like dogs but benefit very little from it, and it's been that way for my family for generations.

"I went off to fight in this war because I thought killing men would be more interesting than breeding dirty animals. Now, I have to go back to our farmstead with no hope of doing anything else. My father is an old man who has known nothing different. But my younger brother is smart enough to be a minister, but all he will ever do is count goats and watch them hump one another."

"And you think the Queen is responsible for this?" Khai asked.

"The Queen and everyone who came before her," Batae barked. "Perhaps the Romans are a curse upon the Amani-aa'ila for their arrogance throughout the years. They have lived like parasites sucking the lifeblood from the people. Now it's their turn."

$$\varnothing \, \gimel$$

The half-dozen vessels of resin simmering in Petronius's plush tent did little to combat the overwhelming odor of burning wood from the hundreds of campfires ablaze within the sprawling Roman encampment. His mobile quarters was an inappreciable version of his estate in Capua—a place he at times missed desperately. With Napata reduced to an ash heap, he felt at least two steps closer to his objective of at least returning to Egypt.

He hoped that the young tribune seated before him could help expedite his plan to march the legions back to Thebes as quickly as possible.

"So, Tribune Marius, there is an important task I am going to bestow upon you."

Cassius Marius drew a sip from the goblet of wine the prefect had poured for him and listened intently. Petronius studied the young man's hawkish eyes. Several times during the Nubian campaign, the tribune had proved himself ruthless and, more importantly, unscrupulous in his methodology in accomplishing problematic commissions. It made him the perfect officer for the assignment.

"It will be my honor, Prefect."

"Wait until you hear it before you esteem it so highly," Petronius said. "I will be leaving for Egypt in the next couple of days with three cohorts from the XXII. We will travel down the river to the fortification at Primis."

"Travelling via the river should speed up the journey," the tribune noted.

"Indeed, and that is the purpose. I intend for us to travel swiftly through the Nile corridor. I want to make certain we arrive to bolster the garrison in the fort. Though the Kushites here are beaten, I'm still concerned about the regiments that splintered from the Queen's army last year."

"Understood," Marius acknowledged.

"The *Cyrenaica* will head north under the command of Tribune Decius Gallus via the Wadi Gabgaba road—the same path we used to get here. They will transport the loot, slaves, and recovered standards and statutes. They should arrive at Primis in about six weeks."

"What of the balance of the XXII?" Marius asked.

"You will be in command of the remaining three cohorts from the *Deiotariana*. You will also return via the river, but your journey will be more meticulous." Petronius arose and referenced a map fastened to a wall. "The greater part of this country's population lives along the Nile. While our withdrawal will be swifter than our entrance, it will also be more visible. I want these people to see the legion that smothered their army. And I want them to see their new masters."

Marius nodded his head in approval. "It should be a rather daunting sight and a convincing lesson to the barbarians. However, I thought you would have opted to press upriver to Meroë. I understand it is the last Kushite city with a semblance of civilization—so goes the rumor."

Petronius folded his arms and stared at the map. "It's no rumor. However, the position of the city gives me pause. Reports say its proximity to the river and the make-up of the surrounding topography make it difficult for a legion to approach it to execute an attack or mount an effective siege."

"It sounds like that would have been a better place for their queen to make her defense," Marius commented. "Their lack of strategic sophistication is most embarrassing. Their understanding must be as dark as their skin."

Petronius squinted at the emblem representing the city of Meroë. Drawing his army further south to Meroë would place him at a severe strategic disadvantage by setting his legions in a nearly indefensible position, with the mighty Nile at his back. It was the sort of trap that he would have set for an invading opponent were this his land. It was a trap he did not intend to March into, no matter who or what was in the city.

"Fortunately, Meroë is not our goal," Petronius finally announced, turning back to Marius. "Our objective elected not to flee there."

"The Queen."

"I received a report from a primus pilus that his unit engaged a band of soldiers designated as the Queen's bodyguard a couple of days ago."

"They knew this for certain?"

"The men wore similar insignia and armor as those who rode with the young prince when he was killed." Petronius retrieved a black leather wristband adorned with gold bands from his desk. It was the first time he had noted a Kushite garment that signified special rank or hierarchy.

"The primus pilus reported that the party was heading west."

"Looking for a way to cross the river to head to Meroë?" Marius speculated.

"Perhaps. However, I have set up patrols along the river on both sides. This should discourage her from making a run south. The

Queen is our primary objective at this point," Petronius stated bluntly, handing the wristband to the tribune. "I am dispatching you with the three cohorts to find her. Fewer men will make you more mobile."

"I assume the goal is to drive her north, and cut off any escape routes to Meroë?"

"No, the goal is to capture her," Petronius said as he returned to his seat. "She is to be the centerpiece on our barge as we sail down the Nile back to Alexandria."

Chapter 11

"My kandace, you must wake up. Someone is approaching."

Amanirenas shook off her slumber to see anxiety etched upon Saiesha's face. The haze of twilight still danced in the western sky, so she reckoned she had not been asleep for very long.

"Romans?" Amanirenas questioned, fastening her sheathed sword to her sash.

"I don't think so. Sabrakmani is talking with them now. They are a few paces down the path."

Amanirenas donned a hooded cloak and covered her head. Her gold-laced leather armor was replaced by a simple kilt that Sabrakmani had procured the day they started hiding in the ancient temple complex. Gone also was the jewel-studded tiara that had adorned her head since the first day she marched at the head of the Kushite army. It pained her to conceal her identity beneath such plain garments, but she did so at Sabrakmani's behest.

As her chief bodyguard predicted, they encountered no one during their time in the abandoned shrine—something she saw as a miracle. In fact, they had not seen a soul since leaving the hideout that morning. Yes, they avoided the main paths, but she always thought that particular region was more populated, given its proximity to Napata. Like Sabrakmani, she speculated that the populace had fled and was in hiding while the Romans continued to occupy the area.

"We fought in the *Shukar* regiment from Kawa," a tall man was saying as four dark figures moved into the light produced by the campfire. The weary looking trio was armed, and all three bore relatively fresh scrapes and abrasions that suggested that they had participated in the conflict in Napata. "I am Batae, this is Pedese, and the quiet one is Khai."

"The *Shukar* has a very good reputation among the regiments," Sabrakmani noted. "It won a great deal of plunder in Philae."

"It *had* a good reputation," Pedese said curtly. "It's gone now."

"The entire regiment?" Amanirenas asked, stepping out of the shadows.

"Chewed up, swallowed, and crapped out by the *Legio Cyrenaica*," Pedese said, his lips turning into a jagged smile. "Hey, you have women here! Beautiful ones at that. Please tell me that you are a priest and that these are prostitutes from the Temple of Amun. I haven't had any in weeks..."

"We're neither," Saiesha said firmly.

"You don't have to be," Pedese said with a wolfish grin. He moved toward her but was cut off by Khai, who was in no mood for the younger man's follies.

"You seem to be more familiar with the regiment than most people. What is it that you do?" Khai asked. Though he had ascertained that the bald man was older than he was, the dim light made it difficult for him to approximate his age.

Sabrakmani studied the man. He carried himself like a pelmes yet bore the insignia of the much lower rank of unit captain. In addition, he wasn't from the same division as the other two, yet they clearly respected him and deferred to his lead.

"I am Sabrakmani, chief bodyguard for the Amani-aa'ila, and this woman is the Queen of Kush, and your kandace."

Batae and Pedese stared at the humbly clad woman and then glanced at one another and laughed coldly. Sabrakmani watched intently as Pedese drew closer to examine her.

"You're too beautiful to be the Queen," Pedese commented. "And waaaaay too thin." He reached for her face, but Saiesha swatted away his hand before he could touch her.

"You again," he said with a devilish glee. "I'll take you first then. It doesn't matter to me..."

Saiesha quickly brandished a dagger that gleamed in the campfire.

"Exquisite blade to be in the hand of a temple prostitute. You must have had a lot of customers before the Romans came," Pedese jeered.

"Saiesha, put it away," Amanirenas commanded. She removed the hood and unfasted the cloak, revealing a thick gold-plated necklace worn only by the Kandace. "I'm pleased you men survived the battle. It was a terrible spectacle..."

"Spectacle? If you're the Kandace, I should disembowel you right here!" Batae exclaimed, unsheathing his short sword. His action prompted Sabrakmani to quickly move by the Queen's side, his hand affixed to his own weapon. "Your battle plan was an embarrassment. Ours was not the only regiment to be destroyed. Do you know how many prisoners the Romans are taking back with them? And for what?"

Pedese quietly lined up with Batae. The menacing duo stood ready to strike, their hatred burning hotter than the fire before them. Sabrakmani stood at the ready. He was confident that he could strike down the two men in three fluid forays; however, he was not sure that he could reach the third man should he brandish a weapon. However, thus far, the man did not make a move.

"Those men gave their lives for the kingdom," Amanirenas said evenly. "They believed in the cause."

"No, woman," Batae retorted angrily, "they gave their lives for Qeren Teriteqas. They offered their lives for a man they admired, and you pissed on their sacrifice by throwing those lives away."

Amanirenas briefly felt Sabrakmani's cold gaze, affirming the harsh words.

"Every call you've made for the last year has been disastrous, and we've paid the price in blood. How many times did you stand and watch after ordering a regiment into the teeth of the Roman legions— only to pull them back like a leashed dog? Philae, Qasr Ibrim, Dakka. All the same.

"Did it occur to you how many wives have lost their husbands?

Children have lost their fathers? Mothers have lost their sons? No matter. This is just a game for your breed."

Amanirenas searched for a response to Batae's words and found none. His words cut through her, leaving in their wake a trail of regret and shame.

"Perhaps death is too good for her," Pedese suggested. "Maybe we should take her to the Roman squad we evaded a few hours ago. She might actually be worth something."

"That will never happen," Sabrakmani announced.

"Sorry, bodyguard, but the way I see it, you might get two of us, but not before the third carves you up like a goat..."

"You men have a choice," Amanirenas stated, fighting to maintain a steady voice. "I've made many mistakes that you've been forced to pay for. But they were mistakes of the heart. And the heart often blinds the mind. And if I could do it again..."

Amanirenas shook her head and managed to avoid the deluge of tears aching to spill over. She locked eyes with Sabrakmani, whose countenance softened somewhat. He offered an empathetic nod to acknowledge her grief. Both of them wondered if things could get any worse.

The tense standoff seemed to last for an eternity—neither side knowing exactly what to do next. To Sabrakmani's surprise, the third man slowly knelt, drew wood from the small stack off to the side, and refueled the fading fire.

"You," Sabrakmani called to Khai, "you bear the sash of the Kerma cavalry unit assigned to the paqar's detachment. Do you know anything of him?"

Khai quietly finished adjusting the wood in the flame, then arose. He shifted his eyes from Sabrakmani to the Kandace. He held her gaze as one would hold another's hand. "I saw him die. It was a soldier's death."

Amanirenas absorbed the news with sullen nod. This time, there was no dam against her emotions, and her tears flowed as freely as the Nile. The vindictive mistress had officially deprived her of her last son. She turned away and silently walked into the darkness.

Suddenly robbed of their rancor, Batae and Pedese shamefully lowered their weapons.

Saiesha glared at the soldiers. "Another mother *has* lost her son," she said to Batae before she disappeared into the darkness in search of the Kandace.

Khai turned to Sabrakmani, who peered into the opaque forest that concealed his queen. The older man looked overburden and tired.

"Every bodyguard that rode with Paqar Jaelen is dead. What happened to the rest of them?" Khai asked, knowing there had to be at least a dozen or more left to protect the Queen.

"Some died getting her off Gebel Barkal. Others getting her away from an abandoned village where the Romans almost captured her." Sabrakmani sighed and sat down a log next to the fire. "They gave their lives for the queen of our kingdom."

"Why?" Pedese spat, kicking a stone into the fire.

Sabrakmani watched the embers flare from the fire and settle in the dirt. Within moments, every one of them faded into a darkened cinder. "Because they believed in Kush," he answered softly, envisioning the face of each one of his dead subordinates. "They believed in their home."

☥ ☥

The moonlight shimmered on the Nile and transformed it into a sparkling piece of jewelry. Amanirenas sat near the river's edge and watched the flowing current drift soundlessly past. Her thoughts shifted mercilessly from Kharapkhael, to Teriteqas, to Akinid, and finally to Jaelen—all of whom now awaited her arrival at some unknown port in the afterlife. She started the ritual prayer unto Osiris at least six times; however, grief always quickly snatched away her desire to continue.

She shuddered to think of what had become of her Jaelen's body. Perhaps the Romans would have mercy and allow them to reclaim his corpse for a proper Kushite burial? She rubbed her arms and drove the notion of compassion from the callous intruders from her thoughts.

The Romans had repeatedly proved that their idea of sympathy was a sword to the neck.

Sabrakmani quietly sat down next to her. Unlike Saiesha, he offered no words of sentiment, only his silent presence. It was a gesture that Amanirenas appreciated, as her mind was awash with a cacophony of thoughts and feelings, and she could not bear to accommodate any more. If anything, she needed to unload them.

"I prayed I would never see this day," she confessed. "How can a mother outlive *all* of her sons?"

Sabrakmani silently entertained the memory of the prince. Unlike his older brother Akinid, who had a temper and was insufferably rash at times, Jaelen was quiet and contemplative, always searching for an answer to the riddle of life. Teriteqas had seen to it that none of his sons were overly attached to their mother in an awkward fashion, and there were times that Sabrakmani perceived a hint of disappointment from Amanirenas that her sons were so independent of her. Nevertheless, her disenchantment always seemed to be quelled by the endless affection Teriteqas had rained upon her.

"Sabrakmani, I killed my son."

"Jaelen was killed by a Roman archer..."

"But I *sent* him to be killed. Just like I did with Akinid. I could have waited. I could have waited for the regiment in Meroë..."

"In which case, an additional 1,050 soldiers would be in Henel as well, and the capital left unprotected. It would have made little difference."

Amanirenas brought her hand to her mouth as if realizing the answer to an ancient enigma. "Every battle—everything I've done in the past year—all I wanted to do was avenge my husband. Was that such a crime?"

"It was no crime. Teriteqas may have done the same."

"I could have ended this in Dakka after Akinid was injured," Amanirenas said ruefully. Memories of her initial efforts to seek peace with the Romans flooded her mind.

While the war took a dramatic turn against Kush upon the arrival of Prefect Gaius Petronius, a brief opportunity to negotiate terms of surrender had presented itself after he had relieved Prefect Gallus. Most of her officers had advised pursuing a peaceful settlement; however, Akinid's death only added to the numerous voices screaming from the grave for her to avenge them. In deference to her anguish and rancor, she used a peace envoy as a rouse and mounted a surprise attack on the new prefect. While bold, the decision led to a crushing defeat for her army. Worse yet was the resulting schism that saw nearly 10,000 men of the *Shukar* regiment depart with General Mshindi and Vizier Pianki, who vehemently disagreed with her escalation of the war. The Kushite army had been hobbled and on the defensive ever since.

"Those men were right. I threw their lives away out of my sorrow. You were right all along, Sabrakmani. I could not see it. I could not see it until it was my son. My *last* son."

Sabrakmani rubbed her shoulder and slowly drew her closer as she sobbed inconsolably. Her body was wracked with remorse and humiliation as the weight of her wanton, reckless use of force against the invaders fell squarely upon her shoulders. Suddenly, she could see every tactical error committed, hear every word of sound counsel she had rejected, and feel every ego she had crushed while storming down her path of vengeance. She found herself in a labyrinth of shame and could not find a way out.

After a moment, she drew away from Sabrakmani and stiffened. "I don't know what to do. Perhaps I am fated to be the last kandace." She thought fleetingly of her young daughter Amanitore. She lamented the many ceremonies and rituals through which she would never be able to guide her. "My daughter. If I gave myself over to the Romans, do you think they would allow her to live?"

"No. That is not their way. Before he withdrew from the expedition last year, Mshindi told me what they would do to you if you were captured. You would be taken to Rome, stripped naked, and paraded through their city in what they call a triumph. You would then be taken to the temple of one of their gods and ritually strangled. Amanitore would be enslaved, and Kush would be ravished for all of its resources."

Amanirenas closed her eyes. She vaguely remembered him describing her potential fate once before, but she refused to acknowledge the prospect. "All the more reason for me to stay away from Meroë. I have to protect her. Some form of the kingdom may live on through her."

"No, you shouldn't go to Meroë now," Sabrakmani said, reflecting on his sudden change of perspective. "I've given this a great deal of thought over the past couple of days. The best thing for you to do is go north and try to reconstitute the Nobatian army. You have to convince Mshindi to keep fighting. The last runner communique from that region placed him somewhere near the second cataract."

"I said a lot of hurtful things to him and Amanishakheto the last time we spoke," Amanirenas said reflectively. "A lot of bitter words spoken from a broken heart. It would be a miracle for them to follow me again."

"Back then, you were a queen blindly seeking vengeance against those who slew her lover. But now you are a mother who has lost her last son in honorable combat. Such a plea will be difficult for Mshindi to ignore."

Amanirenas nodded grimly as she tried to absorb the burden levied upon her shoulders by her own grief. Her refusal to compromise or even listen to wise counsel had placed Kush in a position to receive a death knell. Sadly, it had taken Jaelen's death for her to see how she had allowed her heartache to eclipse the truth that she was not just a queen, but the *Queen-Mother* of the realm. She uttered a prayer of repentance and immediately set her heart upon seeking the wisdom necessary to do for her many spiritual sons what she had failed to do for her natural ones.

"We can start by going to Kawa," she said with humble resolution. "The peshte there was one of my strongest advocates."

"Let's hope he still is," Sabrakmani answered, standing up. "We'll need to go to El-Kurru first. Hopefully we can get some supplies from the pelmes-adab. We cannot get there alone, though. We're going to need help."

Chapter 12

Saiesha hated being outside at night. The biting insects, agitating noises, and general exposure to the elements made her feel naked and vulnerable. However, tonight, the torturous elements of the evening were abated by the unexpected amusement she encountered from the soldiers who shared their fire. Pedese and Batae were an odd couple and an unlikely pairing at first glance. Batae was tall, with short-cropped hair, a beard, and a thoughtful and passionate demeanor. Pedese, on the other hand, was shorter, wore his hair in cornrow-style braids, and was obnoxiously vulgar.

She sat transfixed as the two humorously described embarrassing moments experienced by fellow soldiers of their regiment. From drunken insubordination to fear of scorpions, Saiesha found the entire exchange morbidly fascinating—primarily because the men they spoke of met awful deaths in battle.

When the two became too descriptive and explicit, she shifted her attention to the quiet one. Khai sat across from his raucous companions and stared contemplatively into the fire as if he could see a face among the flames. He was muscular, had a thin beard and his brow had a furrow that seemed to never leave his brown face. Saiesha found his dignified manner attractive, which made observing him that much more pleasurable.

Khai sat alone for the better part of the evening, apparently waiting for Sabrakmani, who was down by the river with the Kandace. Saiesha had overheard the bodyguard ask Khai to remain. However, that had been a while ago, and Saiesha questioned how much longer the other two soldiers would linger in the company of a woman they clearly despised.

Pedese was in the midst of another colorful battlefield narrative when the Queen and Sabrakmani quietly emerged from the shadows. Amanirenas surveyed the scene and then sat next to Khai.

Sabrakmani stood before Pedese and Batae and gestured for their attention. "I understand the two of you are very familiar with the ports along this stretch of the Nile," he said, mainly to Batae.

"Most of them," Batae answered with a shrug.

"While we were down at the river, we were able to see landing torches for several piers down river. Do you think you can identify them?"

"Did you find a boat?" Pedese jeered.

"No, but it would help if I could determine our distance from Kawa. Identifying the ports should give us an idea of how many days we are from the city."

Pedese pondered the man's words. While he was in no particular hurry to return home to his father's presence, he also didn't have anywhere else to go. Moving west was the most sensible action to take at this point to avoid capture by the Romans. He arose and slapped Batae on the shoulder. "It shouldn't be too difficult to identify where we are along the river. Come on."

The three men headed down the path to the river bank, leaving Khai, Amanirenas, and the crackling sound of wood being consumed in the fire.

The soft glow and soothing warmth of the fire lured Amanirenas into a subtle trance, and she found herself fighting off emotional and mental fatigue.

"Your son was very brave," Khai said. His words snapped Amanirenas out of her lassitude. "He was young and inexperienced, but he was bold, and the men respected him for that. The king would have been proud of how he led the final charge."

Amanirenas looked at the soldier and reflected upon his words. "Thank you. You do him honor."

"The prince honored his father whenever he could. The men respected the king, so they fought hard for Paqar Jaelen."

"You say the men respected the king. But did they respect his vision of a free Kush?"

For the first time, Khai turned his gaze from the fire to the Queen. "Men fight for different reasons. Some out of fear of the enemy, others out of fear of the king. I doubt that every man who fought in the war did so to keep Kush free."

Amanirenas tilted her head in curiosity at his choice of words. "You've been educated."

"My father had a limited education and made sure I received more training than he did. I can read and write in both the Egyptian and Kushite scripts."

"I see."

"Do you?"

"What do you mean?" she asked, her guarded response laced with suspicion.

"Do you see what Pedese and Batae were talking about? Their grievances were valid. The vision of a free Kush applies only to the royal and noble classes. Your kind has managed to convince tens of thousands to fight for what only a few hundred will benefit from. Most men fight out of fear of the Amani-aa'ila, not respect for it."

Amanirenas paused and reflected upon her tenure as a warfaring monarch. It was a position she had inherited abruptly and did not want. However, she understood why the war was necessary. She reluctantly admitted that she had spent very little effort over the past year and a half attempting to reenforce the concept of freedom opposed to subjugation. Her musings left her with only one question.

"Why did you fight the Romans?"

The soldier stroked his scruffy jaw and turned back to the fire. "I fought out of fear, but not fear of the qeren. When I was young, my parents had a farm but were in debt. I went hunting with a few others from the village for several days. While I was away, the peshte seized the farm and captured my parents and sister. He had them sold to a Roman merchant in order to clear the debt.

"From that point, I developed a fear of the Romans, as well as what my own people could do given the circumstances. I figured a skilled warrior would never be sold off as a slave. I fight so it won't happen to me."

Amanirenas fought the urge to speak. No words she might summon could bring healing to such a wound. She simply mimicked the soldier and watched the burning wood glow until Khai broke the silence.

"The peshtes and viziers care only about their titles. They have no thought about the people who dwell in the lands they are entrusted to govern. That's why I've never had a family and never will."

"What do you mean?" Amanirenas asked, taken aback.

"I'll never take a wife and have children. Not in this life. It's bad enough that my parents and sister were taken when I was a boy, but to have a wife and children to worry about? That would be too much. It's better to go alone with no attachments."

The words brought a degree of remorse to Amanirenas, who looked away in shame. "And you feel the actions of my family somehow contributed to this?"

"Not the actions of your family, but the way of your family. The way of kandaces and qerens, pharaohs and viziers. They're all the same: self-centered and blind to the people they wound, as well as ignorant to the hurt they cause themselves."

"I think you judge those who rule too harshly. It is a great responsibility..."

"Which demands greater accountability. The fact that people have no choice in who governs them can breed nothing but fear. To know your life is only as valuable as a kandace or a paqar says it is...."

Amanirenas stiffened like an obsidian statute of Isis and drew a sharp breath. The gleam in her eyes told Khai that he had gone too far, and he braced himself for a stern rebuke.

"I have been favored by the gods to come down through a lineage of thriving kandaces and qerens. Some had great insight on how to govern, while some did not. Some were great warriors, others were not. I cannot change what happened to your family, and it's regrettable that you deprive yourself the joy of having one because of what you experienced. But, understand here and now that I value the lives of my people. All of them."

The passion in her voice somehow brought out her striking brown eyes, and Khai suddenly found it difficult to hold her gaze. He nodded silently and returned his watch to the fire.

"My apologies, my kandace. I did not mean to offend."

"Yes, you did," she retorted, folding her arms. "And you have every right to. We have both lived under a shadow, Khai. A shadow of an idea of how the world should work. While it may not seem like it to you, I too have a prison. Nothing has turned out the way I have wanted. I have had to make many decisions, but I have not had very many options from which to choose. I can't escape the role I have to play."

"None of us can," Khai said in a hushed voice. "It must be difficult being a monarch, having to make choices that influence so many people. Me, I lead a unit of twelve horsemen into battle. While I am responsible for ensuring that they do what the pelmes has commanded, I still feel the burden for each one of their lives as they follow me. Two days ago, I lost all of the men under my command, and I feel like my soul has been shredded like a cheap Nobatian shawl."

Khai paused and allowed himself a moment to absorb the wave of grief he had evaded for the past few days. Faces from the dead men in his unit swayed in the flames to an unheard beat. "I can't imagine how you must feel after what you have seen ripped away from you."

"Are you asking how I feel?" Amanirenas questioned, arching both eyebrows. "Because no one has done that. No one has dared to do that! They've hurled accusations at me and questioned my judgment, but no one has asked ... how I felt."

She stopped and corralled the stampeding emotions his statement awakened. For years, no man had expressed concern for how or what she suffered. Every man she had dealt with since her husband's death either needed something from her or expected her to respond and perform as a man would—an expectation that demanded her to abandon the very gifts that accentuated her womanhood. Feelings and intuition were objects every vizier, peshte, and pelmes told her were useless and inept in leading a war against the Romans. Objects she was told had no place in a man's world.

"How do I feel? Does it even matter?" Amanirenas muttered.

"Do claws matter to a lion?" Khai asked after a moment. "Do feathers matter to a hawk? I think feelings matter to a woman because she uses them to do what she is designed to—help a man see what he cannot or does not want to see."

"You don't reason like an ordinary soldier," Amanirenas said, resisting the urge to reveal her growing fascination with him. However, the flame of curiosity was already lit. "Where are you from?"

"Semna, although I don't really call it home. I have not been there in years. I've spent most of my life in military service fighting for one regiment after another."

"Would it matter to you if we lost this war to the Romans?" Amanirenas asked.

"Yes, it would."

"Why?"

"Because no soldier wants to bear the dishonor associated with defeat. No man wants to die for a lost cause."

"Do you think this war is a lost cause?" Amanirenas asked. She studied the man carefully as he pondered his answer.

"Resisting the power of Rome may be a lost cause. However, dying for honor is not."

She nodded slowly in agreement with his assertion. "You asked how I felt about losing an army. My heart aches for them. Perhaps I am guilty of fighting a lost cause for the wrong reasons. But I believe there is still a chance to salvage their honor, as well as my own."

Chapter 13

Petronius was high enough to see a falcon arc through the air and dive upon an unsuspecting rodent scurrying across an open field. The magnificent crimson bird of prey ambushed its target before it could obtain shelter in the crevices of one of the many pyramids covering the landscape.

Petronius counted over fifty of the striking structures—each housing a king or queen of the ancient Kushite Empire. It was not the first royal cemetery the Romans had come across during their long campaign, nor was it the oldest. However, the scores of brick tips rising defiantly from the earth and pointing toward the heavens made it the grandest.

To the north, Petronius could see the mighty Nile rushing silently in the distance, the Kushite holy mountain Gebel Barkal looming ominously on the other side. From his vantage point, the mountain looked like a giant throne awaiting the arrival of some immense deity. In an instant, the Roman commander understood why the greatest of all Kushite kings was entombed on this particular plateau. While the hill was subordinate to Barkal in height, it gave one the sense of communion with the gods of the land and was the perfect dwelling place for the spirits that overlooked the kingdom.

Further to the east, the *Cyrenaica* and *Deiotariana* prepared for their eminent departure. Days before they attacked Napata, the legions had cleared swaths of the dense surrounding forest in order to construct the hundreds of river-going vessels that would transport the legionaries northward. The ships purposed to ferry Petronius's cohorts back to Egypt were already stocked and ready to launch.

In the meantime, Petronius granted himself a few hours to explore their newly conquered territory. In addition to preparing a report for Augustus, the prefect relished the opportunity to indulge his love of history. He was fascinated by the past and took advantage of every chance he had to examine it—no matter which culture it belonged to.

"They have opened the tomb, Prefect," Theodosio Septimus reported. "You may enter whenever you like, sir."

The surrounding pyramids protested in silence, as Petronius became the first Roman soldier to enter the tomb of the man who had at one time ruled all of Kush and Egypt. Septimus followed Petronius into the tomb, along with a Kushite legionary fluent in the ancient Egyptian script lining the walls. The air was dry and stale, and the heat produced by the torch carried by the legionary only added to the discomfort.

Petronius removed his fanciful helmet and studied the text inscribed on the walls. He recognized many of the symbols used by the Kushites, as a great deal of their ancient language was derived from the land he now governed in the name of Caesar. He understood the meaning behind one group of symbols in particular.

"Pharaoh," Petronius said, squinting at the inscription that appeared several times among the engravings.

"Yes, Prefect," the legionary confirmed, gesturing toward the door in front of them. "Within that chamber lies Pharaoh Taharqa, one of the most revered kings in the history of the Nile Valley."

"I've heard of him," Petronius noted in a reflective tone. He turned to Septimus, who was sweating profusely as they stood in the cramped funerary chapel. "He participated in a historic battle with the Assyrian emperor Sennacherib at Eltekeh. The Assyrians were masters of the known world at the time."

Septimus nodded, appreciating his commander's interest in epic militaristic conflicts of the past. "That was more than three hundred years before Alexander, if I am not mistaken."

"Yes. Even though the battle only halted the advance of the Assyrians for a short period, the conflict itself spanned decades. As vast as the Assyrian kingdom was, Egypt became a constant thorn to them because of this man. The Greek historian Herodotus wrote that he was just a boy, but he rallied the Egyptians and Kushites to resist Assyrian rule."

"Were they successful?" Septimus asked.

"The Assyrians ruled with brutality. They eventually put down the Kushites' rebellion and reclaimed Egypt for a while. But it came at a great price. Within a few years, their empire splintered and was supplanted."

"Was this Kushite king responsible for that?" Septimus questioned, looking perplexed.

"No, but he embodied the idea that was responsible for it. The idea of *defiance*. The idea of freedom."

Petronius's thoughts drifted inescapably toward the hunt for the reigning queen of Kush. History was quite clear: the spark of defiance and the notion of freedom were generally entrusted to one individual, who then, if allowed, passed it on to others. The dead monarch in the next chamber was only remembered because he openly defied and resisted the mightiest empire of his day. In doing so, instead of being a footnote in the Assyrian record, an entire chapter in the annals of history was devoted to his role on the world stage. Petronius refused to entertain the thought of Amanirenas somehow obtaining such an improbable status.

"Do you wish to enter the crypt, my lord?" the legionary inquired.

Petronius folded his arms and gazed at the door to the chamber. The memory and legend of the dead Kushite king entombed within the compartment had survived the Assyrians, the Babylonians, and even the Greeks. It was a specter he did not wish released upon Rome.

Petronius slid on his plated helmet and turned to leave. "No. Leave him be."

Chapter 14

"I can't believe we actually have to pay that man!" Saiesha spat vehemently.

"You're no better than anyone else on this trip. You'll have to sit that beautiful rump of yours right next to the heifers for this ride downriver," Pedese replied as he sauntered by her. He paused a moment and surreptitiously seized her plump rear, prompting her to spin around and quickly slap his hand away.

"Did he ask any questions?" Sabrakmani inquired, his eyes affixed on the barge that would transport them to the small village of El-Kurru. Going by boat would shave plenty of time from their journey, as well as help them avoid roving Roman patrols.

"None. All the old man was concerned about was payment," Pedese answered. "The fawn's necklace seemed to make him happy enough."

"Hopefully not too happy," Khai added.

Sabrakmani glanced at Khai. It was the first time the horseman had offered an opinion since agreeing to accompany the Queen's retinue.

"He's right," Sabrakmani said to the Queen. "The necklace may have been too valuable to use as payment..."

"We don't have a choice right now," Amanirenas said evenly, trying to allay her bodyguard's concerns. "Let's get aboard."

☙❧

Cassius Marius was overjoyed to see the first rays of sunlight spill over the far eastern mountain range as the day of his departure from the miserable land of Kush finally arrived. The prefect had departed before sunrise a few hours earlier, and now his own time was nearly at hand. His young aide finished lacing up his armor, offered a quick bow, then departed from the tribune's tent, stopping only to gather a duffle containing Marius's possessions.

The tribune was inspecting the rough map of the Nile Valley he had received from Petronius when two centurions entered and smote their chests in salute. Phoebus Lucullus and Evander Leontius stood at attention as Marius continued to peruse the map. After a moment, the fair-headed tribune returned their salute and invited them to the table.

"I'm making an adjustment to the plan we outlined last night," Marius said, referring to the diagram. "Phoebus, your suggestion of capturing a Kushite soldier and torturing him for information turned out to be a premonition. Last night, one of the patrols brought in a man identified as one of the Queen's bodyguards. Centurion Atticus Camillus has been overseeing the interrogation."

"Hopefully he will give us more to go on," Lucullus said. "It's a vast amount of territory we have to cover with just 1,450 men."

"At the very least, we now have an idea of where she may be headed," Marius reported, noting that Lucullus's armor was still covered with grime and soot from the battle. "We've known for some time there are significant numbers of soldiers from their disbanded northern regiments in the area they call Kerma. We have reason to believe that she may attempt to go there."

Leontius glanced at the map and shook his head. "That journey will take weeks. It's unlikely she'll make it that far."

"I share that sentiment, Leontius, but assuming she is not running aimless like a scared rabbit and Kerma is her goal, we can anticipate where she will go." Marius grinned as he studied the various settlements along the Nile as one would a puzzle. He loved the thrill of the hunt and was anxious to get started.

"Is it still the plan to stop at each city?" Lucullus asked.

"I've modified the strategy. The prefect has left us with three cohorts at our disposal, so we will take a staggered approach. At any given time, one cohort will travel ahead on the river, while two will march on the road that runs adjacent to the Nile, searching the towns and villages. They will alternate at these points," Marius instructed, pausing to point out landmarks denoted on the rough map.

"Tribunes Publius's cohort is already on the river, while Tribune Ventidius is currently leading his cohort up the road as we speak. Their first stop will be a town called El-Kurru. Your centuries will be with me as we set sail in a several hours. Hopefully we will outpace our missing monarch and eventually out flank her as well."

"If Fortune smiles on us, we will catch her in a vice," Leontius said, nodding in approval.

"Gamal Abasi from the evocati ranks will travel with our cohort and serve as interpreter for the expedition," Marius added. "He's Egyptian born and is fluent in the Kushite dialect." Not many dark-skinned men impressed Marius, but Abasi did so thoroughly.

Lucullus lifted a dubious eyebrow and folded his arms. "Tribune, I am honored to be part of this plan, and I understand the significance of capturing this woman. However, what if the natives resist? We will be badly outnumbered."

Marius rolled up the parchment containing the diagram and threw the centurions a bullish scowl—one reminiscent of a schoolmaster annoyed by a foolish question asked by a student who should already know the answer.

"Having at least one cohort on the river every day will help mask our true numbers," Leontius speculated optimistically. "This strategy will make it appear as if there are tens of thousands of us."

"That's correct," Marius affirmed. "News travels quickly throughout the Nile Valley; that much we know for certain. For a primitive lot, the darkies have a rather effective communication network. Having said that, if we crucify the natives by the bushel, they will soon get the message and keep their distance. They may even give us the Queen themselves to stop the bleeding."

"Very well. Let the hunt begin," Lucullus proclaimed with a grin.

🐚🐚

Amanirenas was surprised at how quickly the Nile's strong current moved the sizable barge along—especially given that its primary cargo consisted of cattle and bighorn oxen. An occasional gust of wind bellowed at the back of the barge, propelling it even faster toward its destination. The drafts, however, provided little relief from the relentless early morning sun assaulting them from above.

The insistent rays showered them for at least two hours before Amanirenas could bear it no longer and removed the cloak that covered the black and gold dress she wore. She found a secluded section of the barge upwind of the cattle and leaned against a rail to grapple with her thoughts.

She turned to the south. Every hour she spent on the barge took her further away from Meroë and from her daughter. Uncertainty gripped her like a vice, as she had no idea if the Romans had pressed on southward to Meroë after obliterating Napata or marched back up the northern wadi road that had brought them to the region. She needed to know if her last child was safe, and her motherly instincts urged her to go back.

She bowed her head and petitioned Amun to protect Amanitore. Nothing would be more devastating to her than for the Romans to apprehend and deport the teenager to Rome to be strangled before a mass of vicious strangers. She closed her eyes and tried to shake the perverse image from her mind. Sadly, only when she imagined the thin strap of leather constricting her own neck, forcing blood from her eyes, did the horrific vision of her daughter suffering the same fate abate.

"Are you all right?"

Grateful for the distraction, Amanirenas opened her eyes and searched for the owner of the calming voice. Khai stood nearby, examining her closely. She glanced back across the river and exhaled heavily. The horseman was far more even tempered than the other two soldiers were, but there was something about him that struck a chord deep in Amanirenas. His mannerism reminded her of a sailboat cutting through the opposing current at the behest of the mighty wind. Although progress seemed improbable, it nonetheless came at a sure and steady pace. It was an attribute she longed for now.

"How the gods must love putting us to the test," Amanirenas said, looking away from him.

"Do you speak of rebuilding your army?"

"No. Nothing that simple," Amanirenas replied, a corner of her lip fighting to offer a smile. "I'm talking about motherhood. Everything in me wants to go back and ensure my daughter's safety. The horrific thing is that I may spend the rest of my life not knowing what happened to her."

"I'm sorry." Khai said as he took a place next to her along the railing.

"Sorry for what?"

"For what you're going through."

"What do you mean?" Amanirenas questioned, turning toward him.

"You have a family that you love. People do not see you that way. They see your image on the side of a temple or in the form of a statuette. It's difficult for common people to see the sacred Queen-Mother as a mother with children of her own that she obviously cares for."

"I don't understand why people would have such a callous impression of me or any other kandace. I have feelings as anyone else would," Amanirenas stated, her hands subtly clutching the rail until her knuckles turned white.

"I don't mean to offend, my queen. But the people outside of the palace and noble class have never seen a kandace as a regular person. How many times have they seen a kandace carry a load of laundry to the fuller or fetch water from the river?"

"Servants do those things. Besides, the queen has the burden of leading, and that involves thinking—which is something most common people do not do very well."

"They would if they were taught to think."

Amanirenas offered a dismissive smile. "I'd forgotten. You have been educated. I'm curious, has it made a difference for you?"

Khai raised a questioning eyebrow; however, before he could answer the Queen drew his attention elsewhere.

"See that fisherman over there?" Amanirenas pointed to an old man in a boat anchored not far from the shoreline. The old man methodically cast a net into the water and busied himself by pulling the ropes closer to his tiny boat. "Chances are he is illiterate and has never read an inscription from a parchment. Chances are he has spent his entire life pulling fish from the Nile in that very same spot.

"And chances are he is completely content with the life the gods have given him to live and doesn't care one bit about what is happening in Makoria or Alondia, or who the kandace is, for that matter."

Khai watched in silence and their barge glided past the stationary boat. The old man stayed in view just long enough for them to watch him haul in an impressive catch of fish.

"That catch will feed his family or maybe allow him to barter for clothing," Amanirenas said as their barge turned along a bend in the river. "Either way, it doesn't matter to him that Napata has been burned to the ground. Or that the Queen-Mother just sailed past him on a desperate task to organize the last standing army in the kingdom. Being uneducated and unaware has its advantages."

Khai looked at her and noted the deep frown lines that creased her brow. He knew that she was in her forties, yet at the moment she looked at least a decade older, her face hardened and battered by time and a gambit of intense emotions inextricably linked to her title and position. He searched in vain for the legendary beauty that purportedly captured King Teriteqas with graceful femininity. Nevertheless, he found only the dark, unsentimental face that had driven the once mighty Kushite army to the brink of disaster.

"I agree, my kandace. It probably does not matter to him what the Queen-Mother is doing now. Chances are he's never seen her before anyway." With that, Khai bowed and backed away.

☒☒

Batae was used to the stale odor given off by the massive cattle. To his surprise, he found that the rank smell of the beasts ignited memories of his childhood. For a moment, he saw himself herding the few cattle they had past the droves of sheep on their property. He tried to imagine what life would be like back on the farm. He was less than a day from returning to that wearisome life and wondered if it would be better simply to drift along the Nile all the way to Egypt.

He spun the tip of his short sword on the deck of the barge as he sat on a bench along the railing. His attention drifted from the Queen to his errant fellow soldier Pedese. For the moment, Pedese's attentiveness was pinned on the Queen's young servant, who at times seemed to relish the man's brash focus.

Batae silently wagered how long it would take the intractable young man to set his lust upon the Kandace herself. Batae almost longed for the lad to do so, knowing that the disrespectful action would prompt Sabrakmani to execute the deathly threat he had issued when the two soldiers agreed to accompany them to Kawa. The sum of gold offered by the chief bodyguard warranted at least a modicum of military discipline from Batae. However, the reckless Pedese was another case.

Batae's eyes drifted past the solitairy Queen and across the river. The sails affixed to the mast momentarily impeded his view, however, once they moved, a new vessel came into sight. It was a raft but shaped like none he'd ever seen before. It cut across the water very quickly and possessed a square sail—again, unlike any he'd seen. Behind the strange craft was another, and another, and yet another. Batae rose to get a clearer view, but was met with the alarmed visage of Sabrakmani, followed by Khai.

In an instant, all of them converged on the Kandace—concerned, yet uncertain what to do.

"How many do you think?" Amanirenas asked Sabrakmani. She quickly donned the commoner's cloak to conceal her dress, though she doubted it would do any good.

"I'm not sure. Four hundred. Maybe more," Sabrakmani responded, noting how quickly the vessels cut through the water. It was then that he noticed that each raft was being propelled by oarsmen whose efforts multiplied the wind and the current to move the vessels at a very high speed.

"Bastards are cheating," Pedese cursed.

"We'll have to get to shore," Amanirenas said.

"It isn't going to matter," Khai stated. "They are way too fast, and we would just look suspicious forcing our pilot to run a barge aground abruptly."

"He's right," Sabrakmani noted. "We'll find out in a moment what their intentions are."

Sabrakmani subtly shifted their party amongst the cattle, careful to keep Amanirenas behind him and Khai. The Roman vessels pushed hurriedly past the barge, making it apparent to Sabrakmani that the foreigners had a specific destination in mind.

The Romans passed close enough to them that Amanirenas could hear the dull grinding of the amour as the Romans moved about. She watched like a hawk as the men—many with grimy faces—chattered away in their peculiar dialect and went about their tasks. Only when the fading sound of the oars splashing into the water began to smother their words did she silently exhale in relief.

"Is that all of them?" Saiesha asked, shaking her head. "Where are they going?"

"I think that was a full cohort," Khai noted as their barge rocked smoothly in the wake of the Roman passage.

"Six centuries, from the looks of it," Sabrakmani added. "We may not know their destination, but at least we know what their intentions are." Sabrakmani looked at the Kandace and noted the glimmer of hope in her stony eyes.

"They aren't heading to Meroë," she said with a seedling of gratitude growing within her.

"At least that group isn't," Batae said, scanning the horizon aft of the barge. "But there are thousands more of them out there."

Chapter 15

Amanirenas sat patiently on an ancient brick wall that followed some long-forgotten boundary for at least two hundred *cubits*. Most of the short wall was obscured by overgrown vines, young palm trees, and an assortment of brush. In the clearing before them was a road that led to El-Kurru, a town as old as the wall on which she sat. Scores of people meandered along the dirt road, some approaching the city, while others were on their way to the port leading to the Nile waterway.

The town itself was unassuming and consisted of the standard dry-brick buildings and temples, with the most prominent structure being the Temple of Amesemi. Next to it sat Amanirenas's prime point of interest: the central dufufa and office of the peshte.

She stood up and paced uneasily. She was accustomed to entering cities announced and with a measure of pomp, prompting the officials, most of whom had been appointed by her husband, to turn out in tribute. Nevertheless, Sabrakmani insisted that she wait at the outskirts of the city while he, Khai, and Pedese went ahead.

"Give them more time," Batae said as he took another bite of the large red melon he held. He peered through the soaring palm trees to locate the sun. "They should be back soon."

"The Kandace is not used to waiting or hiding like this," Saiesha declared. "This is her kingdom. This city belongs to her."

"You don't have to remind me," Batae muttered, spitting out several seeds.

"That she should have to evade the very people that worship her is absurd. They owe everything to her...."

Batae took another huge bite from the melon and grinned at the young woman as he slowly chewed the mouthful. The Queen's servant made the same arguments several times with Pedese, and each time she ended up demeaned and insulted in a rude and vulgar way.

"And don't tell me she is to blame for the Romans. She's done everything possible to protect the people of Kush from them," Saiesha persisted.

"She hasn't done everything she can possibly do. Not yet." Batae watch the Kandace for a reaction, but he received none. "She could always give herself over to the Romans. That would be a true act of selflessness on her part."

"I expect such words from the imbecilic Pedese, but I thought you esteemed your queen higher than that," Saiesha said.

"If only the Queen esteemed her own people," Batae said in an accusatory tone. "If only the Queen regarded their welfare to the degree you esteem hers."

Amanirenas turned to the soldier as if he had issued a challenge. She held the man's stony gaze for a moment, absorbing the unspoken rancor tucked away in his sarcastic words.

"How far away are we, Batae?" the Queen asked.

"From what?"

"Your home. I heard you say your father's land is outside El-Kurru." Amanirenas moved closer to the man. "Sabrakmani mentioned you will likely stay here after I conclude business with the peshte."

"That was the arrangement," Batae answered. "He said I would be paid at that point."

Amanirenas nodded. "What are you going to do with the gold?" she asked.

"What does it matter to you?"

"What Pedese will do with the amount he is contracted for is not difficult to imagine. You, on the other hand, are not like him. I'm curious to know how you would spend your portion."

Batae chucked the crimson melon husk over his shoulder with contempt. "If you must know, I will probably use it to pay the taxes imposed on my father by the damn *pelmes-adab* in that dufufa. You have nothing to worry about. The money you pay me with will be coming right back to your coffers."

"You have no idea how the tax and tribute system is set up," Amanirenas said, lifting a skeptical eyebrow. "I do not personally benefit from the taxes you pay."

"Neither do we!" Batae retorted firmly. "While I'm sure they contribute something to your administration, the peshte and pelmeses live very comfortably on the backs of the poor farmers in this district. But that is something you wouldn't notice."

"You speak as if you are a judge over me. Yet, you have no place to do so," Amanirenas stated, her face starting to warm in anger. "I grow weary of you men accusing me over protocols you don't even understand."

"It's not an accusation; it is a statement of fact! I have traveled to dozens of cities fighting this war, and it is always the same. You never saw it because you never took the time. I understand oppression, Your Highness. I understand agreeing to work for a day's wage, but only receiving half of what was promised from the pelmes-adab."

"The Kandace is not responsible for the actions of regional administrators," Saiesha interjected.

"Yes, she is!" Batae exclaimed, rising to his feet. "To the east of this city is a barren section of land hundreds of people live on and try to wrestle some sort of living from the ground. They live in brick huts with palm tree fronds for roofs. Entire families live in a single hut. Have you ever seen how these people are forced to live?"

"I've seen poverty, Batae. But my greater concern is with pushing out the invaders and securing our borders," Amanirenas answered.

"No, your greater concern should be with making sure the administrators you appoint are serving the people instead of raping them. As far as the people on the east side of this city are concerned, you are the rapist—you and your entire family."

"Your contempt is misplaced, Batae. The true transgressors have pale skin and have burned down the center of our heritage. They are the true enemy you choose not to see. If they had their way, they would ship you back to their land as a slave."

Batae let out a soft laugh as he once again reclined on the wall. "Perhaps that's what you're afraid of. When the Romans take over, your kind will be the commoners with little value in their economy. You will be the hidden population no one cares about. You'll be the slaves."

Amanirenas stared blankly at Batae, somehow held captive by his simple words. Her heart quickened as she allowed the image of Roman overlords heartlessly dismantling and disregarding the very system that had cultivated her family for generations.

"The Kandace will never be anyone's slave," Saiesha declared, hoping to shield the Queen from the humiliation the man so blatantly heaped upon her.

"No, she won't," Batae answered, noting the approach of Sabrakmani and the others. "She won't be a slave because she'll be dead. The Romans will see to that—most efficiently."

"If we were under different circumstances, I would have you impaled for the words that have come from your mouth," Amanirenas said, turning back to see a rare grin grace Sabrakmani's face.

"Impaled for what? Speaking the truth? Something you obviously don't want to hear. I'm sorry, my kandace, but you're the one who is blind," Batae retorted.

The smile on Sabrakmani's face slowly melted away as he quickly sensed the tension between the Queen and Batae. "I've arranged a meeting with the pelmes-adab. He was relieved you survived the battle at Napata."

"Very well," Amanirenas said with a nod. "You were concerned about going into the city?"

"We won't have to worry about that," Sabrakmani answered. "We've arranged to meet at a place to the north. Batae, are you familiar with Kuduna Rock?"

"Yes, it's a hill between the city and the northern farmland. It is a lookout point. It will be easy to see someone approaching from a long way off."

Sabrakmani nodded in approval, shifting his eyes between the Queen and the soldier. "Excellent. I have your payment. After you escort us there, you are free to go."

※ ※

Amanirenas vaguely remembered the pelmes-adab of El-Kurru, recalling only that he was older than she and had occupied the administrative post since the reign of her parents, decades before. The man was escorted by three guards, and surprisingly, he made it up the rocky outcropping in no time at all.

"Kandance Amanirenas, praise be to Amun for guiding you through the horrific carnage at Napata. I am Omuro," the man greeted with a bow. "I live to serve you, my queen."

Amanirenas received his greeting with a slight nod, as well as a wave of relief. It had been days since she had been addressed formally, and his gracious mannerisms ushered in a craving for more stable times. "Thank you, Pelmes Omuro. I understand you have served in your position for quite a while."

"Yes, my kandace. Your mother, Amanikhabale, recommended me to the vizier, and I have been here ever since."

Amanirenas glanced at Batae in the background. The soldier was in earshot, but stood aloof, looking north.

"Pelmes Omuro, I trust you understand the importance of the situation that my aide explained to you."

"Yes, my kandace, but the honorable Sabrakmani didn't divulge any details about your intentions. A runner brought the report about what happened at Napata yesterday." The elderly pelmes-adab clasped his hands respectfully and for once looked Amanirenas directly in the eye. "Many of the young men who went to fight in Napata have yet to return, and many here feel that they never will. Up until today, the main question has been whether or not there is still a Kushite empire."

"That question is irrelevant as long as there is breath in my body.

The empire exists, and it will exact revenge for what the Romans have done."

A deep frown quickly enveloped Omuro's aged face. "But how? Not only is your army gone, but support for your monarchy has waned."

"Explain," Amanirenas pressed.

"Even before the battle at Napata, many nobles within this city had expressed the desire to capitulate to the Romans. Many of them understood that this was no longer going to be a war fought by the poor, and that sons of the noble class would now also have to go and resist the Romans. While there are those who are driven to retain the kingdom by a sense of honor, the ranks of those who are willing to exchange the Kushite system for the Roman way has swelled."

"They have no idea what Roman rule would entail," Amanirenas stated firmly.

"Nor do they care, my kandace. They simply want stability," Omuro responded.

Amanirenas shook her head defiantly. "We have to keep fighting. The Romans must pay for what they have done. By the gods, they cannot be allowed to ransack our land and ... kill our loved ones."

"I agree," Omuro said reflectively. "However, there are those in this city who, if they knew you were here, would capture you and give you over to the Romans to curry favor with them."

"Such an action would be useless and foolish."

"Again, I agree, my queen. The gazelle does not attempt to curry favor with the lioness in hopes that it will not be eaten. The lioness stalks and kills by its nature."

Amanirenas studied the dignified old man, noting that he never attempted to gain equal footing with her, instead remaining on a rock face situated below the one she stood on. His choice to stand fast in his position intrigued and impressed her.

"What are your intentions, Omuro?"

"I am an old man, my kandace. I have served this kingdom, served the Amani-aa'ila, served our gods for my entire life. I intend to die in the same posture in which I have lived these many years. I don't know how you can possibly preserve the kingdom that was bequeathed to you, but however you do so, you will have my blessing and humble support."

Omuro offered her a warm patriarchal smile, and for an instant, Amanirenas saw her own father looking up at her. She silently allowed herself to bathe in the warm sensation of acceptance and approval that was found only through the relationship between a father and daughter.

"Thank you, Omuro."

Chapter 16

Tribune Marius was impressed by the artisanship put into the gold and turquoise necklace he was scrutinizing. The artistry and attention to detail rivaled anything produced in Rome, and he instantly decided to keep the exquisite piece.

"A rather conspicuous way to pay for passage on a barge," the tribune said, handing the necklace to an aide. "Store this with my things."

"The merchant said that the necklace was rendered as payment for six people," Gamal Abasi continued, his thick Egyptian accent peppering his words. "Two women and four men."

"One of the women could have been the Queen, and the four men what's left of her bodyguard," Centurion Lucullus proposed.

Abasi took a deep swig from his leather canteen in an effort to beat back the oppressive Nubian heat. "Or it could be more of their noble class fleeing the area using whatever they have as payment."

"Noble class," Marius mocked with a dry smile. After almost two years in Kush, he had yet to see any faction of people that could rightly be compared with Roman patrician or equestrian classes. He paused and pondered both men's assessments. Traffic along the Nile had increased drastically over the past couple of days, since the attack on Napata. It appeared that those with means were migrating southward—deeper into Kush, in the general direction of Meroë.

However, the last report they had had on the Queen had pointed her due north.

"Where was this barge headed?" Marius asked.

Abasi glanced down at the few notes he had managed to capture. "The merchant said it was being piloted ultimately to a village outside of Kawa. However, it was due to stop several times, the first being in El-Kurru."

Marius surveyed the terrain currently occupied by his centuries. Their distance from the river port gave him a slight measure of security, although the wilderness to the east gave him pause. "Lucullus, have the men make camp in the clearing ahead. The timber in the forest ahead should be a suitable source for stockade tonight and rafts tomorrow."

Lucullus offered a crisp salute and then hurried off to issue his own set of orders.

"Abasi, your thoughts on this merchant's claims," Marius demanded.

"These people are anxious. They are uncertain if we intend to kill them or leave them alone. That being said, insecure people are less likely to alienate or mislead a conquering force."

Marius nodded at the veteran's assessment. "Even though apprehensive people are less likely to attack, they are still likely to deceive to protect themselves."

"Yes, sir. I believe the lead from the merchant is a valid one."

Marius stroked his scruffy jaw, a touch of melancholy slowing his movements. "I was looking forward to crucifying some fool Kushite, but none has given me reason. We'll trust the word of this merchant and head to El-Kurru at first light."

☥ ☝

"The river would be so much faster," Saiesha said to the Queen, bemoaning their snail's pace trek as the two of them fought to keep up with the four men prodding before them, kicking up plumes of dust in their wake. "Not to mention cleaner."

Amanirenas fought the urge to order Sabrakmani to slow their pace; however, she knew he was in a race to reach their destination before the sun settled below the western horizon. The chief bodyguard opted to decline Omuro's offer to provide lodging for the evening in El-Kurru in favor of what would certainly be a more inconspicuous billet. While a little out of their way, the place would surely be safer than remaining in town.

With their objective in sight, Amanirenas increased her gait even more to catch a furtive glance of Batae as they approached his father's home. The simple, multiroom dwelling place sat in the midst of a lonely meadow, with only the soft baying of goats drifting through the early evening air. Thus far, Batae's face offered no indication of how he felt about his return home.

The door to the cottage opened, and an elderly black man stepped out to inspect the party that was approaching his dwelling. Even though the man's hair was white and his skin creased with wrinkles, Amanirenas instantly recognized his frame as an older version of Batae's muscular build. The rest of the party slowed to a stop as Batae continued to advance until the older man's eyes lit up with recognition and pride.

"Batae, you've come home," the man said softly as they stood eye-to-eye in the fading sunlight.

"Hello, Father." Before the words fully passed his lips, the older man embraced his son tightly.

Amanirenas smiled for the first time in days. The gods kindly graced her with the opportunity to see at least one family reunited.

☯ ஐ

"The Queen of Kush, in my home!" Malae exclaimed once again as he happily offered his surprise guests more wine. "When I was a boy, I once saw a kandace march past in a parade in Napata. I never thought I would actually have one reclining at my table! I am only sorry that I have no wife and that my house has no womanly touch. It has only been my son Rahman and I for nearly three years now."

"Your hospitality is greatly appreciated, Malae," Amanirenas said before Sabrakmani could respond. It was not customary for a monarch to directly address a commoner such as Malae. Nevertheless, the Queen was still moved by the father's emotional response to seeing his son. In fact, she listened attentively as Batae and his father made an effort to catch up with the events of the last three years.

Sabrakmani excused himself and stepped outside—a further departure from his normal protocol. The night air was still, and a fine mist settled over the meadow. It was the most peaceful scene the bodyguard had experienced in weeks, and he allowed himself a moment to bathe in the coolness of the night.

The door opened again, and within a moment, Khai was standing beside him.

"I take it old Malae is not a threat to the Queen," Khai stated with a slight grin.

"No, the man is simply happy to have his son back. And the Queen is happy to share the moment with them. I figure protocol can lapse for the evening."

Khai drank in the peaceful setting for a while before bringing up the issue that gnawed at both men.

"You don't trust Omuro."

"I do trust him," Sabrakmani responded with a frown. "His underlings are a different matter. The fact that he met us without them says that he disagrees with their views. They would likely turn the Queen over to the Romans."

"Obviously, that's why you wanted to keep moving and not lodge in town," Khai said. Although no one had complained openly, everyone in the group was disappointed when Sabrakmani declined the pelmes-adab's invitation for them to recline in his home for the evening.

"The fewer people we come into contact with, the better," Sabrakmani said, turning to Khai. He appreciated how the younger man thought strategically and was grateful to have a kindred mind to consult. "I'm afraid there are probably more who want to capitulate to the Romans than I thought. I think the safest thing to do will be to stay on the desert road to Kawa. It will take more time than by way of the river, but it should be more secure."

"It would help if we had more men," Khai reflected. "Losing Batae will make things more difficult."

"I've given that some thought as well," Sabrakmani noted, rubbing his eyes as if to brush away an unfavorable sight. "There is one person in the dufufa I can trust. He was a military liaison in Napata for many years. He may be able to provide a few men who can make the journey with us to Kawa."

"That will help," Khai said, glancing back toward the house. To his surprise, laughter bellowed throughout the modest home, suggesting a raucous party in full swing.

"I can't recall the last time I heard her laugh like that," Sabrakmani mused.

"I'm surprised she still knows how to laugh after all she's gone through. She's lost a great deal," Khai said.

Sabrakmani turned his full attention to Khai. Although the darkness made it difficult to read the man's face thoroughly, Sabrakmani was able to discern the growing concern for the Queen that Khai's voice gave away ever so slightly. Amanirenas had indeed lost a great deal. A husband, three sons, and possibly a daughter. The years of campaigning against the Romans had even consumed the extra weight that was customary for a Queen-Mother to carry. As a result, she was much leaner, with well-defined arms and legs. The fragranced and delicate mother and wife had given way to a coarse and caustic warrior who was at times more masculine than a kandace should be. The woman his cousin had married was virtually gone, transformed by war and vengeance.

"We can't let her lose anymore, Khai. She's meant to be a great woman, not a great warrior."

More laugher poured from the house and echoed throughout the misty meadow.

Sabrakmani stepped closer to Khai, as a moth would to a flame. "Teriteqas was a great king because he had a great woman behind him. The Romans took his life, and now they are taking her, piece by piece. We cannot let them turn her into a complete brute, otherwise we will lose everything."

"I understand," Khai affirmed slowly.

"We need to keep reminding her that she was a wife and a mother, and those positions will always outrank royal titles."

As Khai listened to Sabrakmani, he found himself considering his personal vow to avoid having a wife and family. For the first time, he wondered if his decision to avoid an intimate relationship with a woman actually made him less of a man. He wondered just how much of his life he had forgone because of a childhood fear.

"Perhaps we should go back in and join the party," Sabrakmani said, turning toward the door. "Pedese and I will head into town at first light in the morning. Hopefully, we will be back by midday."

Chapter 17

It was like old times to Batae. Unfortunately, it was something he did not wish to remember. At dawn, he joined his father and younger brother as they herded a flock of goats from the barn to clean it. Aside from all the foul places that battle had taken Batae, nothing compared to the scent of a feces-laden barn. Only the company of his father and brother made the task bearable.

Rahman had arrived home late last night—after their guests had bedded down for the evening. He and Batae burnt at least a cruise and a half of oil into the early morning hours as they talked about everything from the cliffs of Kerma to the temples of Napata. Unlike many young men his age, Rahman had no desire to hear about the savagery of battle and instead asked about the customs of the Roman invaders. Batae appreciated the boy's curiosity and did his best to satiate it.

After a while, Malae sent Rahman to escort the goats to a protected part of the pasture. He turned to his eldest son, who continued to rake goat droppings into large piles.

"The gold I gave you last night should cover the taxes against the farm," Batae declared.

"Our taxes have been paid, Batae," Malae responded, watching his son toil with a particularly difficult clump of dung. "The last couple of years have been profitable. It isn't like it was when you left. Rahman is a man now. He works hard and is very good with the accounting. He is a difficult man for the merchants to cheat."

Batae grunted as he managed to pry the dry dung from the ground. "Perhaps you can take the gold and buy him a formal education."

"Don't have to. The pelmes-ate has been investing in his education for the past year."

"The pelmes-ate?" Batae exclaimed. "That corrupt, thieving jackal?"

Malae smiled. "The jackal has a good heart. He wanted to send Rahman to study in Napata; however, the war prevented him from doing so. Instead, he's had Rahman spending time with the Hebrew merchants. They are very good with numbers."

"Hebrews? They'll have him praying to their One God if you're not careful."

"I don't think so," Malae replied with a smile. "We're all hoping things will return to normal soon, but based on what I heard last night, I don't know if normal will ever return to Kush."

"You'll have to ask the Romans about that," Batae said stoically. "They're the new masters of Kush."

"I'm no soldier, Batae, but I can see the look of desperation on the Kandace's face, despite her efforts to hide it. However, she seems to believe there is hope that the kingdom will survive."

"Kush will survive," Batae offered after a moment. "It just won't be the Kush she was given to rule and stupidly lead into the jaws of Anubis. There will be a future. It just won't include her."

Malae sighed. "Then it won't include us either."

"It doesn't matter who runs the kingdom, and you know it. The wealthy crap on people like us the way the goats do on this floor. Afterwards, they kick us to the side smelling like piss."

"Some do, but not all, Batae. Some of them are concerned about the future. I think Rahman is proof of that." Malae grasped the shovel Batae held and gently pulled it away. "Rahman is keen like his mother was. You are smart like her as well. Both of you were meant for more than being goat breeders. Rahman has a chance at being much more. And you have a chance to help him."

"How is that?" Batae asked, looking away.

"I'm an old man. I cannot go out and fight for the Queen. But you can." Malae stopped to clear his throat prompting Batae to turn and face his father. "I wonder what your mother would have thought if she had known that one day, the Queen of Kush would recline at her table?"

"She would have cleaned the walls," Batae said, a tear trekking down his dark cheek.

"Yes, she would have," Malae conceded, wiping the tear from his face. "I know there are more things you want to do in life, but sometimes we are given things we have to do."

"You think I should stay in this war?"

"I think someone needs to fight for Rahman's children and their children after them. Someone needs to help protect the future."

Batae closed his eyes and envisioned the advancing Roman century on the battlefield outside of Napata killing everything it its path as it moved like a single-minded metallic herd. "Father, I don't know if there is a future. These Romans, they're the vision of death."

"I've never seen a Roman before. But I've seen a young Kushite named Batae fend off a lion that threated his mother and baby brother. I didn't think I could've been prouder of you then. But that was before today."

Malae gripped his son's shoulder and squeezed it tightly. "The Queen trusts you. And she needs you."

Batae was about to respond when Rahman rushed back into the barn.

"Batae, one of your companions has returned from El-Kurru."

"Only one?" Batae questioned.

"Yes, he rushed right into the house to talk to the Queen. I think something is wrong."

☥ ☧

Gamal Abasi glared menacingly into the face of Sabrakmani as he awaited a reply from the Kushite. Tribune Marius stood aloof, growing tired of the interrogation and the Kushite's obtuse attitude. The man was bound and flanked by two soldiers who were ready to terminate the prisoner as soon as the tribune issued the order.

"You have been identified as Amanirenas's chief bodyguard by multiple witnesses," Marius stated once again. "Where is the Queen?"

Gamal Abasi translated the tribune's words once again and was again met with a defiant stare. Marius nodded to one of the soldiers, who promptly dug the hilt of his sword into the small of Sabrakmani's back. The Kushite grunted in pain but held the gaze of the man serving as the interpreter.

"As one who works closely with the Queen, I'm sure you understand that we have very painful ways extracting information from our enemies." After the translation went through, Marius nodded again to a soldier, who quickly hurdled a fist into Sabrakmani's face, snapping his head violently to the side.

Dazed, the Kushite recovered and returned his focus Abasi, ignoring everyone else in the room. Blood began to flow profusely from a gash to his lower lip.

"Blood. You're about to lose a great deal more of it," Marius asserted coldly. He turned to leave and gestured for Abasi to follow. The two men left the chambers holding Sabrakmani and marched down the central hallway of El-Kurru's dufufa, a quartet of heavily armored legionaries following them.

Marius stopped in front of a trio of Kushite officials. The tribune locked eyes with the man in the middle. He could not remember the man's title, much less his name, although he understood him to be an underling of what the Kushites called a peshte—a rank roughly equal to a Roman prefect.

"I do believe that man is indeed the Queen's bodyguard. That means that she cannot be too far away. Therefore, we must execute a thorough search for her immediately."

The men looked at one another warily as Abasi translated the tribune's decree.

"If you value the lives of your people, you will make haste to advise them not to impede our search for the war criminal Amanirenas."

The men exchanged glances once again, bowed, and hurried off.

"What about him?" Abasi asked, gesturing to the chamber holding Sabrakmani.

Marius frowned, a tinge of frustration flowing from his visage. "I've interrogated bodyguards before. That man is trained soldier and he will not easily relent. He will die first, so we'll have to make his death a spectacle to be remembered by the others. That's about all he's useful for at this point."

Chapter 18

Khai led the Queen's retinue away from the El-Kurru region at a brisk and steady pace. Judging from the sun, nearly six hours had passed since they had gathered a few supplies from Malae and headed north along the desert road toward Kawa. Despite the brief contention that arose in regard to the route they should take, Khai had managed to convince them that it was best to proceed with Sabrakmani's plan of eschewing the riverway in favor of the back road. He was convinced that the chief bodyguard would never divulge the route to his captors.

Khai looked back at the group every four hundred paces or so. Batae mainly stayed with the Queen, while Pedese opted to bring up the rear. The brash soldier said very little after relaying the details of Sabrakmani's abduction. To his credit, the normally verbose young man succinctly described how the bodyguard had instructed him to wait out of sight while he himself went into a building across the way from the dufufa. There was no way for Sabrakmani to have seen the column of Roman legionaries emerge from the other side of the large admin building.

Sabrakmani came out of the building with another man, but he was hastily pointed out by a young noble standing with a Roman officer. It happened quickly, and Sabrakmani did not resist.

"It was the bravest thing I've ever seen," Pedese said as he described how several Romans had descended on Sabrakmani. His companion had started to protest, but Sabrakmani had uttered something to the man that caused him to slowly back away. Sabrakmani had glanced briefly in Pedese's direction before he was whisked away into the dufufa. "He didn't put up a fight. He just went with them."

Sabrakmani's arrest was a shock, but Khai knew exactly what needed to be done. And though he was stunned when Batae abruptly announced his intentions to continue with the Queen and escort her wherever she needed to go, he had somehow known that the warrior would change his mind.

The Queen was a different matter. She said next to nothing after Pedese's testimony and only briefly debated the merits of using the desert road. Other than that, she was quiet, with the only conversation during their hasty trek northward coming via Batae and Saiesha, as Batae described the purpose of the old road on which they travelled.

At Batae's behest, they veered from the old road down a path leading them through a thick forest that extended for at least a thousand cubits. When they came to a clearing, they were met with a forest of stone monuments, temples, and pyramids.

Amanirenas silently noted the burial ground as one of the last royal cemeteries from the ancient kingdom of Kerma. Her eyes filled with tears, heated with a confused mixture of anger and grief. She paused before one of the more prominent pyramids at the cemetery's heart and slowly ran her hand along the inscription of the structure's adjoining funerary chapel.

When Khai doubled back to find her, her quiet sobs had given way to bitter tears and anguished groans. Saiesha moved to console her, but the Queen swatted the young woman back, wanting to embrace her grief utterly and alone. Pedese watched for a brief moment and then wandered away, his head bowed in reverence. Batae, too, slowly drifted from the scene, quietly followed by Saiesha.

Khai was about to afford the Queen her privacy as well, but instead found himself approaching her. The sobs gradually subsided as he drew near.

"This is the tomb of Sabrak," she said in a hushed voice. "Sabrakmani was ... is ... a descendant of the king in this crypt.

Sabrakmani was so proud to bear this name. He was ... he is ... so honorable and brave."

She turned to Khai, her vision blurred by tears. "He was chosen by my husband over fifteen years ago to lead the bodyguard. I didn't like him at first; in fact, I hated him. He is ... he was ... always so formal, always following rules. But he was ... is ... so dedicated."

Amanirenas leaned against the tomb and tried to compose herself. The effort was short lived as she once again fell into a pond of sorrow. "He always tried to help me understand my duty to the people and not just to my own family. I drew so much from him."

Khai reached out and drew her into an embrace—one she fell into without hesitation.

"He never let me forget," Amanirenas breathed, sorrowfully recalling the many times during the long campaign against the Romans that Sabrakmani had challenged her to look beyond the grief she had for her own family and to consider the greater good of the kingdom. It seemed that he alone was willing to dismiss the vaulted status of the Amani-aa'ila and attempt to corral her fury. It was an act she immensely respected and would miss.

"Now, I'm all alone."

Amanirenas was silent for a long moment as she gathered herself in Khai's embrace. The soldier's slow, rhythmic heartbeat helped her to relax. She drew in a gradual, long breath and then gently pushed away. He briefly glanced at her reddened eyes and noted a fiery resolve that was not there before. He knew at that point that she had somehow accepted her seemingly unending interval in the crucible of life and embraced the change it demanded from her.

Chapter 19

Amanitore felt the storm approaching the city of Meroë. In the distance, ominous dark clouds effortlessly pushed their way past the towering eastern mountains. Even though the late afternoon sky over the city was still blue, Amanitore knew a menacing tempest would soon engulf the region. In fact, she felt as if the storm were coming for her personally.

She hurried down the central corridor of the mansion that had served as her home for the past several months. In her teenage mind, it was a dreary substitution for the lovely palatial home her mother had created in Napata—a place to which she longed to return. Hope simmered in her heart that such would be the case when she received a message from Grand Vizier Matu. Rumor had it that a runner from Napata had arrived earlier with news regarding the war. Her brisk walk became a jog as she anticipated any word from her mother.

She arrived at the meeting chamber to see Matu standing stoically in the midst of four men, three of whom she knew were elders from her mother's war council. The men had arrived in Meroë some time ago and were just as anxious to hear of what had transpired at Napata as she was. The fourth was an exhausted-looking young soldier who was leaning against a table to prop himself up.

The room was silent. The three elders wore sullen expressions and appeared to be waiting for Matu to say something.

Amanitore slowly walked in, and all eyes gradually drifted toward her. Her heart quickened, and she immediately wanted to retreat from the chamber. Before she could move, the grand vizier broke the silence. "Please leave us," he said to the four men. "We'll discuss the details of succession later. The Council of Ministers will need to be convened right away."

The men bowed reverently and left the chamber, each one avoiding eye-contact with the teenage qar.

"Succession?" Amanitore questioned. "What happened to my mother?"

Matu rolled his eyes away from the qar, who moved closer. "There was a battle at Napata. The city was burned to the ground, and many of the temples were destroyed."

"And my mother?"

Matu moved toward the window just in time to see the first drops of rain sprinkle across the open blinds. "The army is gone. The Romans killed most of them, but many just ran away."

"Jaelen was young, but he would never run away," Amanitore said, shaking her head as she thought about the last of her older brothers.

"And he didn't," Matu drew a deep breath. "He's dead."

The weight of the revelation forced Amanitore to sit down on a nearby bench. She looked away in disbelief, but the distant thunder dramatically confirmed what her heart feared.

"My brother is dead," Amanitore said, fearful of the same violent torrent of emotions that had swept her away when her father was killed. She steeled herself for the onslaught that strangely did not come.

"I lost two sons," Matu said sorrowfully as he watched the rain start to cascade from the heavens. "Neither one had taken a wife...."

Amanitore stood up to leave. Perhaps if she left, any additional bad news would simply fade away. However, she knew that would never be the case.

"Where is the Kandace?" Amanitore asked.

"They do not know," Matu admitted. "The Romans surrounded her last known position. A few commanders were able to make their way across the Nile away from Napata. Once the outcome of the battle was obvious, they sent the runner here to Meroë."

"So they really don't know what happened to my mother?" Amanitore interjected, her eyebrows uplifted in hope. "She could have gotten away—Sabrakmani would never leave her. He knows that region very well...."

"They were surrounded by Romans, Amanitore."

The soft rebuke quickly backed the qar down. Even she had heard just how proficient the Roman invaders were once they set themselves to a particular task. Hope had little value or room to maneuver when confronted by 10,000 Roman legionaries.

"Even if she did survive the battle, the army is gone. She would have been all alone." Matu sighed and reluctantly embraced the conclusion that the elders had levied upon him just moments earlier. "With no knowledge about Amanishakheto's disposition in Nobatia, you are the sole ruler now."

Amanitore made no effort to mask her disappointment. "I suppose the Romans will be coming after me now," she said.

"The messenger said that the Romans had fabricated rafts prior to the battle. But there is no confirmation that they've headed southward—or northward. We should receive additional reports over the next few days." Matu said, wrestling with the myriad of thoughts assaulting his mind.

"What should I do?"

"What the Kandace said to do if this happened. Stay here," Matu replied. It was the only thing he was certain of at the moment. However, he was doubtful that the city militia of 1,050 men would do much good against the Romans, should they decide to come in mass.

Yet part of him wished they would. With each passing moment, he grew to understand the rage that slowly consumed Amanirenas as she, too, started to crave the bitter wine of revenge.

"You are the kandace now, Amanitore," Matu affirmed gently. "We are not going to abandon you."

Chapter 20

The Nile was uncharacteristically calm. In the five days that his cohorts had hastily traversed the waterway northward, this was the first time that Gaius Petronius had found the conditions serene enough to make an entry in his log. He sat in an isolated compartment on the river-going barge, his desk adjacent to a window, allowing him to see the western shore pass in the distance as the vessel meandered down the mighty river.

He leaned forward and searched for the words that would best commence his entry, yet all he found was a jumbled collection of tribal names he could not pronounce. His overall assessment of the Kushite sacred city was fragmented and incomplete. On one hand, the city of Napata possessed all of the qualities of an ancient distinguished city: dramatic lore, a royal necropolis, and an array of impressive temples that sat under the eye of a sacred mountain shaped like a crown.

The only thing missing was people. The veteran of countless campaigns against hordes of barbarian clans in the north, Petronius was used to the prospect of killing off entire tribes—primarily because their tendency was to fight the Romans to the last clansman, leaving the invaders with no recourse. Unlike other commanders, Petronius found the process grim, even if it was necessary. The result was always the same: the acquisition of pristine land essentially unmarred because of the primitive state of the former inhabitants.

However, the similarities unexpectedly ceased at that point, as Kush proved to be vastly different. First off, he noted the presence of a rudimentary municipal infrastructure that was standardized throughout the domain. Major towns and villages from Elephantine to Napata shared a common layout, complete with administrative and sacred edifices. The infrastructure was managed by a complex bureaucracy that featured multiple levels of administration, which ultimately terminated with the royal family.

None of this took Petronius by surprise, for upon his appointment, former prefect Aelius Gallus had briefed him, noting that the Kushites had loosely based their governmental structure on the Egyptian archetype. Yet he was surprised by the degree to which the Kushites had adopted and modified the model to what was turning out to be a representation of their own culture, as opposed to Egyptian. Nowhere was this more poignant than the blending of religion, governmental structure, and the royal family. Petronius was particularly intrigued by the concept of the Queen-Mother, who served as the figurative keystone to the entire system. That a king would share his power with a matriarchal figure and a ministerial council astonished him. What was even more amazing was the fact the system had a successful record that went back over a thousand years.

Time gradually slipped past, like the western shore outside. After a while, Petronius reviewed his entry and noted that he had spent most of it explaining how Kush was unlike the Gauls or other tribes the Romans had encountered in the north. He put down his stylus and looked outside in time to see a riverside temple pan out of view.

No one in the Egyptian arm of the Roman government had anticipated the need to march both the III and XXII legions into the heart of Kush. The campaign itself had not been a difficult one, but Petronius could not evade the sense that something was missing—like a cryptic specter lurking in the halls of a dark temple. The Kushite tribes possessed a common language, a common script, a common culture, and a common faith, yet they fought independently of one another, almost with a split personality. Petronius marveled at how ironic it was—as well as how fortuitous.

He glanced northward, his thoughts dwelling on Tribune Marius and his mission to track down the fugitive Queen of Kush. She was the key to dismantling a thousand-year-old system before it realized just how unique it was.

ᚡ ᚨ

Nestled several hundred cubits from the banks of the Nile, Kawa was more than three times the size of El-Kurru and the busiest city in the region. Its position along the river made it the perfect hub for the transfer of goods from the Northern provinces to the southern cities of Meroë and Napata. The city was large enough to accommodate a full governmental cabinet, headed by a peshte who reported directly to the province vizier in Kerma.

The bristling town was enclosed by a stout wall of brown sunbaked bricks that served as an added layer of security to protect the commerce flowing to and from the adjacent river port.

Amanirenas stood on a ridge that provided a picturesque vista of the temples and administrative buildings below. It was her first time seeing the city from an elevated vantage point. In fact, she had never set foot in the town and could only recall offering it a cursory glance from her barge during a trip to Kerma with her husband some ten years earlier.

"How long will it take us to get down there?" the Kandace asked, anxious to meet with the peshte. Surprisingly, Batae's rural path had led them to their goal much faster than she had thought it would. Though her thighs still burned from the constant climbing, and her feet ached from traversing the rock-studded path, she was nonetheless ready for the final leg of this particular journey.

"Not long," Pedese answered. "If we were going straight there, we would make it before the sixth hour."

Amanirenas arched an eyebrow at Pedese, who simply started down a trail leading into an area thick with foliage.

"We have to make a stop at my father's home," the soldier replied dryly. "It isn't far."

Khai stepped into the Kandace's line of sight. "His father is the chief scribe of the province, and according to him, is fiercely loyal to the Amani-aa'ila."

"Do you feel this necessary?" Amanirenas questioned, already formulating the order to go directly to the city.

"I think it wise," Khai said evenly. "The chief scribe should be able to provide insight into the mood of the pesthe and his adjutants. You'll at least know if it is safe to go to the dufufa or if we should go straight to Kerma."

The Queen nodded silently. The stop in El-Kurru had proved that Sabrakmani's fear of disloyal nobles was an imminent concern.

"We discussed it a couple of days ago," Khai added. "It was Pedese's idea."

"I'd forgotten," Amanirenas responded, starting down the path after Pedese, who was hacking through the overgrown tendrils impeding their path. Her mind was so shrouded with grief for most of the trek from El-Kurru that she hardly recalled a word spoken by anyone, let alone the garrulous foot soldier.

𓆯 𓆳

Saiesha closed her eyes and allowed herself to sink into the depths of the fluffy cushions. Tired and aching, she had no objection to drowning in the plush purple couch—if such a thing were possible. She hesitantly opened her eyes and peered around, anxious that the last several hours had been a product of her imagination. Nevertheless, it was true; she and the Kandace were once again in the lap of a luxurious estate. For the moment, gone were the screeching cackles of wild animals and relentless rays of the sun. She had even had the pleasure of a bath, a forgotten treat due to their long trek along the dusty road from El-Kurru.

The Kandace had freshened up as well, and Saiesha was glad to see her queen out of the frayed clothing that had served as her attire for far too long. While the beige and black tunic she now wore was far beneath the Queen-Mother's taste and fashion, it was, to say the least, a welcome upgrade.

Amanirenas stood with Ethaan, their benevolent host, near the entrance to a large courtyard decorated with palm trees and bright red and yellow flowers. Ethaan stood tall and seemed bathed in an aura of dignity that made it difficult for Saiesha to believe he was Pedese's father. The older man was strikingly handsome, with a presence that commanded respect and attentiveness. Saiesha had seen such men at court before, and they often possessed ulterior motives that the Kandace was generally adept at discerning. Yet this man seemed different in a way that made Saiesha monitor his conversation with the Queen, whose look of concern seemed to deepen by the moment.

"You say none of the peshte's administrators can be trusted?" Amanirenas questioned.

"A few days ago, a scribe from Napata met with the senior administrators. He described the bribes the Romans have been making to village and city officials to entice them to capture you and turn you over to their patrols." A wave of shame briefly swept across Ethaan's face. "The new pesthe and the others have agreed to do so should the opportunity arise."

"And what payment is to be made for my seizure?"

"Positions in the new Roman government that will likely be seated in Philae," Ethaan responded, holding the Kandace's gaze. He did so for a long moment, until she looked away in disgust.

"And they believe the Romans will honor any agreements they make?"

"The scribe's reasoning was sound. If the Amani-aa'ila has collapsed, then a new regime must be erected, which the Romans will not be able to administrate themselves. Those familiar with the Roman vassal system understand this is an opportunity to reshape the order of things in Kush."

"The Romans are conquerors," Amanirenas said. "What their legions do not murder swiftly, their senate will strangle slowly. They will take the gold, the food, and the people and will leave Kush an empty shell."

"That may be a fact, my kandace. But no one is left to argue it."

Ethaan grunted as he recalled how quickly many of his associates had embraced the idea of a Kush governed by Roman law.

"Even if something did happen to me, there is still a government in Meroë. My daughter, the council, the high priest, and the grand vizier are still alive," Amanirenas countered, more with her heart than her intellect.

"We don't know that for certain. None of the runners have made it from the south that we know of," Ethaan said evenly. "Furthermore, the scribe pointed out that the first order of business of the new Roman-backed government would be to force the region of Meroë to capitulate or burn it to the ground."

"What else?" Amanirenas questioned, certain that Ethaan was omitting information.

"Any surviving member of the Amani-aa'ila is to be taken to Alexandria and remitted to the Roman governor. There, they will face summary execution or a lifetime of slavery—whichever pleases Caesar best."

Amanirenas turned away and absorbed the news as one would absorb a slap to the face. It appeared that the enemy was not content with simply taking her husband's mistress. The Romans were dead set on transforming it into a vindictive lioness intent on slaying any offspring that did not belong to her.

"The scribe was clear, my kandace. The Romans understand the concept of the Queen-Mother and appreciate your importance as a symbol of Kushite autonomy. They understand that your capture and death will do more than end your regime: It will eradicate the spirit of Kush."

Saiesha sat in silence as she watched Amanirenas wrestle with Ethaan's unsympathetic description of her true plight. In the four years that Saiesha had been in the Queen's direct service, she had witnessed the matriarch run through a gambit of emotions, from love to sorrow to hate. Yet this was the first time the servant had beheld the Queen wrestling against hopelessness and despair.

"I knew there was dissatisfaction and even corruption among the nobles," Amanirenas said slowly, "but I hadn't realized it ran so deep."

The Queen found a chair and lowered herself into it as if she were preparing to be executed. Her thoughts were squarely upon her daughter Amanitore. "Perhaps I should give myself over to the Romans. Perhaps the people of Kush would find it in their hearts to protect my daughter. She could live in Meroë and not be a threat to Roman rule. She could live..."

"With nothing," Ethaan said flatly. "With no honor, with no hope, and with the constant fear that someone might betray her and sell her to Rome as a slave. To kiss the feet of a Roman governor or to bathe the grandchild of a Roman senator. That is how she would live."

"But she would be alive. You are a father, Ethaan. Preserving the life of your child is something you can appreciate."

"I can," Ethaan admitted with care, "but the death of our kingdom will guarantee the death of our children, my kandace. And it will be a slow death—one that will bleed out for generations."

Ethaan settled on a stool next to her. He longed to take her hand, but remained steadfast to the aptness of protocol instead. "You are the Queen-Mother of Kush. Whether or not you are the last one, I cannot say. However, Kush has stood erect for more than ten centuries. If she is to die, let her not do so willingly."

Amanirenas gazed silently at her hands. The years of campaign had converted her once soft and delicate hands that had lovingly raised four children into muscular hooks that now wielded swords, spears, and the reigns of battle-weathered horses. Gone were the even, deep brown tones of her hands. Gone also were the brilliant colors that used to adorn her fingernails. Gone was the extra weight she had so proudly worn since her marriage to Teriteqas. The conflict that had robbed her of her family was now clearly stealing away her womanly assets. At that moment, a firm resolve lodged in her heart. If she were to lose anything else, it would have to be taken away, for she could no longer afford to give it up.

"Kawa was never my final stop, Ethaan," she stated, finally looking the chief scribe in the eye. "My destination is Kerma. I need to find Mshindi, and Vizier Shabakar may know where he is."

Ethaan slowly nodded his head, his smooth black face sharing her newfound resolve. "The general. Word is he and what is left of the *Teriahi* regiment are somewhere northeast of Kerma. But that was months ago."

"I believe I may be able to persuade him to make another stand against the Romans."

"Some might call that a fool's errand," Ethaan said with an understanding smile.

"I'm sure that's what they said to Taharaq when he went against the Assyrians," Amanirenas affirmed with a smile of her own that miraculously withstood the cascade of fear and despair rushing past her soul.

Brushing protocol aside, Ethaan gathered her firm hands in his and squeezed them lightly. They were small but strong, and he prayed that they were capable of bearing the load she was taking up.

"You must leave immediately. I will see to it you have everything you need for the journey. Including a new detachment of bodyguards."

Chapter 21

Yet another small, dusty village yielded no fruit whatsoever. Tribune
Marius surveyed the area with an unimpressed eye and began to rue
the day Petronius had issued him the assignment of tracking down
the wayward queen of Kush. It was the fourth village his cohorts had
invaded since leaving the El-Kurru region, and the report was always
the same. The Romans experienced no resistance to their probes, for
everyone in the village scattered before they arrived. However, this
time, the tribune had surrounded the village before entering and had
actually managed to capture a few people—as wretched as they were.

Marius inspected the lot of twenty or so people, who were secured
by a quartet of legionaries. Upon closer look, the tribune noted that
the lot consisted of nothing but women and a few teenagers. Like the
prior village, nary a man was found.

Gamal Abasi hammered away with his standard battery of
questions, inquiring about a group of strangers traversing through
the region. As usual, the fearful inhabitants were gripped with fear
and offered nothing.

Legionaries combed through the village, rifling through the two
dozen or so brick huts with impunity. Occasionally, a soldier found a
bracelet or something of some inherit value to be looted, but this place
appeared to be too small to offer anything to be desired.

Marius exhaled with contempt. If the vast majority of Kush

consisted of towns like this, then Rome would be better off simply enslaving all of the people and consigning all of the men to the gladiatorial games. Save a few cities, most of the kingdom seemed to be little more than a dung heap.

Finally, Abasi approached the tribune and shook his head. "They said nothing."

"Of course," Marius muttered. "They said nothing, they know nothing, they are nothing."

Phoebus Lucullus appeared suddenly from behind a hut. The fact that his sword was sheathed declared to Marius that there was absolutely no threat in the vicinity.

"There's nothing around here," Lucullus barked, several legionaries trialing him. "Just a shrine to their crocodile god behind those trees. We did not even find anyone hiding in it this time. I think all of the men have run away."

"Or we killed them all at Napata," Abasi commented, rubbing his bearded chin.

"We're not looking for men. We're looking for the Queen," Marius said, folding his arms as he looked at the motley assortment of villagers—none daring to return his gaze.

"Far be it from me to question your tactics, Tribune," Lucullus spoke evenly. "It stands to reason that she would likely avoid large or small villages altogether."

"You're right, Phoebus. She likely took a back road heading north," Marius answered. Neither Publius nor Ventidius had managed to discern her trail as the three cohorts scoured the river and the adjoining road. He was gradually becoming convinced that there was another path leading to Kawa. He was about to say as much when he was approached by a tall legionary with harden eyes.

"We are ready, Tribune," the man reported, smiting his breast in salute.

"We are going to send another message to the government officials we've attempted to bribe in the other communities," Marius said to Phoebus while beckoning to the legionary. He then turned and motioned toward the huddled group of villagers. "That one and ... that one."

The Roman soldier signaled a companion, and together they extracted the two teenage boys singled out by the tribune.

"This method may be time-consuming, Phoebus, but it is necessary and balances out our other efforts."

Within moments, shrieks of pain seared through the village, driven by the harsh cadence of metal being struck by a hammer.

"I understand the need to instill fear among the populace, but isn't there a higher probability that someone in the government will sell her out? That method almost worked El-Kurru when we apprehended the bodyguard. Perhaps if we focused on that..."

"This is a country divided, Phoebus," Marius declared, his voice resonating above the escalating sobs of the horrified Kushite women watching from a distance as the young boys groaned in agony at the hands of their Roman tormentors. "We must work to keep it so."

Marius turned and cast a heartless yet approving eye upon the perverted artwork of his legionaries. He turned back to Phoebus. "The greed of her people will flush her out of the cities, Phoebus. But it's their fear that will flush her out of the bush."

𓏏𓂋

Why would a man want to leave paradise to go fight a war if he didn't have to? Batae asked himself as he followed Pedese and Khai into the stables adjacent to the plush estate that had served as their sanctuary for the past day. The spacious grounds were laden with fruit trees and more color than any part of the surrounding forest. It was apparent that Pedese's mother had made it a point to beautify the grounds to impress upon it a lasting touch of natural elegance before she died.

That the woman of the house had passed away was something Batae needed no one to confirm. Though the estate was picturesque and adorned with art and statuettes from various provinces of the kingdom, the soul of the house was stagnant, for it had no heart to give it life. In fact, there were times that Batae felt as if he were in a plush tomb for the living.

Perhaps that was the main reason why Pedese volunteered to enter the fray with the Romans, Batae thought.

As they entered the stables, they were greeted by Pedese's younger brother Pahor. Although a couple years younger than his brother, Pahor seemed years more mature. At times, the young man's mannerisms and inflections reminded Batae of his own younger brother Rahman, who was roughly the same age.

"These two horses will be the best ones for the journey," Pahor said to Pedese, who virtually ignored the boy as he passed by.

"These will do nicely," Khai expressed, inspecting the straps that would bear the load of the supplies.

"They have strong legs and have no aversion to river travel, so they should be fine whichever route we take," Pahor reported.

Batae furtively glanced at Pedese in expectation of the annoyed sneer that invaded his face when Pahor had referred to the upcoming journey to Kerma. Pedese had made it clear to their father that it was an errand for which Pahor was not suited. The boy had little formal combat training and even less exposure to the sordid men they would surely encounter once they entered the province of Kerma.

Nevertheless, despite his initial retort, Pedese said little after his father expressed his support for Pahor's inclusion in the expedition. Batae could tell that this was simply another chapter in a longer epic between a father and his oldest son.

"Most horses hate travelling on barges," Khai said. "I think they prefer to swim."

Pahor smiled at the comment. "My father said you were a cavalryman from Kerma and rode into battle with Paqar Jaelen at Napata."

"Yes," Khai replied quietly, stroking the mane of the horse nearest to him.

"Have you ever been past the great cataract north of Kerma?" Pahor asked.

"Several times. I'm from Semna."

"I've only journeyed south. My father has never let me head to the northern regions of the kingdom."

Pedese pushed over a few containers as he grudgingly forged through a pouch on a workbench until he found a couple of worn-out bridles. The clamor drew everyone's attention his way.

"There was a reason he restricted you to doing business to the south," Pedese snapped. "And I'm surprised he's forgotten it."

"In case you hadn't noticed, I am a grown man—who is taller and heavier than you..."

"Size means nothing against a Roman maniple!" Pedese stepped forward and glared up into his brother's brown eyes. "You are not ready for this."

"You've been gone a long time, Pedese. You're in no position to judge me, and I don't need your protection."

"You're a fool," Pedese spat, "and not even the gods will be able to protect you. War is not a game you can think your way out of. The best way to do so is not get involved in the first place."

Pahor shook his head. "Why do you even care? I do not understand why you are even going back out. Most men your age are gone. There are available women all over the region. I'm sure they'll welcome you back with more than just open arms."

A long silence filled the stable, and Batae marveled how much self-control Pedese had displayed during the interlude. It was quite the contrast to the arrogant young man who had verbally maligned superiors and fellow soldiers alike during their long years on campaign.

Finally, Khai broke the tense standoff.

"Pahor, we noticed there weren't many soldiers in the military barracks just east of the city's wall. Where are the men?"

"Some went north two years ago with the militia Pedese set off with," Pahor answered, glancing toward his brother. "But a little less than a year ago, another large contingent was reassigned to Kerma and placed under the command of Pelmes Mshindi. But from what I've heard, there is another commander further north who is something of a rival to the Pelmes."

"All other military commanders retreated south with the Kandace last year," Khai noted in an uncertain tone. "Mshindi is related to the King. Who would rival him?"

"The man's name is Amen-Tekah," Ethaan answered, standing at the stable entrance.

"An Egyptian?" Khai asked.

"He has some Egyptian blood from what I understand. He claims he's a descendant of the black pharaohs. It's how he legitimizes his assertion to rule."

"I've never heard of him," Khai said. "Where is he from?"

"Buhen."

Khai grunted. The only place more corrupt than Semna was Buhen. Both cities were known havens for the Blemmey marauders who occasionally raided Egypt. In fact, Buhen was notorious for attracting fearsome Medjay warriors from the Makorian desert regions, who were often hired as murderers.

"Reports from the north say he's managed to draw men away from Mshindi," Ethaan said, stepping into the stable. "The vizier thinks Amen-Tekah may have even been in contact with the Roman detachment in Qasr Ibrim in an attempt to establish himself as a possible vassal."

"But he's likely a thief," Batae commented. "Romans would never trust a man like that."

"Thieves are predictable and easily bought," Pahor asserted, turning everyone's head. "Also, it would make sense to support anyone who rivaled the Amani-aa'ila."

"Indeed," Ethaan said with a slight nod, pleased at the fruit borne by the many geopolitical conversations he had shared with his son.

Pedese's eyes darted back and forth between his father and brother. He then threw the bridles in his hand against the stable wall and broke out in laughter laced with ridicule.

"In summary, the Queen needs to be escorted to her dead husband's cousin—who happens to resent her, just like every other Kushite soldier does, for marching the army into the teeth of an unbeatable foe. In the process, she also needs to avoid this Amen-Tekah, who wants the throne for himself."

Pedese folded his arms and donned the familiar smirk Batae had anticipated would appear at some point. "A jilted lover or a power-hungry black Egyptian. She might well be better off surrendering to the Romans."

"No, my son, she would not." A grim shadow fell on Ethaan's smooth, swarthy face. "Should the Kandace be captured by the Romans, she will be taken to the city of Rome, where she will be stripped naked and beaten. Afterwards, she will be paraded through their city like an animal, wearing nothing but a bronze chain around her neck, while thousands of pale white Romans spit on her.

"She will be marched to a temple, her face painted red, and she will then be strangled with a leather strap. An executioner will twist the strap until her eyes bulge out and blood bursts from her nose and ears."

Ethaan paused and surveyed the four men, each lost in the grotesque visual painted by the elder statesmen. "The last thing the final kandace of Kush will hear will be the roar of the Roman crowd as her neck snaps. Her lifeless corpse will then be discarded on a dung heap outside the city to decay in the open—her bones picked clean by animals. There will be no grave, no pyramid, and no marker to define the resting place of the last queen of Kush. No, Pedese, we cannot allow that.

"We as Kushite men cannot allow such a disgraceful and appalling fate to befall even one of our women, let alone the Queen-Mother. And this is what you men need to convey to Amen-Tekah." Ethaan stepped face-to-face with Khai. "This is what you must convey to Mshindi."

Ethaan slowly pivoted around and found each man's eyes. "I need each one of you to bear this burden and watch over the future of our nation. I need each one of you to *respect* and *protect* the Queen of Kush at all costs."

Chapter 22

The Temple of Amun in the city of Meroë was far less imposing than the shrine dedicated to the ancient god in Napata. While the altar was long and broad like the one that dominated the Napatan temple, this one was bronze and adorned with copper utensils instead of gold. Amanitore silently wondered if the sacred golden items were still in the temple—or, for that matter, if the temple was even still standing after the reported Roman onslaught.

Dressed in her finest golden-laced ephod, the young qar listened as the high priest uttered his prayers to the hulking black statue of Amun-Ra. From what she could hear, the holy man was beseeching the overlord to protect the Amani-aa'ila and bring swift justice to the Roman intruders. It was a prayer that Amanitore had heard dozens of times over the past two years, and she had long since begun to wonder if Amun-Ra even cared about the kingdom's dire situation.

Although she had never participated in or witnessed a battle, Amanitore had both read and heard reports about the savagery perpetrated on the battlefield. Though Kushite warriors were formidable, Roman legionaries were notoriously brutal. In fact, every detail that Amanitore heard about the Battle of Napata forced her to drift farther into a private abyss of despondency—something she had thus far been able to conceal.

Until today.

Two days earlier, another runner from the Napata region had arrived with an update from the battle-worn district. Upon the last report days earlier, the Roman force had divided: one legion heading south, while the other had sailed north down the Nile. The central figureheads of the Kushite government and Amani-aa'ila court had assumed that the legion, which turned out to be the *Cyrenaica*, was heading for Meroë. Most of them, including Grand Vizier Matu, embraced the likelihood that their enemies would have little trouble marching on Meroë and toppling the last substantial city of the empire. Subsequently, a specter of death swept through the city like a blast of hot air from the desert. Most of the nobles had already started to mourn the ancient kingdom, with some well into the process of abandoning their estates. Even with a regiment of over one thousand soldiers protecting the city, no one felt safe.

Yet, surprisingly, another report revealed that the *Cyrenaica* had abandoned their rafts at the great bend and started north up the Wadi Gabgaba Road. No garrison had been left in Napata, and it appeared that the victorious invaders had had their fill of Kushite blood and were content to head back to Egypt with their captured spoils of precious metals and people.

Although relieved, the young qar had far too many questions that needed to be answered. Why did the Romans head north via two different paths? Would they someday return with an even greater force? Did the Romans know that the central government heads were hiding in Meroë, and did they even care? The grand vizier questioned whether Rome even recognized Kush as an actual state, describing how the massive empire probably looked upon them as an assortment of black tribes with no centralized culture to hold them together.

The high priest completed his prayers, approached Amanitore, and greeted her with a curt bow.

"We have done all we can, my qar," the man said in a low voice.

"Then why does it feel as if we've done nothing, Lamal?"

The grey-headed man smiled. "Have you made a decision yet?"

Amanitore fought the urge to roll her eyes. Lamal's reputation for being blunt was well earned.

"No, I haven't," she answered, sitting on a nearby bench. "Matu makes a good argument to remain here and consolidate what's left of the kingdom. He believes we are far enough away from Egypt that the Romans will leave us alone. I can't say that I disagree."

Lamal clasped his hands behind his back. "As the grand vizier, Matu sees things from a political point of view. But there are other perspectives."

"The war council feels that Meroë provides a tactical advantage, and it is easy to defend due to the rivers. That makes it an ideal location to reestablish the kingdom."

"And what are your thoughts?" Lamal asked, sitting next to her.

"My advisors are telling me to abandon everything to the north. But how can I do such a thing? I don't know what's happened to my mother." She stood up and paced in front of the altar. It was a forgone conclusion that the Romans would likely hunt down and kill Amanishakheto when they journeyed north—if they hadn't already done so. While the right of succession to the throne actually fell to her mother's sister, no one believed Amanishakheto would survive for long—especially if she still travelled with her husband, Mshindi. Nevertheless, most of the administration knew Amanishakheto's stand on the conflict with Rome and assumed she would just as soon capitulate to the conquerors.

"Why aren't the Romans coming here?" Amanitore questioned, more to herself. "Jaelen said the Romans had pursued them deep into Kush, to Napata, to kill off the Amani-aa'ila. He said it was their way of cutting off the head of an asp."

"And the rest of the body would then die," Lamal commented thoughtfully.

"The first messenger said Jaelen was dead," Amanitore paused a moment to push back a wall of grief. Coming to grips with the death of her last older brother was a disheartening task. "The second one reported that the Roman force was splitting. By then, they surely knew that many nobles from Napata had fled south to Meroë.

"Now, a third runner reports that the rest of the *Legio Cyrenaica* is heading north on the Gabgaba Road." Amanitore stared at a row of candles as their flames waved jointly to a soft breeze that mange to find its way into the chamber. "It's as if they are disregarding the remainder of the Kushite regime. It's the opposite of what everyone said they would do."

"Perhaps they are pursuing the regime," Lamal said thoughtfully. "The Romans are most thorough. Perhaps Amanirenas is alive and is heading north, and they've divided their forces to intercept her. I suppose they will not stop until they do."

Amanitore slowly turned to the high priest. While Jaelen's death was confirmed, the Queen-Mother's demise was not. "Assuming she survived, why would she go north and not come here to the last regiment of soldiers?"

Lamal smiled and offered the teenager a subdued laugh. "Someday you, too, will be a mother. She would want to protect her daughter and avoid leading the Romans here if she could."

"But the Romans could have done whatever they wanted. There's no one left to stop them. The last time I saw him, Jaelen said the only other regiment of Kushite soldiers would be the *Teriahi* with Mshindi..."

"In Kerma, in the north," Lamal said.

"But Mshindi despises her," Amanitore said, recalling descriptions of the nasty schism between the general and the Kandace. Amanishakheto's bitter rancor toward her sister only served to widen the gap. "He and Amanishakheto would likely start their own dynastic branch of the Amani-aa'ila before helping my mother," Amanitore stated dubiously.

"Doubtful. As I said, the Romans are extremely efficient. Amanishakheto would surely share the fate intended for the Kandace," Lamal reflected. Although skepticism permeated his thoughts, a glimmer of hope managed to spill through.

Lamal was old enough to recall watching Mshindi and Teriteqas both grow into manhood. The two shared many traits besides the same bloodline. Both were intelligent; both could be headstrong and brash. Both were valiant warriors, and both at one point in time had loved Amanirenas—even though one of them had had to let her go.

However, there was one love the men shared that neither would ever relinquish.

The high priest nodded as his fading memory was clear in one detail. "Mshindi may despise Amanirenas for her actions during the war.... But he has always been in love with Kush."

Chapter 23

To torch every third village after passing the third cataract was the plan. To Petronius, it was a modus operandi that instilled fear and work to identify those who were shrewd enough to acquiesce to the new Roman overlords. The method had succeeded in other subjugated segments of the newly minted empire, and he was certain that it would do the same in Kush. It would slow their progress toward Primis to a degree, but Petronius thought the payoff worth the delay.

The first town to be greeted by the barges bearing the cohorts of the *XXII Legio* was Sai. Dozens of the river-going vessels still lined the banks of the Nile, even though hundreds of legionaries had already disembarked and positioned themselves, waiting for orders from the Prefect.

Escorted by a score of soldiers, Petronius made the short trip from the river port to the heart of the ill-fated town. He surveyed the structures like a bird of prey, ascertaining which buildings would be burned, which would be reduced to rubble, and which—if any—would be spared. In any case, the ensuing devastation would not take long to exact, as the town could hardly be considered a city.

"One cohort," Petronius said to his aide, Theodosio Septimus. "Have a second cohort stand guard along the northern perimeter of the ... city. This will not take very long."

"Shall I have the remaining barges continue to the designated campground downriver?" Septimus asked.

Petronius checked the sun's position, which signaled an hour or so past noon. "Yes. The first barges should arrive at the site by the time we finish here."

Septimus offered a crisp salute and then disappeared among the forest of spears held at the ready by Roman soldiers.

The town was dead quiet, obviously abandoned by its inhabitants once it was apparent that they had been targeted by the invaders. Although Sai would be the first town wiped away by the XXII, Petronius had already grown adept at identifying dufufas and temples from his time in Napata and other parts of Kush. He had even developed the ability to distinguish some of the Kushite gods depicted on the structures. While underwhelmed by the scale of the structures he encountered, the Roman governor was nonetheless impressed by the exquisite artwork that adorned them.

"Prefect," a voice called out.

Petronius turned to face the first-spear centurion before him.

"There is something you should see."

⌀◌

The sky was overcast, and the river was quiet. For that, Amanirenas was grateful. The gray clouds provided a welcome relief from the brutal heat from the relentless sun above. However, the light haze that had settled on the river was unwanted, as the fog limited visibility just enough to lose track of the three other vessels transporting the remainder of the Queen's retinue. Khai and Ethaan insisted on splitting up the group of fifty sojourners in order to allay any suspicions as they travelled to Kerma. Thus far, the strategy seemed effective enough, as no one from the two ports they stopped at had raised any questions.

"I think we're making good progress, despite the fog," Khai said, suddenly standing beside her. She noted the look on his face and figured he was only telling half of the truth. While the cavalryman had proven himself an effective leader, he generally struggled when attempting to mask when he was overly concerned about a potentially dangerous situation.

"I don't like being unable to see downriver," Amanirenas said.

"Neither do I. But we can't change the weather," Khai replied, peering into the ghostly mist.

"We can't even see the two boats behind us," Amanirenas commented.

"And that's a good thing," Khai said, turning toward her. He was about to remind her of the strategy they were using to deliberately put distance between each vessel by having each boat set sail half an hour apart. However, the more he studied her face, it was apparent that the inability to see downriver was the least of her concerns. Even now, her attention was adrift in the haze that danced around them, and it seemed as if she were watching an invisible drama unfold before them that only she could perceive.

Despite the consternation etched upon her countenance, Khai was amazed at how radiant she was, particularly against the lifeless gray background. Her beauty was captivating and silently beckoned some deep part of his being.

Before he could turn away, her eyes shifted from the fog and haphazardly caught his stare. The two locked in an awkward visual embrace for a long moment, both coy and embarrassed, but neither willing to relinquish the fleeting pull of attraction and surrender.

"You're concerned about how Pelmes Mshindi will respond to your request," Khai said, allowing reality to invade the personal moment between them. His words prompted a subtle hardness to return to the Kandace's visage.

"No. I'm concerned about how he will respond to me." Amanirenas sighed and offered a subdued smile. "We have a history."

"I see."

"Many of the divisive things that have happened in our family over the past few decades have occurred because of that history."

Khai frowned, determined to find the correct words for his next question. "Please forgive me, but it has always been assumed among the soldiers that you and King Teriteqas were all but inseparable."

He paused as Amanirenas tilted her head in curiosity.

"It was no secret that he loved you very much," Khai continued guardedly. "He wrote proclamations that were read to each regiment describing how we should fight each battle for our families—just as he fought each battle for you. Every soldier in the army knew how much he cherished you."

Amanirenas struggled to find words with which to respond. "I didn't know that," she finally said, managing to wall off the tears and emotions fighting to break through.

"I'm sorry," Khai said, hinting at the inward conflict subtly simmering within her. "I shouldn't have..."

"No. There was no offense taken," Amanirenas said, her calm voice somehow anchoring Khai to his place. "Mshindi and I once had a relationship when we were young, but like so many things at that time in life, it didn't last."

Amanirenas allowed herself a moment to recall the fragrance of her youth, along with the complexities of navigating the idiosyncrasies of her own heart. "But, through it, I met his cousin Teriteqas. Things were awkward at times, but both men were..."

Her words trailed off as she followed Khai's intense gaze. The sun's rays dissipated the river haze enough for them to see at least 150 cubits ahead. The first boat in their party was moored to the side of the river and had been boarded by at least twenty Roman legionaries. The Kandace and Khai could do nothing as the Nile's steady current propelled them out of the fog directly into the Romans' line of sight.

Chapter 24

The foul scent of death struck Petronius well before he saw the bodies hanging on the crosses. The clearing on the far side of the town's central temple served as an orchard of half a dozen trees bearing the dead fruit of Kushite men.

Petronius surveyed the scene, but quickly determined that it was the handiwork of someone other than a skilled Roman executioner.

"The crossbeams are too low," Septimus noted, gesturing to the gruesome sights. "And the base isn't the standard height."

"These men haven't been dead that long," Petronius said as he studied the parched skin of a nearby victim. A dead Kushites' skin maintained a supple appearance much longer than lighter-skinned people's did. "A couple of days at most."

A clamor arose from a nearby shrine as a pair of Roman soldiers emerged with a middle-aged Kushite man bathed in fear. The black man knelt before the Roman commander and began to ramble in his native tongue. Petronius glanced at Septimus, who swiftly summoned the translator.

After a moment, Petronius looked at the dark-skinned Roman legionary for a response.

"Prefect, it appears that this man is the peshte of the town. He begs you to spare their home. He also says that these men are soldiers who fought for the Queen two seasons ago."

"Who killed them?" Petronius asked. The peshte swiftly divulged the answer.

"He says the vizier in Kerma issued orders to punish any man who supported the Amani-aa'ila ... that's the royal family. The man in the middle tried to convince others to keep fighting Romans."

The peshte studied Petronius and made one last desperate utterance.

"He says there are many who would prefer Roman rule to that of the Amani-aa'ila and are willing to fight on behalf their new masters...."

The translator did a double take as he squinted to find the correct words for the peshte's final utterance.

"... Hail ... Caesar ..."

Petronius glared down at the peshte, who quickly cast his eyes to the dirt. The scent of the man's fear nearly overpowered the odor of rotting flesh permeating the area. Petronius looked at the lifeless bodies of the men once more, then turned to leave.

"Tell him to take the bodies down," Petronius said to the translator. "Septimus, order the cohorts back on to the barges. Leave the town be."

𓃻 𓄿

Pedese could tell that the Romans were out of patience. The man who was attempting to interpret the encounter was not familiar with Pedese's dialect and grew more frustrated by the moment. The commanding legionary grasped the hilt of his sword and glared at Pedese with murderous eyes.

The commander's soldiers inspected the barge, rifling through the cargo and shoving the passengers around with impunity. It did not take long before the commander noticed that the men were equipped with swords and daggers. Pedese did not need a translator to know the husky Roman was demanding to know why they were so heavily armed.

"Tell him something!" Pahor exclaimed as more Romans began to appear on the river's edge, preparing to board the barge.

"This imbecile cannot understand my words!" Pedese retorted, getting ready to brandish his own weapon, anticipating the conflict to come.

"Move," Pahor demanded, pushing his older brother aside. He waved his hands wildly to capture the translator's attention. "We are dealers in spices travelling to Kerma."

Suddenly, the translator focused on the young Kushite, hooked by familiar words. The Roman uttered something to his commander and then bellowed a query to the young Kushite.

"We must arm ourselves like this because of the many marauders along the river near Kerma. We have lost two boatloads to the Blemmeys already this season. Now we have to worry about the ex-soldiers from the war. We'll be fortunate to turn a profit this year."

The translator relayed the message to the commander, who snarled in disgust and threw a dismissive wave at the Kushites before leading his troops ashore. Within moments, the Kushites were caught up by the current and whisked downriver.

☥ ☥

Amanirenas stood at the edge of the short pier protruding from the shore. She looked expectantly upstream, anticipating the arrival of the third barge that had been accosted by the Romans hours earlier. She knew that any moment Khai would appear at her side and beckon for her to vacate the overtly vulnerable position, even if it did grant her the best view of traffic along the river.

She peered back toward the shore in time to see the bulk of her bodyguard retinue finishing offloading the other two barges. Their party was fortunate enough to have secured a pier away from the main river port that serviced Kerma, granting them the desired ability to approach the city from a lesser traveled trail. Batae had already taken a few men and ventured toward Kerma to examine the situation awaiting them and to ascertain if any Romans moved among the inhabitants.

Khai drifted into her view, a familiar look of concern etched on his face. Before he could say anything, Amanirenas took another glance upstream, and this time her eyes were greeted with the sudden appearance of the third barge—even though it was still some ways off. Khai, too, saw the approaching vessel and nodded in approval; nevertheless, his look did not waiver.

Amanirenas anticipated that he wanted to reaffirm his opposition to her going into the city, and she waited to see from which direction he would approach his argument this round. She granted the cavalryman more latitude, due to the fact that he now served as her chief bodyguard, but she made it clear that she was still indeed the kandace. She did admit, though, that his reasoning was sound.

Unlike Kawa or El-Kurru, Kerma had a fully functioning governmental apparatus with a complete complement of peshtes, scribes, and other administrators, who often travelled to Napata. As a result, travelling in the city would not be like traversing through the bush, as there were far more people who could identify her.

"I just sent Saiesha and a couple others to see if they could secure lodging for the evening," Khai reported.

"I thought you would have had us make camp outside of the city," Amanirenas said.

Khai glanced downriver toward the busy port. He had lived in Kerma for part of his youth, and he knew every section of the outlying region. "It will be safer for us to lodge in one of the surrounding villages. The last thing we want to do is fight a gang of marauders."

Amanirenas nodded. There was no doubt that her new bodyguard retinue could repel a band of thieves, but it made perfect sense to avoid conflict of any kind as long as they could.

"I sent them to one village in particular," Khai noted as she started to retreat from the pier. "The people in that community are trustworthy."

"Good. We'll need a place to go after I meet with the vizier. I may not have a favorable reception from him," Amanirenas admitted, thinking about the last time she laid eyes upon Shabakar. It was just after her husband's funeral, and she had been emotionally raw, taking offense at any criticism levied toward the king. Shabakar had voiced a demeaning thought and then drawn a sharp rebuke from the widow Queen.

"Then why go to him?" Khai asked tensely, trying to maintain an aura of respect. "I still don't see why we don't just head east..."

"He's a corrupt man. Ethaan and you have said as much and ... I know as much," she said, shaking her head subtly as if ruing an unwanted memory. "My family is responsible for that corruption, and I have to answer for it. I have to see for myself how deep the sickness runs."

"Though it isn't my place to say, my kandace, I respect your conviction, but is gaining that knowledge worth the risk associated with the effort?"

Amanirenas studied Khai's face and noted that there was more etched upon it than the concern of a soldier or even a bodyguard. She esteemed his unspoken thoughts and decided to honor them with an explanation. "The vizier is family. Shabakar is the king's cousin. The greatest thing I risk is further dishonor."

The two of them turned to see Pahor jump from the barge to the pier and retrieve a line to secure the vessel.

"Khai," Amanirenas called as he started to head back up the pier, "I do appreciate your concern. Sabrakmani would have had the same uneasiness."

Khai bowed slightly in acknowledgement before turning to help secure the barge.

Chapter 25

It was the third hour of the day, and Tribune Quintus Publius was inspecting the perimeter of his camp with a keen eye. Just as he had done for several days, the tribune examined the moat and jagged stockade, circumventing the serrated palisade that enclosed the encampment. Although he was completely satisfied with his camp's defensive posture, he refused to allow hubris to erect a false sense of security within himself or the men under his command. Despite the fact that they had met with almost no resistance during their hunting expedition from Napata to the outskirts of Kerma, the fact they were trespassers in a foreign land and were vastly outnumbered was never lost on Publius.

The presence of the Roman encampment on the opposing side of the Nile seemed to garner little attention from the people who inhabited Kerma. Like the people in most of the villages the Romans had come across during their sojourn down the Nile, the local Kushites seemed wary of conflict and mainly avoided the Romans—with the exception of the opportunists.

Publius made his way back into the camp and decided to peruse the subdivisions reserved for the additional cohorts from the *XXII Legio* that were due to arrive any day. Although their time at the location was uneventful, he silently looked forward to the day when Marius and Ventidius would march through the gates with nearly a thousand more legionaries.

Nevertheless, the unspoken truth was difficult to avoid. He had no dread of the Kushites since the battle in Napata; they offered him nothing to fear. The further north the Romans travelled, the more fragmented the Kushites became, resembling a motley collection of city-states that lacked an apparent head. Brandish a few gladii in their presence, and even the very scent of resistance dissipated like a plume of smoke.

A soldier approached Publius, saluted, and then extended a worn parchment. The tribune took the note, knowing it was the report from the detachments patrolling the landing stages that serviced Kerma a couple of miles away. He slowly made his way back to his tent as he carefully studied the second of the three daily reports sent from the unit.

Uneventful, Publius thought. *Uneventful is good. Very good.*

A second soldier entered the commander's tent and presented another parchment.

"News from the detachment patrolling the city," Publius said, hoping for a report similar to the one from the pier detachment. The unit assigned to the city often made use of operatives from among the natives, and from time to time it requested money with which to purchase intelligence from the more sophisticated Kushites. Publius was surprised at how easily and cheaply most of the Kushites were bought. However, thus far, their bribes had yet to pay off with any helpful information.

Then, for the first time in several days, Publius's heart skipped a beat.

This would not be an ordinary day after all.

"And this report was written two hours ago?" Publius asked.

"Yes, Tribune," the soldier replied sharply. "I brought it across the river with all haste."

"Very well." Publius turned to an aide who was busy in another section of the tent. "Junius, alert the forward guard. We're going across the river to the city immediately."

"Welcome, Kandace Amanirenas," Shabakar offered with a bow. "The city of Kerma greets the Queen-Mother with love and affection."

Amanirenas nodded, her eyes affixed to the vizier's. The two studied one another for a long moment. The vizier was alone in his office and seemed unsurprised by the Queen's unannounced visit.

Khai stood behind her, surveying the room. The office was plush, decorated with all manner statuettes of Apedemack, Set, and several other Egyptian deities. The dufufa that housed Shabakar's workspace was large and doubled as the city's temple to Amun-Ra. The fact that so much traffic flowed through the northern section of the building gave Khai pause. Nevertheless, he and Batae had mapped out an escape route through the facility should they need one.

"My complements to the young man you sent to arrange our meeting," Shabakar said. "He was very convincing and well-spoken."

Amanirenas thought briefly of Pahor and how much the young man favored his father, both in sensibility and in words. "It may not have been standard protocol, but we have to take certain precautions," Amanirenas said.

"I understand completely," Shabakar responded. "We heard rumors that you had survived the battle in Napata. But to have you here is an unexpected honor."

"It appears you have additional guests as well," the Queen stated. "When did the Romans arrive?"

"Almost a week ago. They have an encampment on the other side of the river."

"And you choose not to attack them?" Khai asked.

"I'd expect such a question from a soldier," Shabakar said, scrutinizing Khai. "They've given us no reason to attack them...."

"They march through the streets of Kerma and patrol the landings along the river as if this were a Roman outpost," Amanirenas asserted. "That's more than enough reason."

Shabakar glared at her with a subtle slippage of contempt discharging from his gaze. "Yes, we can attack and overwhelm them, just as your man here points out. However, they are but the vanguard for at least two more cohorts—and it is only a matter of time before they arrive. That, to me, is more than enough reason to let them alone. Perhaps if you and Teriteqas had followed that course of action, there would still be a Kushite Empire."

"Kush is not dead," Amanirenas said firmly.

"No, my kandace, you are not dead. The kingdom, on the other hand..." Shabakar shook his head and turned away. "I'm afraid the kingdom died with my cousin, and your attempts to exact revenge for his death only resulted in a slower bleed out."

"There was more at stake than revenge," Amanirenas said. "And there still is. There is a thousand years of Kushite history to honor and generations of freedom to preserve. We can still drive them out."

Shabakar slowly turned to face the Queen. "My cousin loved you. It is because of that love that I will tell you this. The Romans here are hunting for you, and you will find no refuge among the nobles in Kerma."

Khai fixed his gaze on the vizier as his heart slowly started to race in anticipation of Shabakar's next sentence.

"I'm not here to seek refuge, Shabakar," Amanirenas declared evenly.

"I didn't think you would accept if from me, even if I offered it," Shabakar commented with a thin smile. "Therefore, I recommend you head west. The Romans might not follow you into the Great Desert."

"Do you truly believe that's best?" Amanirenas asked, stepping forward like a lioness moving toward it prey. "That hardly sounds like something you would have said three years ago. Where is the man who fought so hard against receiving this appointment? You were so convinced that your talents would be wasted this far from Napata."

Shabakar rolled his eyes away from her. "Say what you will, Amanirenas. However, you have no option. The kingdom is gone."

"So you just accept Roman rule? Allow their laws to supplant ours?"

"You've left us no choice!" Shabakar shook his head and composed himself. "However, they will leave eventually."

"Only after they've plundered the land for gold, food, and slaves," Amanirenas declared. "They see us as inferior, and no one will be spared from their disdain. That is the Roman way."

"No, certain Kushites will be immune," Shabakar said.

"It appears he's already made an arrangement," Khai commented, his protective instincts fully engaged.

"Is this man your new advisor?" Shabakar mocked.

"Have you made an agreement with the Romans?" Amanirenas pressed.

"It is a matter of survival," Shabakar replied with a slight nod.

"And our people?"

"*Our* people will adapt," Shabakar stated. "It's no different than the policies enacted by your father to preserve the Amani-aa'ila. My agreement with the Romans is simply a way to preserve the way of life granted to me by the royal family."

Amanirenas fought through the wave of disgust washing over her. "You don't understand the Romans the way I do."

"Lest you forget, Amanirenas, it was your husband who took Kush to war against them, not you. It is doubtful that you *know* as much as you think you do."

"The Romans believe themselves to be masters of the world. They see you and me as little more than dark-skinned slaves to be bought, sold, traded, and whipped. They'll discard anyone who no longer serves their purpose."

"Sounds familiar, does it not?" Shabakar said with a slight laugh. "It was the mantra of the Amani-aa'ila for generations." He started to add to his comment, but then examined her cold glare.

"Tell me, what do you intend to do? You are a queen with no army—nothing more than a religious figure. A warrior queen who has won no wars."

Amanirenas met his subtle taunts with a silent gaze that challenged his manhood and any assertion of courage.

"You should leave while you can. Perhaps one of the Jewish villages will have compassion on you."

"I'm not the one who needs compassion, Shabakar. I guarantee that the gods will remember this day. I will not let them forget your cowardice. And when the day comes, you will pay."

A knock on the door echoed through the office, and a one of the

Queen's bodyguards stepped in. The man whispered something to Khai, who immediately turned to Amanirenas.

"We have to go. Romans have entered the dufufa."

"I've heard they intend to strangle you in the temple of Mars, their god of war," Shabakar mused as he sat down behind his desk.

"We have to resist," Amanirenas asserted. "We cannot let Kush fall."

"Go west, Amanirenas," Shabakar uttered. "There's safety in the desert."

"I'll die first." With that, the Kandace and her bodyguards swept out of the room, leaving Shabakar alone with his thoughts.

"Perhaps you will," he grunted.

Chapter 26

Sweat rolled into Batae's eyes as he anticipated the unknown. He stood at his post just beyond the dufufa waiting for Khai to lead the Queen from the building's southern-most entrance. The soldier he had sent in to alert Khai to the approaching Romans was the first to emerge, but he stood fast at the doorway, attempting to keep the pathway clear.

Batae watched apprehensively as he counted no less than twenty Roman legionaries forcing their way into the dufufa's western entrance, while an additional ten made their way to the rear. Within a heartbeat, Khai emerged from the building with Amanirenas, two additional bodyguards bringing up the rear.

Instinctively, the Queen picked up her pace from a brisk walk to a light jog. Batae waved them over, and within moments the six of them melded into the crowded streets of Kerma. Batae glanced behind them and noted that at least two legionaries had caught a glimpse of their escape and were in pursuit, with a third turning to signal the others.

Amanirenas knew where they were heading, grateful that Khai had insisted on mapping out an escape route beforehand. Her blood flowed like raging Nile waters hurdling toward a cataract as she dodged merchants, women bearing loads, children, and anyone else impeding their path. She heard Khai's heavy footsteps directly behind her and did not bother to turn to identify their pursuers.

They took a sharp turn and dashed into a dense section of foliage off the main pathway. Slowed by the vegetation, Amanirenas turned to inspect what was happening behind her and was met by the face of Akfoor, one of her new bodyguards.

"Where are the others?" Amanirenas asked.

"We must keep going, my Kandace," the young man answered, reaching pensively for the Queen.

Before Amanirenas could respond, the clang of clashing metal shattered through the greenery. She squinted past the trees, but only saw streaks of swinging blades flashing through the foliage. She began to back up as Akfoor led her away, but her progress was frozen when a death shrill saturated the air ... followed by another.

The two pushed through the vines and branches until a tributary running toward the Nile cut off their path.

"We have to go further south," Amanirenas said, fighting the disorientation brought about by the blanket of green dominating her view.

"This way," Akfoor called, spotting the wooden bridge spanning the stream, which measured roughly eight to ten cubits. Sword in hand, the young man hacked through the tendrils toward the bridge until a sharp blade protruded through the greenery and sliced his forearm.

Akfoor stumbled back, but quickly recovered to block the slash of the Roman gladius bearing down upon him. The legionary swinging the sword pressed his attack, intending to drive the young Kushite into the water behind him. However, Akfoor spun adeptly to the right, quickly reversing the situation.

Annoyed, the Roman arced the gladius above Akfoor, bringing his full weight down upon the smaller opponent. The violent blow forced Akfoor back against a fallen log, and the young Kushite struck his head against a tree, his sword tumbling away as he blacked out. Amanirenas reached for the Kushite's weapon and assumed a defensive posture as the Roman moved away from Akfoor.

"Tu venis ad me cum ferreo canis exprimamus," the white-skinned soldier uttered menacingly. He advanced toward Amanirenas, raising his two-edged weapon with the intent of repeating the stroke he had made against Akfoor.

Amanirenas braced herself for the impact, imagining her legs to be like the great colonnades that supported the Temple of Amun-Ra in Napata. She swung her sword upwards to meet the Roman gladius. She gnashed her teeth as the two pieces of steel met, sending a fiery shock down her spine. Nevertheless, her arms withstood the strike, and the Roman stepped back, his face bathed with irritation.

Before he could reposition for a second parry, Amanirenas initiated one of her own, thrusting forward, then swinging right, and then left. Her speedy moves surprised the Roman, driving him back a couple of steps. Angered, he baited her into pressing another attack. As she stabbed forward, the Roman sidestepped the blade and delivered an open-handed slap across her face. A loud smack echoed through the trees as the fierce jolt sent her lurching blindly into the vegetation.

"Stultus meretrix," the Roman shouted.

Although the pain sizzled through her body, Amanirenas somehow managed to stay on her feet, keeping her eyes fixed on the enemy. Before she could recover and confront him again, a Kushite spear sliced through the air and past the Roman's helmeted head.

The legionary scanned the background for the would-be assailant.

With his eyes removed from her, Amanirenas swiftly lurched forward at the invader. Her sword serrated his amour and disappeared deep into the Roman's chest. The man dropped his gladius and gasped for air. Before he could make another move, his eyes slowly fluttered and rolled back into his head. As he hit the ground, Batae leaped from the foliage like a leopard.

"Good thrust," he commented. After inspecting the lifeless Roman, Batae pulled the sword from the man's chest. "Can't believe I missed him so badly."

Amanirenas helped Akfoor to his feet and handed the young man back his sword.

"Where are the others?" Amanirenas asked Batae.

"They're fighting off several Romans. We have to get to the rendezvous point."

Batae guided a disoriented Akfoor toward the bridge. As they left, Amanirenas stood over the dead Roman's body and studied the twisted look on his face. She then reached for the gladius lying haplessly at his side. The foreigner's weapon was heavy, but extremely balanced. It was not dissimilar to the one her son Akinid had retrieved from a dead Roman two years earlier.

She took one last satisfied glance at the dead legionary and then hurried after Batae.

☒ ☒

"You would have saved us a great deal of time if you had detained her when you had the opportunity," Tribune Publius stated as he glared at Vizier Shabakar. Although his Greek was limited, the vizier understood the Roman's critical tone. Nevertheless, he allowed a Kushite interpreter to facilitate the conversation.

"I understand your concern, but everything happened so quickly," Shabakar said, settling into his chair. He hadn't even had a chance to leave his office before the Roman barged in. "Your troops stormed through the compound and flushed her out before we could react. Your disregard of the fact that this is still an administrative center is offensive."

Publius frowned at the statement as the interpreter finished processing the words into Greek. "Your daily operations here do not concern me. I currently have one objective, and that is to apprehend the Queen. Our agreement hinges solely upon your ability to help us in that endeavor. To be clear, your full cooperation will influence our decision on how much of this city, if any, will be spared when the rest of the legion arrives."

Shabakar let the interpreter drone on as he held the centurion's heartless gaze. He slowly ran his hands along the top of his desk in an effort to keep from balling them into fists. A slight nod was his only acknowledgement of the Roman's threat.

"Did you manage to find out any useful information? Surely the two of you discussed something of value."

"The Kandace is a stubborn woman. She can also very shrewd. She gave me no clue as to what her intentions are."

"Her intentions are simple," Publius said. "She is on the run. The only question is on the run to where?" Publius allowed the question to hover between them for a moment. The Kushite let the words dangle until he saw the ire starting to build in the invader's eyes.

"I told her to go west."

"Why?"

"I suggested that your forces would not pursue her into the Great Desert."

"Your advice was inaccurate. She will be pursued until Caesar decides otherwise. And he is not in the practice of allowing deposed monarchs to wander about their former kingdoms."

"She is one woman, weary, isolated, and soon to be forgotten. She's is no threat to your master."

"That is not for you to determine," Publius said as a pair of legionaries entered the Kushite's office.

"We have a report, sir" one of the men stated crisply.

Publius raised a hand and gestured for them to leave the room. Before he turned to follow them, the tribune addressed Shabakar once more.

"There is one other thing you need to remember, Kushite. Caesar is your master as well."

Chapter 27

Amanirenas studied the ornate hilt of the Roman gladius she had acquired from her attacker earlier that day. The grip was hard to the touch and appeared to be made out of a substance similar to elephant ivory. She ran her fingertips lightly along the double-bladed weapon to its sharp tip. She grimaced ominously and wonder how many lives—Kushite or otherwise—the weapon had violently extinguished. Though the blade was covered with a light film of grime, it possessed enough luster to reflect the quivering flames of the fire that warmed the courtyard of the modest compound serving as their refuge for the evening.

Saiesha sat next to her queen, staring aimlessly into the fire. Aside from a brief story of how she came to be in possession of the Roman weapon, Amanirenas had said very little since arriving at the hiding place designated by Khai. Pedese reported that Khai and several others had not made it back to the first gathering point after confronting a handful of Roman legionaries outside of the dufufa. Saiesha was certain that the Queen was concerned about them—Khai in particular.

Per the plan, the remaining thirty men from the new bodyguard contingent had escorted the Queen to the enclosed compound, which consisted of eight or so structures. Several of them were actual homes, though only two were occupied.

The bodyguards quickly went to work setting up patrol details both within and outside of the compound. Saiesha appreciated their efforts, and for the evening, she actually felt safe.

"He's so blind," Amanirenas said to the flames.

"My queen?" Saiesha stammered, the Kandace's statement jolting her back into the moment.

"Shabakar's hatred for me blinds him to reality." She dropped the tip of the gladius into the fire. "He said he would accept Roman rule, and it would be no different than the reign of the Amani-aa'ila."

Amanirenas lifted the scorched blade from the yellow flames and studied it. "That a man can be so consumed with rancor toward one family that he would sacrifice a nation and his own dignity. For such words to come from a vizier..."

"Not just any vizier," Saiesha said. "He was blood to the qeren."

"Blood doesn't matter when you refuse to live by principles," Amanirenas said. "My mother told me that a kandace must live by convictions, not preferences. True rank and privilege are only esteemed as long as one's honor is sustained."

The Queen shook her head and mused upon the many times she had violated her mother's maxim since Teriteqas died.

Saiesha smiled faintly, for while she preferred to be back in Napata, her convictions tethered her to the Queen and a thoroughly inconvenient situation. Her smile soon faded into a frown as she pondered the Queen's words. It was one thing for a pelmes-ate or a scribe to turn his back on the Amani-aa'ila, but for high level administrators like viziers and peshtes to do so denoted a significant lack of faith in the royal family—or in Kush itself.

"Do you think others feel the same way as Shabakar and are willing to forego Kushite sovereignty?"

Amanirenas drew a shallow breath and hated the answer that came to mind. For nearly 250 years, royal succession had come down through her family lineage. Sadly, scarcely a member of their dynasty was remembered for doing something great and contributing to the prominence of the Kushite Empire. At best, a ruler may have constructed a temple or two. At worse, more than a few of them had simply funneled the wealth of the provinces into their personal treasuries, leaving state business undone or poorly executed.

"I have to change how they feel," Amanirenas reflected, turning toward Saiesha. "I may not be able to change how they feel about me, but I have to find a way to change how they feel about Kush."

A commotion arose in the distance as a dozen or so men emerged from the dark and filed through the gate into the compound.

Judging from the reactions of Batae, Pahor, and the others, Amanirenas surmised that it was the remainder of the bodyguard troop. She made her way to the group, greeting each one with a smile that communicated her relief and gratitude at their safe return. She peered around for Khai and was immediately accosted by a sense of dread when she could not find him. She was relieved when her eyes finally found him talking with the older Kushite man and woman who appeared to be the owners of the compound. Amanirenas watched as Khai embraced the couple and then headed her way.

Amanirenas greeted Khai with a nod as the cavalryman offered her a bow.

"They've pretty much kept to themselves since we've arrived," Amanirenas said. "They obviously respect you a great deal. They had no objection whatsoever to our entrance when Pahor mentioned your name."

Khai glanced back at the couple, who had already disappeared into their abode. "That was my uncle and his wife. My mother grew up in this complex."

"They have my gratitude," Amanirenas offered as she subtly studied Khai. His tunic was covered with blood, and he was clearly fighting exhaustion. Although she wanted to send him off to rest, one question burned in her soul, and she felt obligated to ask. "How many men did we lose?"

"Three," Khai answered. He named the men who had died that day and noted how the news seemed to squeeze the life from her as if she were caught in an unrelenting vice.

"Thank you," she said softly as she turned toward a darkened portion of the compound. "Thank you all."

"Batae told me what happened after we fled the dufufa. He told me about the Roman."

Amanirenas stared into the black forest dominating the area beyond the compound wall but said nothing.

"Are you all right?" Khai asked as he drew closer.

"That was the first one," she replied in a hushed voice. "That was the first man I've ever killed by my own hand." She rubbed her fingers together as she recalled the morbid sensation of the sword carving through the Roman's chest, and for a moment she could smell the pungent odor of the man's final breath wafting into her face.

"I never realized how hard it would be," the Queen said, turning toward Khai.

"Taking a man's life is never easy," Khai said.

"Killing the Roman wasn't the difficult part. Living with the memory of doing so ... That is proving to be ... difficult."

She locked eyes with Khai and saw in them a reservoir of compassion. Moreover, his silent response propelled her further into his gaze until her heart started to flutter. The emotional sensation confused her momentarily, skewing her thoughts. For an instant, sanity was briefly restored to her irrational world, and she could see herself walking through her garden in the cool of the evening in a colorful gown that massaged her skin. For the slightest of moments, she felt *alive*.

Nevertheless, the specter of mayhem descended upon her and resumed its place. She turned back toward the darkness.

"But as difficult as it may be, I will do it again."

Khai watched her start to walk away but remembered that there was one piece of news he had waited all evening to deliver.

"My queen," he called walking toward her, "we were gone so long because I had to visit a man I served with in the militia before he was transferred to the Nobatia regiment."

Amanirenas stopped and faced him inquisitively.

"He's been in contact with a man whose caravan provides supplies to the regiment. The word is that Mshindi's army is beyond the second cataract, just outside of Semna."

Chapter 28

Quintus Publius stood at attention as his superior officer paced through the command tent like a caged predator. Marius's fair-skinned face was beet red, and Publius knew it was not due to the sun's harsh rays. Centurion Lucullus and Gamal Abasi stood off to the side, waiting to see how their commander would respond Publius's report of the previous day's affairs.

"Five legionaries were killed?" Marius questioned, breaking the foreboding silence.

"Yes, sir," Publius answered. "Our soldiers reported that there were at least seven to eight men assisting her as she fled from the dufufa. Our Kushite operatives report that there were as many as fifteen men in the group she traveled with upon her arrival to Kerma."

Marius stopped and faced the tribune. "An administrator in El-Kurru said there were three or four men with her—and we captured one of them." Marius ran his hand through his sweaty dark blonde hair as he recalled the day the obtuse bodyguard had been crucified.

"They could be relatives or unwitting sympathizers," Lucullus mused.

Marius studied Publius ominously. "Did you follow my orders upon your arrival?"

"Yes, sir. We crucified four prisoners. They're hanging on crosses just the east of the city," Publius reported.

"Perhaps you should have placed them in front of their temple," Lucullus said.

"We had the vizier's attention the day we arrived," Publius added. "The crucifixions made sure of that. He was very receptive to our offer."

"But the message wasn't received by everyone," Lucullus said. "She went from four men to at least fifteen. People are still willing to help her."

"Worse yet, they're probably still willing to believe in her," Marius declared as he unhooked his pugio and slammed the ornate dagger on a desk. He rubbed his eyes and shuffled through a litany of thoughts. His cohort had arrived at Publius's camp two hours ago, and he had yet to remove his amour or even have a drink.

"What did the ... vizier say when you interrogated him? Surely he had something to contribute for his sake," Marius said.

"He told her to go west and into the desert. However, he believes that she likely went east, possibly even north, past the cataract."

Marius walked over to a map suspended on the wall of the tent. "If this map is accurate, there's nothing much to the east."

"That is correct, Tribune," Abasi affirmed. "Much of it is either grasslands or barren desert."

Marius silently nodded as he recalled the path they had taken through some of that flat, bleak land a year earlier as they had pursued the Queen's forces when they were retreating south to Napata. "She would have no cover whatsoever for miles."

"They couldn't have gotten far if they left last night," Lucullus offered.

"If she went that way," Marius said beneath his breath. "What's beyond the cataract falls to the north?"

"An assortment of small villages. A few ancient Egyptian military outposts," Publius answered, glad he had taken the time to study the attributes of the region. "Reports say that there is a rather large one here near the town of Semna. It is said that Kushite marauders use it as a base of operations."

"How many days would it take to make that journey?" Marius asked.

"For us, five to six days," Publius answered. "The locals say that this is the largest cataract falls on the Nile, and it will take us time to navigate the steep paths around it. It will be especially tough this time of year because of the low water levels."

"It would be a gamble," Lucullus warned. "What if she really did go east? If we are wrong, she will have a good chance at making it to the coast. From there, she can go to Arabia or even make it to Parthia...."

"Possibly," Marius said, stroking his jaw. He studied the chart penetratingly and allowed his predatorily instincts to guide his thoughts to a verdict. "If she wanted to make it to the Red Sea, then she would have backtracked long ago. It's still more logical for her to go north to try and link up with the Kushite forces there. So we will go north as well."

"The prefect should arrive at Primis by then," Publius said, estimating the distance between the two plots on the wall map. "Hopefully any Kushite forces in between the cataracts are still focused on his progress north."

"Quintus, your cohort will cross the cataract falls tomorrow to continue the pursuit. Do what you can to locate and capture her, but proceed no further than Semna," Marius said, his eyes darting from a blot representing Kerma to the one on the map labeled Semna. "I will remain here and await Ventidius. I need to pay a visit to Kerma before we join you."

𓅱 𓋴

Amanirenas heard the mighty cataract waterfalls before she actually saw them. Upon their arrival to the great drop-off, she could hardly believe her eyes. The Nile rushed along like winding snake and then disappeared, leaving nothing but a cloudy mist with a distant roar echoing through it. The Queen tried to find words to describe the sight, but she could not. She stood in silent awe of the raw power assaulting all of her senses at once. It took a moment for her to notice Pahor standing next to her.

"I've never seen these falls before," the young man said with wide eyes.

"I have. But I'll never get used to the sight," Amanirenas said. She looked at her youngest bodyguard and smiled. She had grown to appreciate how his intelligence and forward thinking supplemented their group. The young man's astute ability to negotiate had proven beneficial multiple times already. She was convinced that Kush would arise from its dark labyrinth on the backs of such young men.

She walked over to Khai, Batae, and Pedese, who were huddled in a final conference. "Are we ready?" she asked, struggling to be heard over the raging falls below.

"I still don't think this is the best course of action," Pedese said, shaking his head. "If we split up, we divide our forces. If we divide our forces, we have less chance of surviving an attack."

"We wouldn't survive an attack, period, idiot!" Batae ranted. "The goal is to make it to Semna."

"In one piece!" Pedese retorted.

"Damn coward. The girl is braver than you are," Batae lectured as Saiesha joined the group.

Amanirenas put up a hand to quell the squabble. "We all agreed on the way here that splitting up the group was the best way to throw off any Romans who may be pursuing us. When they arrive and interrogate the caravan dealers and merchants along the riverways, they will have to make a choice about which party to follow."

Khai nodded in affirmation and turned to Saiesha. "You have to give the merchants reason to believe you are the Kandace."

"I've been with the Queen-Mother for a long time. I'm sure I have some of her mannerisms down," Saiesha said with a smile.

Amanirenas grasped her servant's hand and squeezed it affectionately. The two shared a momentary glance that seemed to stretch an eternity. Saiesha's selfless service had never been lost on Amanirenas, but this could potentially be her greatest sacrifice. If the young woman was apprehended by the Romans, she would likely suffer the humiliating fate that awaited the Queen of Kush at the hands of her enemies.

"Batae, we will wait until you and the others blend in with the caravan before we hike down the path along the cataract," Khai announced. He kept one eye out for Pahor, who was off making arrangements for Batae, Saiesha, and half the bodyguard to join a large caravan scheduled to take a land route toward Semna. The journey would take at least a week to reach the city—if not longer.

"Sell it, but don't be too obvious," Khai said with an affirming nod. Batae offered a smile to acknowledge the cavalryman's rare attempt at levity. "Once we've cleared the cataract below, we'll seek passage to Semna via the river."

"With any help from the gods, we'll all die swiftly," Pedese muttered. Batae gave the shorter man a shove, grateful that they would not be travelling together this time around.

Pahor emerged from the bushes and offered Amanirenas and Khai a nod of affirmation.

"This is it," Khai said calling the bodyguard troop together. Within a moment, he and the Kandace were surrounded by a group anxiously ready to depart. "We discussed this the entire way here. The gods willing, we'll rendezvous on the twentieth of Mechir at the Shrine of Amesemi outside Semna. Follow your assigned rolls and..."

Amanirenas gently gripped Khai's shoulder. The soldier stopped and acquiesced to the Kandace.

"It will be a while before we are all together again," Amanirenas said, mainly to the assembly preparing to depart with the caravan. "The ancestors are grateful that you have sacrificed so much to preserve the Kush they've bequeathed unto us. But I want it known that I am grateful for the sacrifices you have made for me."

Chapter 29

Kerma was by far the largest population center the Roman invaders had attacked since sacking Napata—a fact that stimulated the soldiers all the more. Gangs of legionaries prowled through the streets of Kerma in search of anything valuable enough to loot or something remarkable enough to destroy. Of the two dozen or so freestanding structures in the town, most were either engulfed in flames or reduced to rubble by the ropes and tackle of ravenous Roman soldiers.

Nevertheless, there was a marked sense of frustration among the ranks, as they were met with little to no resistance from the natives. The streets were void of Kushite bodies because no Kushites were to be found as the Roman war machines stormed ashore and into the city. Several centuries were dispatched into the surrounding forest, only to find empty villages and unoccupied shanties and storage sheds.

The central dufufa was one of several structures left unscathed in Kerma. Following orders issued to him by the prefect weeks earlier, Tribune Marius guardedly filed into the dufufa to inspect what he could of his enemy's culture. His prolonged expedition offered him many opportunities to analyze Kushite governmental and religious organization, and the prefect expected a full report of the tribune's experiences at the larger population centers. Marius complied with the order, convincing himself that he was simply engaging in a study of the culture and people that populated the newest province of the Roman domain.

He bypassed the dufufa's administrative wing and pressed down a central corridor to the temple annex. He removed his helmet as he entered the shrine—both in an effort to defeat the humid air and in deference to the gods whom the chamber honored. The education afforded to him by his conquest revealed that the Kushite gods were not dissimilar to the deities revered by the Romans, Greeks, and Egyptians. Although he by no means saw himself as a devout man, Marius fully embraced the thought that the world was indeed governed by an omnipotent power that transcended man's trifling struggle to control his own destiny.

The Roman tribune drew near to an arrangement of extinguished candles that were clearly in place to provide light for the perusal of a document that no longer occupied the empty space before him. The sunlight flushing through a set of overhead windows drew his eye to a shelf of neatly rolled parchments. As he approached the documents, Lucullus entered the shrine.

"Forgive me, Tribune. But you wanted to be informed if any city officials were apprehended."

Marius gave his aide a cursory glance. After a moment, he put his helmet back on and headed toward the central corridor. "Who is he?"

"The man claims to be the governor of the province," Lucullus answered.

"Who captured him?"

"He wasn't actually captured. He came in from the forest and more or less surrendered."

The two officers exited the dufufa and were greeted by a cloud of drifting ash. At the bottom of the stairs stood a quartette of legionaries standing guard over a tall black man adorned in an ornate ephod and matching headdress.

Lucullus summoned the interpreter, who met them as they converged on the Kushite.

"You are the vizier?" Marius questioned. The black man tilted his head in curiosity as the interpreter translated the question.

"Yes. I am Shabakar. I govern the region from Kawa to the second great cataract. I was appointed by Qeren Teriteqas."

"I am Tribune Cassius Marius, commander of all Roman forces in the region. Do you understand my title?"

"I do," Shabakar answered. "But what I do not understand is why you burn what Caesar wishes to rule?"

"Shabakar?" Lucullus voiced. "Tribune, this is the man Publius wrote about in his report. The one who helped our soldiers nearly capture the Kandace when she was here the other day."

"It appears I failed to render enough assistance," Shabakar said in Greek, surprising the interpreter by using the primary administrative language of Egypt. "My city was to be spared if I cooperated. Is this how Romans honor their word?"

"Watch your mouth, boy," Lucullus ordered. "You can very quickly find yourself hanging on a cross."

Shabakar averted his eyes to a street lined with burnt-out husks that just a day before had teemed with merchants and traders from all over the region.

"Why have you come here?" Marius asked in Greek. "What did you hope to accomplish?"

"I wanted to see if you intended on pursuing the people into the wilderness."

"As a reward for your assistance, orders were given not to destroy the estates in the nearby hills," Lucullus said. "Being the vizier, I assume one if not all of them belong to you."

"I may be the vizier, my lord, but I cannot govern a city that has been burned to the ground. This is not what I negotiated with Publius."

"Tribune Publius had a different mission," Marius stated. "His orders were to capture the Kandace, and those orders came from me. My orders are to do the same, as well as to subjugate the land of Kush and exact retribution on those who orchestrated the attacks on Primis and other sites in Egypt—and those orders come from Caesar."

Shabakar fought to keep his breathing steady and focused his attention on the dufufa behind the Roman commander. He was grateful that the governmental edifice still stood erect in the midst of the destruction wrought by the invaders. He did not know why the tribune had spared the building, and he did not care. He was only aware of his growing desire to secure the preservation of the sacred structure, which served as a link to Kush's majestic past. Indeed, the Romans were no different from how the Kandace had described them.

"Your point is well taken, though," Marius continued. "We have no intention of pursuing your people beyond the city. Someone must remain to rebuild Kerma for the glory of Caesar."

"Most gracious, my lord," Shabakar said with a nod.

"Escort him out of the city," Marius commanded the legionaries. Shabakar surveyed the ruined city, then glanced at the tribune before turning to leave with the soldiers.

"Rather bold," Lucullus said as the five men disappeared down a path leading into the woods.

"He's more presumptuous than confident," Marius countered. "He had expectations that were not met. Publius made promises that gave him a sense of entitlement."

"Surely the Kushite doesn't see himself as an equal deserving of status within the Roman order?" Lucullus mused.

"Perhaps he does," Marius stated as he headed back inside the dufufa. "He was important enough to receive a visit from a queen who is being hunted by a force occupying his city."

"It was a waste of her time. If he didn't have anything to offer her before, he definitely doesn't now."

Marius arched an eyebrow at the comment, and he silently admitted that her actions had confounded him the moment he had read Publius's report. For her to walk past a detachment of Romans and into the office of a man who had already struck an accord to betray her was beyond audacious.

More disconcerting to Marius was the report that she had taken up a sword and fought and killed a legionary. While others viewed it as a fortuitous strike by a desperate woman, he saw the action as an act of courage beyond her sex. He found himself dwelling on Prefect Petronius's constant examination of the Kushite concept of the

Queen-Mother and how the imagery of a warrior queen was woven into the fabric of the kingdom's long history.

He turned from Lucullus and reengaged his perusal of the shelved parchments.

"I am not anxious about what she may have obtained from the vizier, Lucullus. However, I am concerned with what she may have given him. It may be something more difficult to kill in the long run."

Chapter 30

Saiesha appreciated the caravan's methodical pace along the ancient path. The ensemble of two hundred or so travelers and pack animals was in no particular hurry and could move only so fast. This being the case, Saiesha often found herself enjoying the walk and even managed to befriend a few of the children in the caravan.

Their two days on the road had proved uneventful, just as Khai had predicted. Outside of the incredible vistas painted against the sweeping blue sky, there was nothing spectacular about their journey. In fact, at times, Saiesha caught herself imagining what life would be like being with a nomadic caravan permanently. However, it never took long for an enormous winged insect buzzing by or a lethal pit viper slithering along the trail to snap her out of the preposterous fantasy.

Nevertheless, despite the thus far uneventful two days, she sensed something in the air. Batae's usually dreary mood had flat out turned dark a few hours ago, and as of yet she had been unable to find out the cause of the shift. His pace was usually slower than hers and placed him toward the rear of the caravan. Yet today, he led their inner group of twenty-two people and had spent more time than usual speaking with each of the bodyguards. She watched him for a while and then decided to approach him in an effort to get some information.

"Slow down," Saiesha called as she caught up with the towering dark soldier. "You haven't walked this fast since the night we left El-Kurru."

He glanced down at her and grunted, an irritated grimace twisting his normally austere face.

"Batae, what's the matter? You've been on edge all day."

"The caravan will be veering off the main path tomorrow, down a road that will take us further east. They're deviating from the original route."

"Is there a reason why?" Saiesha asked, not really wanting to hear the answer.

"The foreman has received multiple reports about marauders along this road, so he's decided to take one that treks further east. He thinks it will be safer."

"What does that mean for us?" Saiesha responded with a slight sigh. Marauders were bad, but Romans were worse. "How far will it take us from Semna?"

"It could add a week to the journey," Batae replied.

"The Kandace could be long gone before we even get there...."

"I know," Batae said sharply, looking toward the western horizon. "We have to stay on this road, so we're going to separate from the caravan in a few hours. I've already told the men."

Saiesha nodded apprehensively. She was unsure if twenty-one men—well-armed as they were—would be enough to dissuade a callous band of raiders from attacking them. Nevertheless, she decided to say nothing.

"How long have you been serving the Kandace?" Batae asked with a notable shift in tone. The question caught Saiesha off guard and she actually had to think about the answer.

"Just over ten years. I was originally acquired to help with Amanitore when she was a child. But the Kandace ended up changing my main responsibilities."

"I have no idea what that feels like," Batae stated.

"What?"

"You said you were acquired. I keep forgetting you're the Queen's slave. What does it feel like to be someone's property?"

"I've never looked at it that way," Saiesha replied. "The Kandace has always been very good to me."

"I'm sure you've had a very privileged life, but it doesn't belong to you. You can't make your own decisions."

"My life is better than what it would have been," Saiesha countered. "I've received an education..."

"That should make it worse. I'm not a learned man, but I think being educated would mean that you actually had an understanding of the limitations on your life."

Saiesha shot the man a disdainful look, a sense of disbelief growing within her to think she had actually found him attractive. "You think too much for a soldier who raised goats."

"No, I just have a lot of questions about this senseless world I live in," Batae muttered. "I'm fighting against being enslaved by the Romans while protecting a government that enslaves its own people."

"I can understand your confusion," Saiesha said slowly. "But from what I understand, the Romans would probably force you to become a slave called a gladiator—someone who has to fight in front of crowds for a living."

"I'm familiar with the term," Batae said, recalling the many times Kushite soldiers were warned about being captured alive by the Roman legionaries. It was well known early on in the war that some of the captives had indeed been sent back to Roman Egypt to serve in what was called the gladiatorial games. "At least those men have the chance to fight."

"My point is, there are worse things than being a slave to the royal family," Saiesha said.

Batae noted her frown had diminished somewhat. "Yes. The only thing worse than being a slave to the royal family is accepting it."

Chapter 31

Tribune Publius sat outside of his tent, staring at the brilliant full moon dominating the night sky. The cackles, howls, and screams from the surrounding wilderness echoed over the protective palisades and into the Roman camp like an unrelenting wind.

Publius had long since grown accustomed to the nightly serenade and even tried to associate certain animals with specific cries. From time to time, he sent legionaries into the forest to capture the beasts to confirm his predictions, often placing bets with the other officers. It served as a good diversion to pass the hours of searching and waiting. Every member of the cohort under his command was ready to engage an enemy that seemed dead set on avoiding them at all costs. The heat and constant toil associated with their mission only served to worsen the monotony of the situation.

The tribune pondered the dream he had the previous evening. During the hazy vision, he had been visited by a messenger from Mars who had promised him that the undesirable and unprofitable journey was drawing to an end. As a result, the tribune was certain that something was about to change.

"Tribune," a voice called.

Publius looked up to see First Spear Centurion Justus Cyprian standing next to him.

"We've received a report from the reconnaissance scouts," Cyprian said.

"I don't want to hear another insipid account about merchants and barges...."

"You want to hear this one from them."

"Just tell me, Justus."

"Very well. A group of twenty or so people have been spotted...."

"Another one?"

"Yes, tribune, however, this time several people match the descriptions we were given in Kerma. And only one of them is a woman."

Cyprian examined his commander as he pondered the information.

Publius arose suddenly and entered his tent. He studied the map that served as their guide, mentally measuring the distance from their current location to Semna. They were still a couple days ahead of the cohorts led by Marius and Ventidius.

"How far away are they?" Publius questioned.

"Their last position was seven miles away."

Then, as if Mercury himself had delivered a message, the tribune spun around to Cyprian. "Prepare a light detachment for a swift deployment at first light. I want you to lead it. It's time to end this chase, Justus."

☒ ☒

Amanirenas hacked away at the darkness with the Roman gladius. Although it was heavier than a traditional Kushite iron sword, the tip of the blade sliced through the night air efficiently and felt more like an extension of her arm than a weapon grasped in her hand. Timber in a fire a few cubits away crackled softly and provided the dim light illuminating her exercises.

Portions of a training routine she had learned as a teenager flashed through her mind as she swung the sword. Soon she began to envision an opponent dodging her parries and launching counters to her rapid thrusts. The imaginary Roman drove forward, blocking her blows with a *scutum*. The large shield protected him from eyes to shins, making it all but impossible for Amanirenas to strike any sort of bodily blow.

She gritted her teeth and swung the blade with every bit of might her tired muscles could muster. The Roman nonetheless withstood her punishing onslaught and peeked from behind his shield with eyes that mocked her futile effort. In a fit of rage, Amanirenas elevated the gladius, brought it down violently, and spun to the left. She executed her maneuver faster than the Roman could reposition the scutum, leaving him vulnerable for a split second. She drew back and lunged forward...

"My kandace, the scouts have returned with a report."

Amanirenas snapped from her contest with the specter and faced Khai. The cavalryman held his distance until she lowered the Roman weapon.

"If we continue by way of the river, we should arrive at Semna by noon tomorrow."

"However, you think we should approach by land," Amanirenas said resuming her bout with the invisible opponent. "How much longer will that take us?"

"Another day," Khai responded, watching as the blade flashed reflections of the nearby fire. "There is one stop outside of the city I would like to make."

"If you think it necessary," Amanirenas managed to say in between breaths. Sweat started to moisten her forehead as her jabs and thrusts intensified.

Khai started to retreat from the clearing but stopped short. He quietly studied the Queen's movements. It was not the first time she had guided herself through such a routine since acquiring the Roman weapon, and, like before, she burned far more energy than she needed to.

"Your form is off," Khai said across the fire. Amanirenas stopped and looked at him inquisitively. "Shorten your strike angle and let the blade do the work."

She applied his advice and silently resumed her practice, a grim look of determination covering her face. She kept going until she noticed his gradual approach.

"Grip the handle higher," he said, reaching for the sword and guiding her hand closer to the base of the blade. "It will help you deliver a stronger blow at a closer range."

Khai took up station behind her and methodically guided her arms into position with his own. "Romans are trained for close-quarter combat. You won't have time to widen the angle of your swing. Getting a higher grip will..."

"Allow me to deliver a stronger stroke much faster," Amanirenas said, becoming acutely aware of the change in temperature as the feeling of the steady warmth of Khai's body, as opposed to the oscillating heat from the fire. Her heart fluttered wildly for a moment as his muscular arms closed in around her.

"His eyes were brown," Amanirenas said, reaching for the first thought she knew would divert her feelings. "The Roman I killed in Kerma. His eyes were brown. I've seen them every night in my dreams."

"Taking a life in one-on-one combat is different than fighting on the battlefield. It is much more intimate." Khai's eyes drifted down to the Kandace and rested in the curly locks of her dark hair. Their bodies were close enough for him to feel the rhythmic rise and fall of her shoulders as she breathed.

She tilted her head and came face-to-face with his square chin, bristled with short, dark whiskers.

"I find myself repulsed but wanting to do it again. As if I were trying to defend my children," she said in a hushed tone.

"In a way, you are," Khai affirmed, struggling not to meet her lost gaze. "You're the Queen-Mother."

"After every battle, Sabrakmani always made it a point to subtly remind me that I was a woman. As if I would ever forget. He would have Saiesha adorn my room with flowers or something feminine."

"I'm sure he was trying to prevent the enemy from forcing you to forget that there is a soft and beautiful side to you. That warfare isn't the sum total of who you are," Khai said slowly.

Their eyes locked suddenly and demanded a long, pregnant pause—each of them wanting to deliver a message, but uncertain of what should be said.

Finally, Amanirenas found the words to complete her original thought.

"He said killing was a task unsuited for women. Not because women were unable to kill, but because the very act took more from the woman than it did from the victim."

Khai's muscles tensed as he fought the mounting desire to close the short distance between them. His arms were already closing in around her, and he felt powerless to stop them. "I think we all lose something when we take a life. But we do what we must to survive."

"I didn't want to fight them," Amanirenas said coyly. "I wanted to give them the Northern provinces. It was so unbefitting of a Queen-Mother."

"No," Khai answered in a firm but soft voice. "It was very becoming of a woman who wanted her family and her life intact."

Amanirenas softly exhaled and relaxed, allowing herself to rest in Khai's firm gripped. As she did so, she gradually felt the strong, steady cadence of his heart. She slowly diverted her eyes to the fire.

"What do you see when you look at me?" the Queen asked softly, "A haggard warrior queen bent on revenge, or an old dried up woman who has for some reason outlived her family?"

"Neither," Khai answered, his eyes drifting to the fire as well. "I see a courageous, determined woman fighting for what she loves."

"But I don't love Kush," Amanirenas confessed, her voice peppered with shame. "It's taken so much from me."

"I've never thought you loved Kush," Khai said as he relaxed his grip on the sword and slowly running his hands along Amanirenas's arms. "I believe you're fighting for your family."

"My ancestors?"

"No. Your descendants. They are the ones that need you the most. They're the ones crying out to you from the future. Fight for them."

Khai summoned all of his fortitude and reluctantly drew himself away from the Queen. He took a few paces past the fire and then looked back—their eyes locking once again.

Chapter 32

Batae barely had time to react. A dozen sword-wielding Romans swirled through the forest like ghostly apparitions released from an unseen tomb. Two bodyguards were cut down by javelins before the rest of the troop could take up a defensive posture.

Several of the Kushite guardsmen rushed to meet the Roman onslaught, while the remainder hurried Saiesha down the forest path and toward a rocky outcropping. Batae knew it was a futile action but felt obligated to maintain the ruse a moment longer and hopefully grant the Queen's brave young servant a chance to escape. Nevertheless, even that minuscule amount of hope faded away when he saw at least two dozen additional Romans emerge from the wooded section ahead of them.

Although gripped by sudden fear, Saiesha hastily followed two bodyguards up a rocky path away from the desperate fight below. Certain that she would likely be captured, she fought off the cold grasp of anxiety and turned to face her pursuers. She brandished the ornate dagger that Amanirenas had given her days earlier, intent on inflicting a lifelong scar on the first invader that came near.

Batae managed to kill two legionaries before determining that there were at least fifty Romans in the vicinity. He located Saiesha and decided to make his final stand between her and the Roman vitriol, determined to extinguish the royal line in the cruelest manner imaginable. He swiftly made his way to her and the two bodyguards at her side. At least a dozen of the Kushite guardsmen read his actions and followed suit.

Respect and protect. If they couldn't do it for the Queen of Kush, then they would do it for the lone black woman threatened by a hostile force.

The men reached Saiesha and turned to confront their fate with honor and a determined sense of purpose. However, instead of engaging an advancing horde of pale invaders, they were met with the confounding scene of the Romans retreating into the forest for cover. A steady stream of spears soared overhead toward the legionaries; claiming a few lives but mostly driving the fighting force into the trees.

Although stunned, Batae still expected the tenacious enemy to mount a charge; however, when he saw where the multitude of spears had been launched from, he uttered a prayer of thanksgiving to Apedemack. At best guess, at least two hundred armed Kushite men stood at the top of the rock-strewn bluff.

The bodyguard troop instinctively continued up the ridge toward the Kushites. Saiesha smiled brazenly, for even she knew that as long as the Kushite force held the high terrain, the Romans wouldn't dare venture into the open.

"Who are these men?" Saiesha asked Batae as they struggled through the jagged boulders. "Are they marauders?"

"No," one of the bodyguards replied before Batae could respond. "Some of them wear the sash of the Sai tribes, while others bear the shields of the Makorians. These are likely men who serve under the warlord Amen-Tekah."

Saiesha flashed Batae an inquisitive glance, hoping for confirmation as they edged closer to the assemblage of men.

"We're about to find out," Batae muttered.

𓆸 𓃣

Saiesha was amused and terrified. While she was overwhelmed at the fierce loyalty displayed by the soldiers who attended Amen-Tekah,

The Queen of Kush

she was decidedly underwhelmed at the slovenly dressed chubby man sitting before her. The black and red commander's tunic he wore looked more like a tablecloth draped over his portly body, and the curly beard covering his dark, round face looked as if it hadn't been trimmed in months. Despite the conflicting sensations rolling around in the pit of her stomach, she was proud of the fact that she had managed to conceal her contrary thoughts and kept a straight face while Batae explained their situation.

There was a continuous flow of men in and out of the large roundhouse that apparently served as Amen-Tekah's headquarters. The man may have assumed the elite title of Grand Vizier, but he certainly did not act like one; nor did he act like a pelmes or any other military officer. The blatant lack of martial discipline quickly began to wear Batae's patience thin as he was interrupted several times as men walked right up Amen-Tekah and started an entirely different conversation.

Batae finally managed to complete his account after what seemed like hours. He waited silently for a response from Amen-Tekah, who took a swill from the goblet in his hand and then stared at him blankly.

Saiesha was about to ask a question when the heavy man commenced a very long and very loud belly laugh.

Batae glanced down at Saiesha and then back at Amen-Tekah, who, for the first time since they had arrived, stood to his feet.

"Your story is very amusing," Amen-Tekah remarked after composing himself. "So the Kandace is alive and is looking for Mshindi." The comment triggered a round of laughter from the dozen or so men in the roundhouse. Batae assumed that most of them were want-to-be nobles who were actually well-off marauders.

"I'm afraid she's come all this way for nothing," Amen-Tekah said as the mirth finally died down. "She would have been better off going south after her army was pummeled. There is nothing for her here. Mshindi is a coward, and Kush is dead."

"Kush still lives as long as the Kandace is alive," Saiesha asserted.

"Oh, it speaks!" Amen-Tekah said, his eyes fondling Saiesha's shapely form. "It's been so long since we've had a choice young beauty grace our company. How well does she lick toes?"

169

"I am in the employ of the Queen-Mother of Kush, you fat f..."

"Lord Amen-Tekah," Batae interjected before Saiesha could finish, "I'm a soldier and know nothing of politics. I care only to protect my home, and that is why I have fought the Roman invaders for the past two years. They bleed and die just like we do."

"Only we've been bleeding and dying a lot more than they have," someone heckled, prompting another round of laughter that taunted Batae.

"The Queen-Mother is going to stand and fight..."

"No, she's going to lie down and beg!"

"Interrupt me again," Batae stated resolutely, grasping the hilt of his sword. He scanned the room as his threat was met with silence.

"So, what are you asking for, soldier?" Amen-Tekah asked, sitting back down. "My men saved your lives today. What more do you want?"

"Your men fought well against the Romans. They looked as if they've engaged them before."

"Some of them have. Many of them served under Teriteqas. But once he died, they lost their motivation. Most of them are young opportunists. There are even a few Medjay warriors here."

Batae was impressed and nodded. "You have well over a thousand well-armed men here."

"You do have a soldier's eye," Amen-Tekah said with a smirk. "However, we fight for our own lands, not for the Amani-aa'ila."

"Then you fight against the Romans," Saiesha asserted, ignoring Amen-Tekah's lustful gaze.

"It's true there have been hundreds of Romans heading downriver over the past few weeks, but none have stopped to attack Semna. They seem preoccupied. With your queen in the vicinity, now we know why."

"Then why do you have such a large force?" Batae asked.

"The peshte in Semna hopes to curry favor with the Romans. He's actively hunted and executed anyone who refuses to renounce the Amani-aa'ila. He hangs them on crosses like the Romans would, they say. Many of my men are religious and believe that doing such a thing would prevent their souls from entering Henel."

Amen-Tekah paused as a handful of the men in the roundhouse grunted in agreement.

"You mentioned Mshindi earlier. What about him?" Batae asked.

"The cowardly jackal," Amen-Tekah jeered with glee. "He stays away from Semna. His army roams to the east, beyond the second cataract. He won't fight for the Kandace but continues to allow her sister to occupy his bed. He's a lost soul."

"What do you mean?" Batae questioned, trying to make sense of the warlord's words.

"Pelmes Mshindi is a man without a kingdom," Amen-Tekah continued. "He's broken away from Vizier Piankhi."

"Why?"

"It's simple. Piankhi wants to be the one to negotiate with the Romans when the time comes and hopes to be named grand vizier of Nobatia, Kerma, and Makor. Last I heard, he was held up in a fort near Qasr Ibrim."

"Selfish bastard," Batae cursed.

"Indeed, and that's what Mshindi thinks. He can't serve under Piankhi while he himself is still married to a member of the Amani-aa'ila," Amen-Tekah replied.

Batae glanced around at the men occupying the large circular meeting hut. All of them nodded in agreement with Amen-Tekah and murmured amongst themselves. Finally, Batae saw them for what they were: spineless, wanton thieves waiting for a chance to cannibalize a kingdom that had endured a thousand years. Nauseated by their venal temperament, all he could think of was leaving their presence.

"Like I said, I'm a soldier, and I don't care for politics. If you believe your way is best, then the gods be with you. As for us, we will continue on our way to Semna. We have business there."

Amen-Tekah released another fit of laughter. "You impress me, soldier. I am inclined to conscript your men and ... have my way with your woman ... But I am interested in seeing what Mshindi's response to the Queen will be after all this time. Therefore, I will send you on your way."

Chapter 33

"Khai! We feared the worst when we heard the news from Napata. It's good to have you home again."

"It's good to be back, Uncle Ra'Shaar," Khai said, allowing himself to absorb the warm feeling associated with home. The village in which he had grown up resembled an oasis and was flanked by numerous palm trees. The bustling sound of livestock filled the air, although nary an animal was in sight. "There were times I had my doubts."

"I'm sure," Ra'Shaar said, shaking his head. He recalled the countless hours that he and his wife had prayed for Khai's safekeeping during the long war. "And I want to hear all about it."

Ra'Shaar stepped back and scrutinized his nephew with an approving eye. "You look so much like your father."

"You would know," Khai said as he offered a rare smile. "How is your family?"

"My family? It's your family as well, and they'll be overjoyed to see you! All of your cousins have taken wives. Two have even given me grandchildren."

Khai nodded at his uncle's evident contentment. Ra'Shaar did what he could to be a father to Khai after his family was abducted, and it was Ra'Shaar who had given Khai the substantial amount of money needed to purchase his first horse. Even though his uncle had tried to convince him not to join the militia, Ra'Shaar had provided nothing but support once the young man had made up his mind.

"Beatha will conjure us up a grand feast," Ra'Shaar said as he gently grasped Khai's arm and started up the path through the village. Khai took two steps and then stopped.

"I'm sorry, uncle. I don't have the time right now."

"Why not?"

"Of course, I came here to see you, but what I really need is information."

"What information could you possibly need from me?" Ra'Shaar asked with a perplexed smile.

"You've always had a good working relationship with the pelmesate in Semna. I need to know ... the political climate in the city."

Ra'Shaar raised his eyebrow as he studied his nephew. Khai had always been a difficult person to read, but today he was different. "Things seem chaotic. A peshte runs the region on behalf of the vizier in Kerma. Instead of the Romans, he's constantly fretting about a rogue pelmes with an army not too far beyond the cataract to the north. You probably served under him during the war."

"Mshindi," Khai said with a nod. "Does he come into the city very often?"

"Never, from what I hear. I think he's at odds with every administrator in the region."

"Even Piankhi?"

"Him and another rogue man named Amen-Tekah. He has about a thousand or more men and claims rulership of Nobatia and Kerma."

"I've never heard of him before," Khai said.

"Just another warlord trying to pick up the pieces of a shattered kingdom. Although they've come close a couple of times over the past few months, he and Mshindi have yet to clash on a battlefield. Mshindi and Piankhi, however, have had a couple of minor conflicts."

"Kushites fighting Kushites, while Romans rove freely up and down the Nile," Khai muttered in disgust.

"The pelmes-ate tells me the Romans have announced that they'll be setting up a vassal in Korosko. Piankhi, Amen-Tekah, and a handful of others are vying for the position. But I don't believe the Romans will do things the way they're expecting them to."

"Nor do I," Khai said.

"What's your interest in such matters?" Ra'Shaar asked. "When you left, you were a cavalryman. Now you speak like a peshte. Since the Queen-Mother is dead..."

"The Kandace is with me," Khai announced in a subdued voice. "She wants to mount another assault on the Romans to drive them out. She needs Mshindi's help to do it."

Ra'Shaar sighed heavily and cast a wary eye at his nephew. "Khai, the war is over. The Romans have won."

"The Kandace doesn't see it that way, and neither do I."

Ra'Shaar looked askance. "I don't understand, Khai. Why do you of all people believe the Amani-aa'ila is worth fighting for?"

Although he was taken aback momentarily, Khai deemed his uncle's question a valid one. Yes, the Amani-aa'ila had likely profited in some fashion at the capture and trade of his family. Yes, royal policies of commission and omission had contributed to the toxic environment that existed and had allowed such abductions to take place throughout Kush with impunity.

Kush could be vile, and Kush could be wicked. However, in the end, Kush is ultimately what the people allowed her to be.

"The Kandace has convinced me that it is," Khai said.

"How?"

"She could have fled to Meroë," Khai said, shaking his head as if wresting with an irrational thought. "She would have been relatively safe there. She could have gone east or even west, but she didn't. I was wrong about her. Everything she's done has been out of love for something greater than herself. Even fighting the Romans."

Ra'Shaar tilted his head and, for the first time in a long while, he was able to read his nephew. "It appears she isn't the only one with a love in her heart for something greater," he said admirably. "There's no need for you to go to Semna. I can tell you where Pelmes Mshindi is right now."

✇ ✇

"What do you mean, a rogue group of Kushites?" Tribune Publius demanded, standing eye-to-eye with Centurion Cyprian.

"They came out of nowhere. We had the Queen cornered, and then these soldiers just appeared," Cyprian reported evenly.

"So, now they are soldiers?"

"They had to have been," Cyprian said with a slight frown. "They were disciplined in their approach and how they launched their spears. They were obviously well trained."

"They were likely marauders," Publius stated, his hot breath bathing Cyprian's face.

"Perhaps. But they outnumbered us and had the advantage of high ground. I didn't want to risk losing more men, particularly since we know so little about this region."

Publius glared at the centurion for a moment and then turned away. "I will not argue with your rationale, Justus. However, you were so close to ending this forlorn pursuit." Publius filled a goblet with posca and offered it to his fellow officer. Cyprian accepted the beverage yet refrained from drinking.

"Tribune, I'm concerned that those Kushites were part of a larger hostile group. Whoever they were, they are now providing shelter to the Queen. This now complicates matters for us."

"Indeed. We have to change our tactics," Publius commented. He removed his galea and raked his sweat-drenched hair with his hand. "We can no longer afford to dispatch single centuries. From this point on, we move as a cohesive unit."

"Yes, sir," Cyprian responded, grateful that he had not had to expend much energy convincing his commander to follow the sensible course of action.

"However, we need more information." Publius called for the praefectus castrorum, who quickly appeared and stood at attention.

"There are at least twenty men in our ranks with dark skin. Find them and have them report to me immediately."

The officer saluted crisply and hurried away into the encampment.

Publius turned toward Cyprian. "By Jupiter, I was hoping to have more to show for our efforts before getting to this point. We're running out of time. Marius will be here in a couple of days, and I want this woman apprehended before he arrives."

Chapter 34

The Shrine of Amesesmi sat in a lonely clearing just beyond the east bank of the Nile. Semna sat on the opposing side of the river, scores of boats perched at the docks leading to the city. Unlike the neighboring ancient Egyptian fort, the shrine itself was peaceful and rarely received visitors other than pilgrims fulfilling vows made unto the wife of the war god Apedemack.

Amanirenas studied the temple from the cover of the nearby forest. The towering trees gave her refuge from the late morning sun and provided her with the opportunity to examine the shrine's unique architecture. She reckoned that the structure had been erected some four to five hundred years ago—a testament to Kushite engineering.

The striking contour of the building jabbed at her heart, as it painfully reminded her of how very little she and Teriteqas had actually constructed during their reign. Together, they had commissioned only a handful of building projects in Meroë, and some of those had been put on hold indefinitely due to the conflict with Rome. She hoped that Kharapkhael would someday take up the mantle of creating Kushite edifices that would endure for centuries, but now that dream would have to take another form.

Her thoughts shifted to the path leading east toward a nearby mountain range. Just beyond the hills was her objective: the last standing army in Kush. Yet looming higher than the mountains was the specter of a persisting debt, demanding payment in full.

"You're still worried about it," Khai said. Her head spun around as the sound of his voice snatched her from the contemplative state.

"Worried about what?"

"The general."

Amanirenas surveyed the area and noted Khai was indeed alone.

"The others are around," Khai said, anticipating her concern. "I have several groups waiting along the road. We should spot Batae and Saiesha's party as they approach the shrine."

"I hope they weren't delayed," Amanirenas said.

"That look on your face has come and gone several times over the past couple of days. I know you're anxious, but I believe you'll be able to convince the general to fight for Kush."

"If only it were that simple," Amanirenas said with a sigh.

"I'm just a soldier, and I have a limited knowledge of what motivates men politically. But Mshindi is a soldier as well. In the end, I believe he'll put aside the differences you two have and fight."

"Mshindi may be a soldier," Amanirenas said as she sat down on a fallen log, "but he's still a man with a heart. A heart I was not too kind with at one point in the past."

"And you think he bears a grudge against you? Surely it doesn't override his sense of duty."

"And it never did in the past. He was completely loyal to my husband. He never let any bitterness show. Even after I arranged for him to be assigned a command far away in the Northern province." Amanirenas paused and measured the amount of regret issuing through her voice. Her comfort level with Khai had grown by leaps since they left Kawa, yet she was still guarded as to how much to share with him.

"And then there is Amanishakheto, his wife ... my sister. I've wronged her as well. There is little reason to believe family will count for much in the coming days."

"I understand less about relationships than I do about politics," Khai said sitting next to her on the log. "I've never allowed myself to care about anyone for fear that it would cloud my thinking and make me less decisive. Soldiers can't afford that sort of burden.

"Once a soldier has an objective and an order, things are very simple, and fear, worry, and regret don't matter. There is no past, no present, only the objective and the order. Perhaps that's how you should look at this. Lay the emotions aside—focus only on the objective."

"Spoken like a man," Amanirenas said serenely, fondly recalling a similar conversation with Teriteqas. "It's easy for a man to categorize emotions as if they were tools to be stored on a workbench until they are needed. But women aren't like that. For us, emotions, sensations, people, and experiences are all interrelated. What happens to one influences how we feel about the other."

She placed her hand on top of Khai's and gave it an affectionate squeeze—a gesture that took him by surprise. She quickly allayed his concern with a warm smile.

"You are right, though," she added, her eyes drifting toward the east. "There are times when one needs to be singular of mind. To ignore how things are related and cut away the distractions. That seems to be the only way to properly make war and win a real battle."

"After Napata, I was finished with fighting. I wanted no more to do with the Amani-aa'ila. Something died in me when I saw the paqar go down. When I came across you, all I saw was more death and waste, and for the first time in years, all I wanted to do was go home."

"What changed your mind?"

"Sabrakmani," Khai answered with a nod. "He was convinced that you should try to preserve not the Amani-aa'ila, but the nation of Kush. The notion that we are many tribes making up one family— and all of the families are important. That's what changed my mind and my heart. I believe that Pelmes Mshindi and his wife will listen to that."

Khai gently place his free hand atop hers. His heart slowly started to race as he gradually locked eyes with her. Almost instantly, he encountered a deposit of strength and dignity that radiated throughout her soul and into his.

"I believe they will," Amanirenas affirmed tranquilly, losing herself in the depths of Khai's conviction. "You honor your family, Khai. I believe your father would be very proud of you."

The quiet moment was torn asunder by the sudden sound of heavy footfalls. They both looked across the clearing and saw Pahor running up to them.

"My kandace, it's the other group," Pahor exclaimed, trying to catch his breath. "Batae and Saiesha. They've arrived!"

⚘ ⚘

Legionary Akil Chuma raced through the Nubian forest like a leopard. He dodged branches, rocks, and even snakes as he sliced through the foliage with the sole purpose of delivering the gift the gods had dropped into his lap. While the prize was not necessarily for him, he would indeed benefit from the result. He hurdled the trunk of a massive tree and relished the thought that his name would forever be associated with the capture of a black queen that had incited rebellion against Rome. He would stand shoulder to shoulder with the first spear centurions of the *Legio Deiotariana* as they paraded past the forum during Petronius's triumph—a common honor granted to legionaries who distinguished themselves during a campaign.

He finally reached his objective and slowed down as he came upon the stockade protecting the Roman encampment. Mindful that he still wore the garb of a Kushite merchant instead of a veteran Roman legionary, he raised his hands and recited the password enough times to avoid any misunderstandings. The sentries protecting the porta praetoria gave him a brief inspection and then waved him through the gate.

Once in the camp, Chuma again broke into a sprint, rushing by the armory and skirting past other soldiers on his way to the command tent. The closed flap and lack of a posted guard announced that the tribune was not in his tent. Panting heavily, Chuma tried to divine where the tribune might be during the hora quinta. On a whim, he headed in the direction of the sacrificial altars.

However, as he rounded the corner of the command tent, he nearly collided with the tribune's personal guard.

"Tribune, I have news," Chuma blurted as he pushed past the sentinel.

"What is it, soldier?" Publius asked, heading into the command tent without breaking stride.

"We've found her."

The tribune spun around, suddenly recalling that the Egyptian legionary was one of those sent out to track down the Queen. "Are you certain?"

"We followed a party to a shrine on the east side the river."

"So? They could have been anyone."

"Yes sir, but these people fit the descriptions given by the legionaries that engaged the hostiles a few days ago. There were a dozen men travelling with a lone female." Chuma paused, noting the tribune's growing interest. "While at the shrine, they met up with a second group—most of whom were deployed in the surrounding vicinity, serving as a security detail."

"Continue," Publius said, folding his arms.

"The object of their security ring was a woman—and everyone in the party deferred to her."

Publius nodded in approval, his lips forming a thin line. "Where is she?"

"About an hour away. But they are being tracked by a team of our scouts. We'll be able to monitor them for at least two days if necessary."

"No," Publius voice was full of resolve. Marius was only a day or two away, and sound judgment pined at Publius to await the other two cohorts before proceeding. However, an insatiable desire to end the miserable hunt burned far too hot within him. "We'll leave immediately."

Chapter 35

The half-day journey was not as difficult as Amanirenas had thought it would be. The mountainous terrain was tamed by a well-worn path that gradually inclined as it meandered through the diminishing forest. The Queen's heart rate increased steadily as they drew closer to their destination.

"We're making better time than I thought we would," Khai said from somewhere in the rear.

"Yeah, I just can't wait to die," Pedese commented flippantly. "Only the third time this month I've walked into the jaws of death." His words seemed to diffuse the collective nervousness of the group, as many of them smiled at the soldier's remarks.

Even Amanirenas found herself reacting to Pedese's comments with a weary grin. At the moment, she welcomed any thought that would deter her mind from constantly rehearsing the forthcoming meeting with the general.

"How long?" the Queen asked Khai.

"We should see their encampment as soon as we clear the hills up ahead."

Amanirenas nodded and willed herself to pick up her pace, which, in turn, forced the retinue to do the same. She focused on the hills ahead, longing to see a regiment of Kushite soldiers once again. She silently prayed to whichever god would listen for irrefutable wisdom and golden words to convince Mshindi—or whoever would take heed—to take up arms against the Roman invaders as opposed to other Kushites.

Batae's report about Amen-Tekah, the self-proclaimed grand vizier of the region, gnawed at her like a leech. Splintering into tribal factions governed by competing strongmen guaranteed the demise of the Kushite Empire. Her father had frequently predicted such an occurrence if respect for the Amani-aa'ila should ever wane. To him, maintaining power was expressed through a simple progression: Work for their adoration first—if people love you, they'll do anything for you. Work for their respect second—people will at least obey a ruler whom they honor. Work for their fear last—people who are in dread of you dare not plot against you.

Amanirenas was in the process of determining the best way of recapturing the respect of the soldiers in the valley below when the salvo of arrows whistled overhead and indiscriminately darted the trees to their left. The bodyguard swiftly took up a defensive posture, Pedese and Batae assuming the point position and being the first to draw their weapons. Khai stepped in front of the Kandace, who instinctively drew her sword.

Respect, the Queen thought, peering through the forest for the first Roman she would attempt to dispatch.

Another volley of arrows streaked from the foliage.

"They're shooting over our heads," Pahor stated, sweat dotting the sides of his head.

"The damn Romans want her alive," Batae said, squeezing the hilt of his weapon in preparation of the bloodletting to come.

Amanirenas stole one last glance toward the eastern hills—hope of seeing the last Kushite army ebbing away with each heartbeat.

So close...

While the foliage concealed them, Khai perceived that the stalkers now flanked them to the left and the right. In fact, he was certain that they were moments away from having them surrounded.

"How many?" Saiesha breathed, clutching a dagger.

"A lot," Pahor answered calmly.

Khai narrowed his focus to the area deadhead. "These aren't Romans," he said, maintaining his weapon at the ready.

"Makurians," Batae asserted.

"It's their style," Pedese responded. "They were always good at ambush."

Out of nowhere, a dozen black men armed with spears and short shields appeared before the bodyguard troop. Before Amanirenas could finish counting them, three dozen more emerged, slowly inching forward as if tightening a noose.

"Kandace Amanirenas," one of the men called.

The Queen moved to step forward, but Khai stopped her before she could.

"Identify yourself," Khai demanded.

"Kalamar. I come in the name of Amen-Tekah, the grand vizier of Kerma and Nobatia."

Amanirenas glanced at Batae, who offered a slight nod to confirm that the man was indeed familiar.

"What do you want?" she asked as thirty to forty more men filtered in from the forest—completely encompassing her party.

"Simply put, you."

☒ ☖

Batae and Khai followed Amanirenas as she was led into the large, brown brick house situated in the midst of a walled compound. The rest of the bodyguard troop was herded to a holding section of the complex that Pahor immediately recognized as a pen designed to house cattle.

As they entered the house, Khai immediately assessed the assortment of men inside. Of the dozen or so, only a handful even looked like they could be mistaken for soldiers, while none of them possessed a prayer for passing as nobility.

The fattest and darkest man in the room wore a colorful tunic and the headdress of an Egyptian priest. Khai grimaced at the disagreeable sight and concluded that they were finally face-to-face with Amen-Tekah.

"Welcome! I am Amen-Tekah, the grand vizier of Kerma and Nobatia," the large man said, rising from the stool serving as his makeshift throne. "I've waited a long time to meet you."

Amanirenas surveyed the dreary room in silence. When her eyes finally fell to Amen-Tekah, the fat man wore a grin that reminded her of a wild hyena.

"This is Kandace Amanirenas, the Queen of Kush," Khai announced.

"I know who she is," Amen-Tekah barked with a devilish smile. "The nobility of Kerma welcomes her."

"For a grand vizier, you have a poor understanding of formal protocol," Amanirenas said, stepping forward. "A vizier always meets the Kandace outside and escorts her in. And he never introduces himself. To do so is a sign of disrespect."

Amen-Tekah laughed, his deep baritone voice filling the room. "You must forgive me. My advisors failed to educate me on the appropriate way to receive a kandace—likely because they've never met one before!"

The chamber erupted with a cascade of mocking merriment. Amanirenas entertained their mirth for a moment before brandishing a broad smile of her own.

"Fair enough, because I don't recall ever appointing you as the grand vizier of anything. A royal appointment must be confirmed by the Council of Ministers and then consecrated with the appropriate sacrifice in the Temple of Amun-Ra. Otherwise, it is illegitimate."

"Maybe so. But as you can see, I have more swords and spears than you do. So I can call myself pharaoh if I want. However, I believe the Romans would call me a proconsul or a governor." Amen-Tekah reseated himself on the stool, his protruding gut spilling onto his thighs.

"Anyway, I had your man followed," he said gesturing to Batae. "You were simply too ripe of a fruit not to pick for myself. Perhaps the Romans will make me governor of all Kush once I turn you over to them."

"That's an empty likelihood, and you know it," Amanirenas

stated, her piercing gaze somehow driving Amen-Tekah's smile away. "I've heard you're from Egypt. If that's true, then you know they'll never accept you."

"And why is that?" the large man asked with a serious tone.

"The Romans adhere to a strict command structure, starting with the principes. Your appointment as a governor would be scrutinized by the Roman Senate." Amanirenas paused to examine the befuddled expression on Amen-Tekah's face.

"Augustus Caesar may be a young ruler, but he is sensible enough not to make appointments that would be a source of ridicule by influential men in his government."

"You act as if you know this man," Amen-Tekah said dismissively.

"I know him well enough to say that he would never approve of making a lowly criminal that used to herd camels through the desert a vassal of a hostile province. If they knew I was your captive, the Romans would take me from you and not even bother to ask."

"You speak as a desperate woman without the cover of a man. You have no options, and your words carry little weight," Amen-Tekah declared.

"You're correct, Amen-Tekah. I am desperate. But my desperation is not for myself." She slowly clasped her hands behind her back. "I am desperate to preserve Kush and everything passed down to me from previous generations. I am desperate to prevent Rome from ravaging this land as they've done to Egypt. They will take our gold as surely as they've taken Egypt's grain.

"But our true gold isn't that which is quarried from the mountains— nor is it the bounty taken from the Nile. The true gold of Kush is the people in it. The Romans will take the people and make slaves of them. Every generation of Kushites from now on will live on bended knee before Caesar until we're forgotten."

Amen-Tekah shifted his weigh from side to side, all sense of mirth evaporated like a dry savannah lake during the late summer.

"You've seen it before, Amen-Tekah," Amanirenas continued, watching as her audience drifted one by one into wordless conversations with haunting memories.

Amen-Tekah recalled the hefty taxes levied on his trade by the Roman regime. Excises that turned a once-lucrative endeavor into a futile effort to garner even a small profit. The Roman tax system had driven him seemingly overnight into the criminal existence that now overshadowed his life. And although he was good at it, theft and marauding were not his first preference.

"Your words have gained weight in this short span," Amen-Tekah said with a sigh. "The Romans are like a plague. They take, take, take, and give nothing back but a dried and withered corpse. It is a grim prospect." He frowned and rose to his feet. "And you want to go to Mshindi and try to convince the fool to fight the Romans again?"

"No, I want you to come with me."

Amen-Tekah laughed. However, this time he was the only one. "He'll kill us both."

"Perhaps, but at least he'll kill me first."

The hall exploded with laughter. Even Batae was entertained until he received an unyielding glare from Khai.

"Such spirit. I've always taken pride in my ability to identify courage, even when it is veiled by foolhardiness," Amen-Tekah said. "You are worthy of a noble death, Queen. And yes, I will escort you, even if it is to Henel."

Chapter 36

The village of Kor sat nestled among a cascade of soft rolling hills. Mshindi had no idea for how many centuries the hidden town had served as respite for caravans and traders sojourning between upper and lower Kush or how many thousands of travelers it had greeted as they completed the arduous trek from the east. Part of him felt bad that the once-charming settlement now served as the makeshift home base for the *Teriahi* regiment. Outside of the fort in Qasr Ibrim, it was perhaps the final Kushite military facility in the kingdom.

He stood next to the window of his personal chambers on the second story of the village's central dufufa. This vantage point offered him a prime perspective on the village, as well as of his encamped army that was occupying most of the surrounding region. The villagers busied themselves with their everyday tasks—most of which were now dedicated to help support the 2,500 men that made up his portion of the Nobatian regiment. Nevertheless, the people seemed to embrace the soldiers—partly because their presence served as a major deterrent to the Blemmeys and other lawless tribes in the area.

There were times that Mshindi wished that their sole purpose were to fill the role of the local police force; however, he knew this was not the case. He looked beyond his army at the horizon, where the swirling clouds were lit aflame by the late afternoon sun. Somewhere out there, a shift had taken place.

Even before the runners had arrived more than a week ago with news of the Roman victory at Napata, Mshindi had somehow known that an angry Roman storm from the south was heading his way to engulf the assemblage of Kushite manhood before him. His suspicions had been confirmed at least twice as they received information that the Romans had burnt several settlements as they headed down the Nile on their return trip to Egypt. While Mshindi doubted the invaders would venture far enough inland to engage his force, he could not help but think about the major cities of Qustul and Korosko. Under the Amani-aa'ila, his regiment had been the designated sentinel for the region, yet here they were stowed away in a small village in a hidden valley and estranged from their appointed vizier, Piankhi.

"Up, up," a soft voice demanded from below.

Mshindi looked down and smiled.

"Yes, Mara," he said, picking up his two-year-old daughter. The little girl brushed her hand against the stubble on his chin.

"Rough," she delivered with a frown.

"Yes, I know. I don't look or feel like a general today. Your mother insisted I take a day off. And your mother always gets her way."

Mshindi kissed the little girl and then put her down. She immediately shot toward her mother, Amanishakheto, who cradled another child as she sat on the bed.

"If that were true, we'd be back in Korosko right now," Amanishakheto sassed playfully.

"It wouldn't be safe."

"I know that," Amanishakheto muttered shaking her head. She glanced at the baby in her arms. "She's never known anything more than this dufufa or this trivial village."

"I'm sorry," Mshindi responded, turning his attention back toward the distant horizon. "It's been over a week since we received the news, and I still don't know what to do. Amanirenas, Jaelen—both dead."

Amanishakheto grimaced at her sister's name. Their last private conversation nearly three years earlier had proven to be prophetic in nature. Predictably, Amanirenas had allowed her passion to escort her judgment, and now the kingdom was fragmented, and the Amani-aa'ila was next to collapse. She had no idea of Amanitore's fate—nor did it matter from a legal perspective. Upon the deaths of Amanirenas and her last surviving son, divine rulership fell to Amanishakheto.

Although she envied her older sister, she had never imagined that the burden of being kandace would fall upon her, and she found herself more conflicted than ever. In the span of two years, the Roman army had marched into Kush and beaten them soundly on their own soil. Her husband's regiment of 2,500 men was no match for the garrison in Primis, let alone the Romans returning from the southern campaign.

Although Mshindi was in command, final word on their next course of action was subject to her dictate. She pondered capitulating to the invaders, an action she had stressed to Amanirenas three years ago. However, she knew that Mshindi would never entertain the thought at this point. The Romans would view Amanishakheto as the kandace, apprehend her, and execute her in a humiliating and violent fashion. She knew that her husband would die before allowing such a fate to befall her or their children.

"We're still waiting to hear back from our scouts about the Roman garrison to the north. The arrival of those cohorts last week was a bad omen," Mshindi was saying, his eyes still affixed to the western horizon. "Oh, I'm sorry, we agreed there would be no talk of war in this room today."

Amanishakheto tendered him a forgiving smile as she arose with the baby.

"Well, since you've already broken the agreement, I think the best option may be to avoid the Romans altogether and go east."

"You would no longer be a queen. It would be the end of the Amani-aa'ila. Kush would die," Mshindi said.

"I wouldn't be a queen, but I would still be your wife. And these would still be your daughters."

Mshindi surveyed the three of them—his family. He had spent the vast majority of his life in service to Kush—fighting her battles and protecting her borders. Now she was pitted against an unbeatable foe, and he was tired. He longed for the simplicity of a life spent living by the river and growing crops on a nearby farm. One word and the *Teriahi* would be disbanded, with 2,500 men returning to 2,500 families. The Romans would pass through the region none the wiser and head home with their victory. Dignity would be a small price to pay for survival.

"What of Vizier Piankhi in Qasr Ibrim?" Amanishakheto pondered. "What would he do?"

"Whatever he wants. However, he'd be wise to abandon the fort," the words rolled bitterly from Mshindi's mouth as he thought about his strained relationship with the regional vizier. Ever since they had withdrawn from Amanirenas's forces, the vizier had been making subtle hints that he intended to negotiate with the Romans as a government independent of Kush when the time came.

"Amanirenas never did trust him. Even before the war," Amanishakheto said. "Appears she was right about him."

"Enough about Piankhi. Do you truly wish to leave? The decision is yours," Mshindi said, caressing Amanishakheto with his eyes.

Before she could answer, a knock at the door sounded through the bedchamber.

"Yes," Mshindi answered.

Amanishakheto's personal attendant opened the door. "Commander Olaeto with an urgent message," she said, quickly giving way to the muscular soldier behind her.

"Yes, commander?"

"My lord, we've received word via the homing falcon from the cataract watchtower. A large contingent of Amen-Tekah's men is headed in this general direction."

"What is that fool doing this time?" Mshindi groaned.

"There's more, my lord. Three Roman cohorts have entered and navigated the cataract."

"We knew more would come," Amanishakheto commented.

"Yes, my lady. However, one cohort has veered off and is moving east very quickly. And if they continue in that direction, they will arrive here within a day."

"How did they find out about this place?" Amanishakheto asked.

"We're not sure, but they could be stalking Amen-Tekah's group. The last report calculates that the Romans will intercept them within the day, at which point they will be less than an hour from us."

"Perhaps he made his deal with the Romans and he's leading them here," Mshindi said. He dismissed the commander and allowed himself one last brief moment of peace. He glanced at his wife, and the two shared a long gaze that conveyed more than either one of them could say in an hour.

The decision of whether to abandon the fight or face the invaders one last time had been made for them.

Chapter 37

Publius despised jungle warfare. Lying in wait and ambushing an opponent ran contrary to the Roman military ethos drilled into him since the first time he had lifted a gladius. He preferred to battle in an open field, giving him the opportunity to see the full strength of his adversary. However, the current terrain afforded him little choice but to stalk his prey in the bush and wait for the best moment to strike.

The reports from the reconnaissance patrols had proved fruitful, and the Queen of Kush was marked. It mattered little to Publius that she now journeyed with roughly 150 armed men. Her destination mattered even less to him as he issued silent hand signals to the company of 450 legionaries hidden amongst the trees and foliage as they waited for the Kushite troop to enter a plot of land clear enough for them to mount a methodical charge.

Within moments, the Kushites would enter the three-way vice manned by the four centuries under his command. Although the other three commanders had voiced concerns about the stealth approach, they understood the significance of the opportunity and agreed to the unorthodox maneuver.

Publius ignored the warm sweat rolling into his eyes from his galea, careful to keep the red plume atop his helmet beneath the large leaves providing him cover. He savored the gradual buildup of stress as anticipation of the strike ascended like the early evening moon.

Saiesha was completely baffled by the character that was Amen-Tekah. The man possessed not a drop of noble blood, but somehow managed to exhibit every disagreeable trait of a conceited, entitled minister. His deep voice seemed to shake the leaves from the very trees, and he was none too shy about speaking his mind. He complained constantly about Mshindi for reasons Saiesha was yet to fathom. From what she could gather, the general and his army represented the last vestige of law and order in the region and stood as the sole impediment to Amen-Tekah's unchecked control of the northern trade routes.

Thus far, Pahor had done an admirable job of occupying the hefty strongman with anecdotes of the political strife that had marred the regions south of the third cataract falls. The young man's efforts kept Amen-Tekah and his endless list of hollow complaints away from the Kandace, which was appreciated, as the distraction allowed her walk well ahead of the self-proclaimed vizier.

"We've only a couple hours of light left," Khai said to Amanirenas as they approached a clearing in the forest. "We're still about an hour away."

Amanirenas responded with an optimistic nod. While their unexpected detour at the hands of the "grand vizier" may have derailed their timetable, it did have the agreeable effect of building their contingent of allies. Yet, as she looked around at the assorted clutch of men that followed Amen-Tekah, she saw what amounted to a band of finely dressed mercenaries, criminals, and thugs maneuvering for prime potion at a gaming table.

By some miracle of Isis, she was able to convince Amen-Tekah to leave the bulk of his force at their basecamp and take only one hundred or so men as they sojourned to Kor. The last thing she wanted was for Mshindi to feel threatened by the sudden appearance of 1,000 men sworn to fight for a hostile rival.

Nevertheless, despite his unceremonial decorum and lack of anything resembling formal etiquette, Amanirenas was grateful for Amen-Tekah's cooperation. His presence boosted her belief that people were willing to defy Roman superiority and fight for Kush and their own way of life.

Saiesha breathed a sigh of relief as the party finally emerged from the forest into a clearing of waist-high grass. At least now she only had to avoid the snakes on the ground instead of the ones concealed among the vines and tree branches. All was quiet in the peaceful glade—even Amen-Tekah had ceased talking and appeared to appreciate the gentle scenery before them. She followed a red falcon as it gracefully sliced through the air above the tree line ahead.

The bird veered swiftly to the left—cutting out of the path of an iron projectile launched from the dense foliage about sixty cubits ahead. The javelin arced and impaled itself in the torso of the Kushite on point. Before he hit the ground, at least a dozen more Kushite soldiers were skewered in like fashion. The bodyguard retinue promptly ushered the Queen and Saiesha into the center of a defensive sphere.

Amen-Tekah's men instinctively elevated their shields and created a living barricade against the threat that emerged methodically from the forest before them.

Khai had seen the Roman maneuver twice before—once in Philae and again in Primis. Now, as then, he was utterly astounded at the precision, skill, and discipline demonstrated by the legionaries.

Guided by the steady cadence of a whistle, the Romans slowly emerged from the trees, line by line, until it became apparent that they were purposely forming the shape of a spearhead aimed directly at the heart of the Kushites. All the legionaries in the front line of the formation extended their pilum from behind their curved shields.

A handful of Amen-Tekah's men rushed past the defensive sphere around the Kandace and charged the Roman configuration with a hearty battle cry.

"No, don't!" Khai shouted repeatedly. However, their angry bellows drowned out his warnings.

"The spears! Watch the spears!"

Furious, Amen-Tekah urged the warriors forward, yet those who were not impaled by the Roman lances were repulsed by the interlocking shields and forced off to the sides.

"We have to get the Queen out of the open," Pahor exclaimed. "Head to the tree line on the left!"

"No!" Batae sounded, "They've outflanked us." Even as he spoke, Romans systematically filed from the tree lines to the left and right of them.

Before Khai could even issue the order to retreat down the path they had come down, the Romans quickly formed a skirmish line two men deep on both sides—drastically reducing their only opening for escape. However, the legionaries did not advance, but rather held their ground, with their pila extended beyond the red wall of their shields.

The marching Roman phalanx continued its slow advance, forcing its way into the Queen's defensive circle. Amanirenas drew the Roman gladius she carried, wiped the sweat from her eyes, and focused intently on the cadence driving the Roman encroachment. She took several deliberate steps forward, her weapon pointed at the invaders.

"What are you doing?" Pedese screamed at her without thinking. She turned to him and quickly yanked the spear he was carrying from his grasp. The soldier resisted briefly and then let go, a perplexed sneer covering his face. "Crazy woman."

Suddenly, the bursts from the whistle sped up, and as it did, the outermost lines of the phalanx slowly swung ahead, gradually giving the formation a right and left wing.

Amanirenas narrowed her eyes and scanned the deadly configuration like a hawk. The enemy's constant undulating movement, paired with the swaying spears and swords, made it difficult, but at last she found the prime objective. She sheathed her sword and repositioned the spear in preparation to launch it into the hive of Roman legionaries.

Tribune Publius observed the skirmish with growing satisfaction as Centurion Cyprian's century executed the phalanx maneuver. The legionaries did an exceptional job of deploying the wings—disallowing the Kushites to slip around to the sides of the formation. Anyone who tried was swiftly cut down. The original number of 150 or so Kushites that had entered the clearing was dwindling by the moment. Some of the foolish dark-skinned beasts impaled themselves on the sharp iron shanks of the Roman pila like meat as they attempted desperately to break the formation.

"Close," tribune ordered to the awaiting optio.

The soldier briskly relayed the command to the rest of the century. He then flashed the corresponding hand signs to the centurion who commanded the century on the opposing side of the field. In the wink of an eye, the dual skirmish lines formed by the centuries shifted their position and closed the gap behind the Kushites.

Publius was about to order the perimeter centuries to engage when he noticed that the phalanx had abruptly stopped its advance. The screeching communication whistle was silent, and he immediately probed the field for Cyprian. He quickly located the centurion, lying on his back with a spear protruding from his neck. Although the man convulsed for a moment, his movements quickly faded.

The Kushites quickly took advantage of the paralyzed formation and rushed to attack the edges. Publius almost laughed at their valiant effort.

"Advance," the tribune commanded coolly. As the order spread down the line and across the field, Publius glimpsed one of the two black women who had entered the glade with the Kushite soldiers. The woman rather heroically charged the nearest wing of the phalanx swinging what looked like a Roman gladius.

"That must be her," Publius speculated, all mirth drained away. "Black dog." Less than fifty paces away, he altered his direction and headed directly for the Queen.

Chapter 38

Pedese managed to stay clear of the iron-tipped Roman spears until one of Amen-Tekah's men inadvertently shoved him directly into the path of the formation's left wing. Even though Pedese balanced himself, he still stumbled into the wall of shields and caught a thrusting gladius to the shoulder. Suddenly, a huge hand grasped his neck and jerked him away before the Roman could pull the sword back and fire another thrust that would have certainly pierced his chest.

"By the gods, have you forgotten how to fight these bastards already?" Batae shouted, hurdling Pedese aside. "Attack the edge!"

Pedese watched as Batae took an angle, drove his spear in between the shields and then literally pried the legionaries apart. He quickly exploited the resulting gap by slamming his massive body between the two men, causing the formation to fold momentarily while the Romans hustled to regroup. However, by the time they did, Batae had managed to kill one legionary and maim another.

Amen-Tekah saw the maneuver and hastily adapted a version of his own. The bulky warlord seized two spears, wedged them between two frontline Romans, and then drove his large body between them. Several Kushites rushed into the ensuing gap, further destabilizing the formation. Several interior lines of the phalanx started to fall back; however, they had nowhere to go.

Khai almost started to entertain the prospect of survival, but then caught glimpse of the nearly 200 Romans starting to close in. Soon, all hope would be choked off. He quickly relocated the Kandace, who was engaged with a legionary who had broken away from the phalanx.

The Roman launched several calculated thrusts at the woman, but failed to pin her. She was incredibly nimble and danced around the enemy, searching for an opening. Khai rushed to her aid but was intercepted by a crushing blow from a Roman shield.

Amanirenas spun around the legionary and sliced his leading leg, managing to gash his calf. The Roman appeared to lose his balance but recovered and swiftly stabbed at the woman, inflicting an acute wound to her leg. The Kandace absorbed the gouging, elevated her gladius, and swiftly brought it down on the Roman's still-extended arm—severing it at the elbow. As the man went down in agony, she repositioned her blade and plunged the tip into his back at the base of the neck—quickly ending his tortured screams.

Amanirenas wiped away the blood that splattered across her face and was immediately confronted by a vindictive bearded Roman wearing the red crest of a tribune.

"Quod occideris postremus Romanorum," the man roared, his gladius pointed at her ominously. However, he did not advance, but rather made a directional gesture with his free hand.

Before she could respond, Amanirenas was all but surrounded by several legionaries who carefully boxed her in. She glanced back at the demonstrative officer, who approached guardedly.

"Tu praemium petat," he uttered with a sadistic grin.

Amanirenas instinctively engaged the nearest Roman with a fierce parry. Ignoring her tired arms and the throbbing wound on her leg, she silently swore she would meet death before they captured her.

She thrusted fiercely at one legionary and missed. Another Roman struck her dead in the face with the hilt of his gladius, hurdling her into the long grass. She landed on her back but instinctively rolled over to her hands and knees, a jolting pain piercing through her body with each movement. Her vision was blurry, and she could scarcely make out the strands of grass in her face.

"Colligunt usque eam," she heard the tribune command.

Amanirenas pawed blindly at the nearest person, her mind drifting between a dark void and the raucous reality swirling around her. However, she immediately felt another blow pound mercilessly against the side of her head. She lost all sense of balance, and a warm liquid ran down her face. Dazed, her stomach quivered violently, followed by a swift eruption of bitter fluids as she vomited profusely.

For a long while, darkness was all she could see. She welcomed the tranquility it offered and found it difficult to resist the quiet haven that beckoned her. Yet, every now and then, voices and strange noises interrupted her solitude. Some of the voices even sounded familiar.

"No prize for you today, Roman!" someone exclaimed.

Amanirenas couldn't make out who the person was—nor could she understand the cacophony of clashes and yells that seemed to grow louder.

"Sunt plures Kushites post nos!" someone trumpeted in a strange tongue.

A momentous rumble, growing like the sound of an approaching deluge, trailed the words.

Amanirenas could sense footfalls all around but had neither the strength nor the inclination to raise her head or open her eyes to investigate. Even when she tried to move, a firm hand gently held her down and silently discouraged any more effort to do so. The shouts and noise grew closer and louder, like a driving rain, until they gradually blew past.

"The Kandace, my lord," a faceless voice uttered.

"Impossible..."

The Queen opened her eyes and could only discern several ghostly figures staring down at her.

"It's a very bad wound," one voice said.

"She's going to lose it," said another one.

Amanirenas closed her eyes and focused once again on the encroaching darkness. This time, she decided to float away on the gentle tide of peace flowing through it.

The last thing she heard was the soft sobbing of a young lady—then there was the darkness.

Chapter 39

Quintus Publius stood at attention, his eyes affixed to the map that covered the tent wall behind his commanding officer. Even as Tribune Marius continued with his stern rebuke, Publius stood in disbelief at how far ahead of schedule the other two cohorts were in their arrival. Publius anticipated at least two more days before the other Romans caught up with them.

"What is your explanation?" Marius demanded.

"I saw an opportunity to capture the Queen and fulfill our mission," Publius stated plainly, assuming the tribune was likely already aware of the sordid details of his startling defeat, which had been brought about by a separate force of Kushites that literally appeared out of nowhere. "The intelligence was good. I had her within my grasp."

"The strategy you employed to apprehend the Queen is not in question. Your lack of judgment is, however."

Publius stiffened up at the comment, a gesture that did not go unnoticed by Marius.

"I had a sufficient force to engage the soldiers travelling with the Queen. They were no match for four centuries. I could have captured her with three."

Publius paused to recall the events that had transformed certain victory into a bewildering beating. The sudden rain of Kushite spears from the trees—followed by hordes of black men darting from the forest like angry bats. The Kushities attacked the phalanx formation's defenseless rear flank, causing them to break ranks prematurely, resulting in the death of nearly every Roman caught in the middle. Fortunately, at least one centurion had a better perspective and sounded a general retreat—a move that spared at least three of the four centuries from certain demise.

"How many soldiers attacked your force?" Marius asked, turning to study the map behind him.

"I didn't have a chance to count them," Publius replied stoically.

"Where did they come from? What tribe were they affiliated with?" Marius queried tersely.

"Their clothing was different than those who were with the Queen...."

"You don't know." Marius voiced, spinning around. "Say it! You don't know! You took your forces into a region you knew nothing about and were ill-prepared for what you encountered."

"I beg your pardon, sir, but that is the mission you gave me. We accepted that risk when we set out down the Nile. I regret losing 150 men, but it revealed that there are still hundreds of Kushities willing to fight."

Marius drenched a cloth in a nearby basin of cool water. He patted down his face slowly, trying to extinguish his anger in addition to combating the warm air.

"That line of thinking was applicable in Kerma and in the southern regions. But not here. Taking calculated risks to reach an objective is part of being in command. But it must be worth it. The soldiers that ambushed your centuries were likely what's left of the Kushite regiments we faced two years ago."

Publius silently recalled how the Kushite army had been whittled away when the III and XXII legions had started to drive into the heart of Nubia. The force that once outnumbered the Romans three to one had disappeared in droves, and Publius, like most other Roman officers, assumed that fear of facing Roman steel again would permanently hold those men at bay. However, if that was not going to be the case, the tribune welcomed the challenge.

"I see my error, sir," Publius said, anxious to move past his miscalculation. "This leaves us with one option. We have to go after the men who attacked us..."

"No. That would invite another disaster. Remember, Publius, your loss of so many men tarnishes my honor more than it does yours. The loss will be avenged, but it shall be done so efficiently," Marius said, turning back to the map. "The terrain of this region does not play into our favor. The surveyors report the landscape along the Nile from here to the second cataract is a mixture of jungle and rocky enclaves. There could be thousands of former soldiers along the river."

"Are you proposing we veer east, back along the wadi we used to enter Kush? Doing so would draw out any belligerent forces when we cut through the forest region into the eastern plains."

"Perhaps."

"Marius, I might add that it's better for us to engage and eradicate them while we are here with all three cohorts. Otherwise, we risk them becoming an infection that will never go away."

"I understand, but this new development leaves us with but one sane option." Marius knocked an empty goblet from a nearby table. "We must go to the fort in Primis and inform the prefect."

Publius looked away. Prefect Petronius would no doubt want a detailed report of his encounter with the Kushites, forcing him to relive the pitiful fracas once again.

For a long while, Amanirenas's memory of the battle came only in flashes of fragmented images with no sound. The images never made sense: Roman shield, Kushite spear, blood, and—Mshindi. Nevertheless, things slowly began to come together. She was immensely sore but forced her body into an upright position anyway.

It was then that she realized that she was in a real bed nestled in a plush room fit for a queen. A cool breeze fluttered into the chamber via a large open window. Her clothing was clean and bore a fresh floral scent.

"Take it slow, my kandace."

Amanirenas turned her head, expecting to see Saiesha, but was surprised that the simple motion was not enough to bring her faithful servant into full view. Only when she adjusted her torso could she see Saiesha.

"My eye," Amanirenas gasped softly, reaching for her left eye, only to find a garment there. She traced the cloth around her head and felt suddenly overcome by nausea. Saiesha rushed to her side as she stood up and nearly fell back down.

"No!" she cried, rising again. "No! They've taken my eye!"

Amanirenas pushed Saiesha away and struggled to move forward. Anguish, fear, hatred, and remorse blended to flush the pain from her body and fuel her drive to walk. After a few steps, she crumpled to the ground, tears streaming from her right eye and slick, dark fluid oozing from beneath the bandage covering the left. She sat up and wept profusely, refusing to imagine what the grotesque contortion that was her face looked like.

She sobbed until her tears ran dry and her heart went numb. However, when her own moans finally subsided, someone else's softly filled the room. The familiar voice transported Amanirenas back through time—before the war, before marriage, before every ceremony and sacrificial ritual that made her kandace. All the way back to childhood.

Amanirenas opened her eye and found Amanishakheto embracing her the same way she had when they were little girls intent on weathering a fierce emotional malady. The less Amanirenas cried, the tighter her younger sister's embrace became.

Within moments, Amanirenas found herself comforting Amanishakheto, swaying gently back and forth as she had done so many times decades ago.

Chapter 40

The medicine administered to Amanirenas by the healers every few hours could not compare with the euphoria she felt while holding her infant niece. Amanirenas spent most of the day rocking baby Katrea to the tune of the many songs she used to sing to her own children what seemed like a lifetime ago.

Occasionally Mara, Katrea's two-year-old big sister, ran up to her Aunt Amanirenas, demanding that she put the baby down and shift all attention toward her. Amanirenas was impressed by her niece's fiery personality and thoroughly entertained by the way the little girl mimicked her mother in both word and deed.

Amanirenas wished the day could last forever. It reminded her of a moment in time when she was a mother not to a kingdom, but to a simple family unit that she nurtured daily with her own heart and hands. Memories of motherhood flooded her thoughts like a river. The recollections were vibrant and pure, with the good far outnumbering the bad.

The door opened and Amanishakheto entered, followed by a healer bearing a kit of medicine and clean linen. Amanirenas sighed and begrudgingly delivered Katrea into Amanishakheto's waiting arms. She then sat down on the bed and shifted her body, granting the healer full access to the nasty abrasion on her left leg.

Little Mara settled down on the floor and watched with extreme fasciation as the healer went to work on her aunt's leg. Amanirenas smiled at the gaping expression that filled the child's face.

"Is it feeling any better?" Amanishakheto asked.

"Not really, but at least I can walk on it now."

"Well, it has only been a day," Amanishakheto said with a faint smile, relieved that her sister looked much better than she had the day before. "I think the rest has really helped."

"Not more than your children have. They are so lovely. And Mara here acts just like you."

Mara's eyes inquisitively darted from her aunt to her mother. Satisfied that nothing was being asked of her, she focused back on the healer as he continued to redress Amanirenas's wounded leg.

"It is so peaceful here. It reminds me of Sanam," Amanirenas said.

"Yes, I thought that as well when we first arrived. There is an orchard behind the marketplace just like the one mother grew in Sanam. Even has the same fruit."

"Are there any llamas?" Amanirenas asked impishly.

"Oh, gods, no! I was terrified of those heinous creatures!" Amanishakheto exclaimed, shaking her head. "They were worse than camels! They would spit and..."

"They would eat anything," Amanirenas sassed, trying to restrain from breaking into a full fit of laughter. "Remember the time one ate part of your ceremonial gown, and mother made you wear it anyway?"

"Ugh! That was soooo humiliating! I think I had father slaughter that beast afterwards."

"You asked, but he never did it."

"What?"

"I convinced him to spare the animal and send it somewhere else," Amanirenas admitted, ignoring the discomfort caused by the healer cleaning a minor wound on her right shoulder.

"Ohhh, Renas! And you wonder why I've been such a bitch to you over the years!"

"I know; I've earned most of it," Amanirenas responded.

"No, you've earned all of it!"

The sisters giggled lightly and then exploded into full laughter that echoed through the bedchamber, both amazed at how much the other had changed in the last three years.

The laughter continued until the healer removed the blindfold coving Amanerinas's left eye. As the final bandage was detached, little Mara arose and quickly retreated to her mother's side.

"No, baby, that's your aunt," Amanishakheto said softly to her daughter, striking her cheek. "Give her a kiss. It will make her feel better."

Mara gingerly stepped toward her aunt, her eyes fixated on the swollen black-and-blue aura surrounding the disfigured socket containing a now dead eye. The healer paused as the little girl slowly reached up and drew Amanirenas's head down low enough to plant a kiss on the swollen side of her face.

Amanirenas whimpered meekly as her niece traced her fingertips tenderly along her aunt's enflamed cheekbone. The little girl smiled and then swiftly embraced Amanirenas, who drew her in and clutched the child as if she were a precious jewel dropped from the heavens. She felt much better indeed.

After the healer had finished, a servant entered the chamber to help Amanishakheto take the children for their noon nap. Amanirenas stood at the window, watching the people below tend to their various tasks. Many of them were soldiers and were likely fully aware of the Roman threat lurking beyond the rolling southern hills like an audacious lion fearful of no one.

She practiced fixing her gaze on objects near and far in an effort to become acclimated to her lack of depth perception. Although her vision now seemed flat, with everything appearing on the same level, she was surprised to see how quickly she was able to focus and process images with her single eye. Instead of being blurry, the colors were deeper and richer—particularly yellow and green. In addition, her sense of smell seemed sharper than before. Even her hearing was more sensitive and in tune with whatever she focused her eye on.

A knock at the door drew her attention from the window.

"Enter."

Khai stepped in bearing a vessel of luscious red berries. "My kandace," he said with a bow.

She smiled and accepted the bowl, the sweet scent of the treat teasing her nose. "Thank you."

"You're looking better," Khai said, happy to see her up and walking about.

"So are you. I'm glad to see that Mshindi at least gave you a change of clothes."

"I needed it. That and a bath and shave."

"You look good," she said, stroking his smooth face with the back of her hand. "How are the others?"

"Batae's been eating nonstop, and Pedese's been complaining nonstop. Like myself, they've finally bathed. The others are fine as well."

"And Pahor?" the Queen asked, full of concern.

"He's getting better as well. His injuries are going to keep him out of the next few battles, but they haven't stopped him from asking a hundred questions a day."

Amanirenas grinned as she envisioned the core of her bodyguard troop—each with his individual quirk that made him special. Only Khai had been permitted to see her during her two days of her recovery.

"Now tell me what's really happening," Amanirenas requested as she slowly sat down in a decorative chair. "I spoke briefly with Mshindi last night. It was more of a cordial greeting than a military briefing. We've yet to really talk. Please give me the details."

"Simply put, Amen-Tekah's men would just as soon fight Mshindi's regiments as they would the Romans. There have already been a few fistfights here and there. The forces have been separated, with Amen-Tekah's men placed on the west side of Kor."

"Why is there so much animosity between them?"

"Most of Amen-Tekah's men are commoners or worse. Some of them were even imprisoned in Kushite jails to the north and managed to escape when the war started going badly two years ago. On the other hand, many of the commanders in Mshindi's regiment are nobles, and some even served in the police detachments in the northern cities.

There's a lot of mistrust between the two camps, despite the common enemy."

"What about Piankhi?" Amanirenas asked. "I have my sister's opinion. But based on what you've heard, where do you think he stands?"

"No one seems to be sure. After they withdrew from the expedition last year, he and Mshindi disagreed on how to deal with the Romans. Piankhi thinks he can broker an agreement with them. But Mshindi is highly skeptical."

"Just as a soldier should be," Amanirenas said as Khai sat down in the adjacent chair.

"And what of the Romans? Is there anything new from the scouts?" she asked.

"Yes, there is," Khai answered, a sudden darkness blanketing his countenance.

"What is it?"

"The cohort that attacked us linked up with two other coming from Napata, one of which burned Kerma a few days earlier," Khai reported.

Amanirenas shook her head and thought ruefully of Vizier Shabakar, wondering if the shortsighted man had survived the torching of the city.

"The three cohorts have since sailed down the Nile. Mshindi believes they are likely headed to the Roman fort at Primis."

"And they made no effort to come here?" Amanirenas asked with an even tone.

"No. In fact, it's like they had no idea we're here."

"What do the others have to say about it?"

Khai clasped his hands together and frowned. "Mshindi is thinking about dividing his army into several regiments. A couple staying here, a couple going east."

"Basically, disband the *Teriahi* and run," Amanirenas interjected.

"Yes. He has no desire to confront the legion at full strength, and I can't say that I blame him after what happened in Syene, Philae, and Dakka."

Amanirenas's face was stone cold. She could not deny the accuracy of the accusation history made against them. Every encounter she had had with the legions at full strength had resulted in a sound defeat for her. Nothing she could do could rewrite the deflating experience the Kushite regiments had received over the past two years.

"What of Amen-Tekah?" Amanirenas asked, searching for some optimism.

"He isn't afraid of the legion. Then again, he is not a military man and does not have the sense to be afraid. He thinks we can simply ambush them."

Khai's comment wrenched a faint smile from the Kandace as she recalled how the portly warlord and his minions had fearlessly pummeled away at the fierce Roman phalanx formation.

"Mshindi believes that Piankhi will stay in the fort at Qasr Ibrim and then send an envoy to the Romans at some point," Khai reported.

"How many men are in that fort?"

"About 800. They're the other part of the *Teriahi* regiment. But there's no way he can hold a fort against 5,000 Romans," Khai said.

"4,500 men," Amanirenas whispered.

"What was that?"

"We would have a force of 4,500 men. If we could just bring it together." Amanirenas stroked the linen fold over her left eye as she pondered their situation, as if it were one of the mathematical equations she had studied in her youth.

"That's fewer than we had in Napata. Not nearly enough to defeat a legion in the open field."

"You don't understand," Amanirenas said as she stood to her feet. "We'll never defeat them, and I don't believe overwhelming them with numbers should be the goal. I've already made that mistake."

"Then what?"

"We need to send them a message." She turned to Khai, who had risen to his feet, a myriad of questions perched upon his tongue.

"We need to send them a very convincing message that cannot be misunderstood."

Chapter 41

P ahor bathed in the peaceful warmth of the campfire as he watched the western sky gradually shift from soft shades of yellow and orange in response to the sun's steady decent. Dawn and dusk always captured his attention, prompting him to stop and consider the mechanics governing both heavenly events. The very sight of it made him forget how mangled his right arm was as the result of a Roman's gladius.

Though he had been taught from an early age that Horus manipulated celestial occurrences, deep within, he refused to believe that the Egyptian sky god was that powerful—or even existed at all. The many hours he had spent with the Kandace over the past month had only reenforced his feelings. She was by far the most educated person in their party, and even she harbored reservations about the gods—something he found extremely provocative, given that most of Kush embraced her as the offspring of the goddess Isis.

The sky had grown dark enough for him to assume his nightly study of the constellations when his brother Pedese appeared and sat on the other side of campfire, a plate of seared fowl in one hand and a Roman's galae in the other.

"Counting the stars again?" Pedese jeered while biting off a piece of meat. "I hope you've eaten. They're about to run out of food over there. It's not like when we were in the bush. There are way too many mouths to feed now."

"I'm fine," Pahor responded, tossing a small rock into the fire. "Any word on the Queen?"

"Khai said she's getting stronger. Even said she walked out of her room today. The woman is tough as a palm tree trunk."

Pedese paused and recalled the first time Batae, Khai, and himself had happened upon her outside of Napata. He had thought she was nothing more than an emotional heifer with a royal pendant affixed to her neck. However, the fact that she was willing to endure the hardship of traversing the harsh Kushite backcountry to convince a handful of men to fight for a dying nation had won him over long ago.

"Rank is given, but respect is earned," Pedese said.

"*Respect* and *protect*," Pahor mused, recalling the charge his father had issued to the handful of men who had set out to escort the Kandace from Kawa to their current location. "I heard she's blind. Is that true?"

"She lost her left eye," Pedese replied, thoughtfully fondling a dry piece of meat before throwing it into the yellow flames. "I saw the Roman going for her, but I couldn't get to her before the pale bastard struck her. I was too late...." He lifted up the Roman helmet and watched as it reflected the dancing flames from the fire. "But he lost more than an eye over the matter."

"It's a miracle any of us survived that," Pahor reflected, ignoring the throbbing pain from his own wounds.

"Yeah, but a bunch of us didn't," Pedese noted, thinking about the handful of bodyguards who had died protecting the Kandace during the Roman ambush. All of the men were from his hometown, recruited and employed by his father. Some of them he had grown up with and knew quite well.

Pahor studied his brother, still not used to hearing such serious words flow past his lips. He had heard the furnace of war was capable of purifying the heart of any man who experienced it, and his brother was living proof of that.

"Father is extremely proud of you," Pahor said, poking the fire with a stick. "While you were gone, he couldn't stop talking about you."

"Of course he couldn't," Pedese said flippantly.

"I wouldn't lie to you. I just wish you would drop the pretense and accept who you are."

"And who am I, Pahor?" Pedese retorted as he rose above the fire. "You and father act as if I have something I need to live up to...."

"And you do. But you always run away and..."

"What is that?" Pedese inquired, point down the road that led toward the heart of Kor.

A slight rumble gave way to the harsh thuds of a half-dozen hooves pounding against the path. There was still just enough sunlight for Pahor to see the lead rider.

"That's a vizier," Pahor noted as the men galloped past. "I recognize the tunic."

"Piankhi," Pedese said. "I'm sure he's arrived to see the Queen."

"Pelmes Mshindi thought he'd never leave the fort," Pahor said.

"What did I say about respect being earned?" Pedese uttered. "This just got real interesting."

"Why am I not surprised by what I see? Over 5,000 Roman legionaries two *iters* away in the fort at Primis, and the two of you sit here and entertain the fantasy proposed by the kandace of a fading dynasty."

Piankhi's voice reverberated through the meeting chamber like the Egyptian gong at the Isle of Philae summoning the masses to prayer. The short but stocky vizier carried himself as if he were the tallest man in the room. His flawless red and gold tunic was tailored perfectly to fit his athletic form, and only the grey peppering his beard and short hair betrayed the fact he was likely the oldest person in the chamber. His fiery eyes darted across the table at the four people seated before him until they eventually rested upon Mshindi.

"One month ago, we agreed you would track down this criminal and end his reign of terror, yet here you are consorting with him," Piankhi berated.

"You call me a criminal?" Amen-Tekah spat, his harsh Egyptian accent grating against Piankhi's ears. "For years, you syphon off all of the grain from Egypt, as well as imposing a tax on the fish drawn from the Nile. It wasn't until your soldiers went off to fight the Romans that the poor in this region were able to fill their bellies without worrying about your soldiers and police applying the whip and snatching the food from their tables! If anyone is the criminal, it's you!"

"What do you plan on doing, Amen-Tekah? Killing me right here?" Piankhi taunted arrogantly. "You can try, but I doubt your fat ass can move fast enough."

"Take a sword, little monkey, and let's put your judgment to the test. Fat versus cowardice."

"Enough!" Mshindi demanded, glaring at both men. "Piankhi, I don't believe you came all the way from the fort to exchange insults. You're far too calculating for that. As for our agreement, things have changed considerably since then."

"Be that as it may, Mshindi. More Romans have arrived, and I am the only person in this room they may even consider listening to."

"We're aware of the three cohorts," Mshindi started.

"Cohorts?" Piankhi questioned with a laugh. "There's no way you would know this, but the *Legio Cyrenaica* arrived at Primis a few days ago. They marched from Napata along the Wadi Gabgaba Road."

An eerie silence fell upon the room as everyone contemplated the revelation.

"Why are you here, Piankhi?" Amanirenas asked firmly.

"I heard of the hostilities between rogue tribes and Roman soldiers," Piankhi answered, more to Amen-Tekah and Mshindi. "I came to talk sense to these men. I cannot negotiate with the Romans if Kushite soldiers are killing their legionaries."

"Who authorized you to negotiate with the Romans, Piankhi?" Amanirenas asked. All eyes fell upon her as she sat at the ceremonial head of the table. She was a bit gaunt, but her voice was firm, and her one brown eye as steady as that of an archer.

"My husband presented your name, and it was I who made the ritual sacrifice in the Temple of Amun-Ra to confirm *and* bless your appointment. The Romans will deal with me and no one else."

"Your courage is commendable, Amanirenas, but your time has passed, and the future of Kush is no longer in the care of the Amani-aa'ila," Piankhi said as he shot a glance at Amanishakheto, who sat next to her sister. "Teriteqas provoked this beast, and you prodded it on with a hot branding iron when you went to Egypt with 20,000 men. You sealed your fate long ago. Caesar will not stop until they've captured both of you, dead or alive.

"And now you slaughtered at least two centuries a few days ago? Roman honor will demand they seek vengeance and atone for a loss of that magnitude. Their senate will accept nothing less. The only hope Kush has is for me to go to them and negotiate a settlement."

"You mean surrender," Amanishakheto remarked.

"I'm sure your family will see it that way, but for the rest of the kingdom, it is a way out of an unwinnable conflict no one wanted in the first place."

"That's the first thing you've said this evening that I can agree with, Piankhi," Amanirenas started resolutely. "I was one of those who never wanted this conflict. I tried to talk my husband out of getting involved. I even ... I even told him to let the Romans have the Northern provinces if it would satisfy them."

The Kandace allowed her confession to linger around the table for a moment. "I was willing to sacrifice part of the kingdom—the part of the kingdom governed by you—not to spare the rest of Kush, but to spare myself from the *possibility* of losing what I already had. Not my crown, not my palace, but my family."

Khai and Batae, who stood a few paces behind the Queen's seat, silently glanced at one another, both recalling the night Amanirenas had learned of the heartrending death of her youngest son and how she had lamented her daughter's dubious future.

"Up until our last evening together, I tried to convince him that it wasn't worth it. But he said that we had to be resolute and stand firm for the sake of our ancestors, as well for as those who are yet to come. He felt that his manhood hinged upon what he allowed the Romans to do.

"So he went, and he died for that conviction. Filled with wrath, I hated the Romans, but I hated Kush more because he had died for it instead of me. In my rage, I used the army as a hammer to bludgeon the Romans, and I was wrong to do so."

Amanirenas looked squarely at Mshindi, her eye issuing an unspoken apology for the many times she had disregarded his council.

"Hundreds of men and families bore the expense for my error, and I will bear that debt for the rest of my life. I will never be able to pay it off, nor should the gods allow me to do so."

Amanirenas frowned as her voice faltered and tears pooled within her eye. No one at the table moved as she struggled to compose herself. Amanishakheto did nothing to prevent her own tears from spilling onto her cheeks.

"My brothers, I have sinned, but the truth is undeniable. Just as it is impossible for the cheetah to remove its spots, it is also impossible for a man to contain the wind. The Romans are conquerors, and they would have attacked us eventually. As soon as Cleopatra's dynasty was exterminated, they were going to come for us: a country full of gold and plump with people. Make no mistake, we *were* their next conquest."

A contemplative silence dominated the room. Each person felt the need to respond, but no one possessed the adequate words to address the circumstance.

"What do you propose?" Mshindi questioned.

"We attack them. But we have to do it together," Amanirenas asserted, her eye decisively rolling toward Piankhi.

The vizier scowled shamefully at the Queen. "If that's what you really wish to do, you don't need me. It's a simple matter of loyalty. The 800 men in that fort will follow Mshindi to Henel and back before they follow me anywhere. All I can really offer is a way to negotiate a settlement."

"Piankhi, you've administrated this region for years. You know how the Romans view us. They believe us inferior. For Kush to have a chance, we need you," Amanirenas replied, standing. Her action prompted everyone else to rise as well.

The once-belligerent vizier surveyed the three people who stood resolutely with the Kandace. Despite his pride, his experience with the Romans testified to the validity of Amanirenas's argument. Any pretense he had of garnering respect from the invaders was a simple fantasy that needed to end. He nodded silently and then rose.

Khai and Batae once again exchanged a quiet glance, neither man wanting the moment to slip into the past.

Chapter 42

Marius's high rank afforded him the luxury of an actual room located in the central building of the Roman fortification. The space was stoic; it contained a simple cot, a desk, and a closet housing the tribune's equipment and few personal effects.

The tribune sat secluded in his room and busied himself with the task of compiling the logs and notes he had kept since departing from Napata. Although he had made an oral report to the prefect the day he arrived at the fort, Petronius made it clear that he wanted to review the tribune's logs documenting the actions taken by Publius leading to the loss of so many Roman soldiers during one engagement.

Marius occasionally drank from the half-empty canteen of water next to his notes as he contemplated the prefect's subdued response to the apparent failure of his mission. Marius had expected his commanding officer to berate him for failing not once, but twice, to capture the Queen. In fact, during the quick march to Primis, Marius had braced himself for the grim prospect that his career in the Egyptian province was likely over.

As he stood up and tugged at his torso armor, a bent blade of shieling displaced sometime during their excursion through Kush scraped against his arm and intensified his hatred of the African campaign. He was weary of the exasperating Kushites and their parched, worthless land, and he was ready to strike a decisive deathblow to whoever resisted Roman supremacy.

He took a swig from the canteen and then tossed it aside, grateful for the breeze flowing into his room through the window above the desk.

"Isn't it a bit early for that?"

Marius threw an indifferent look at Tribune Decius Gallus as he stood in the doorway. The younger man removed his helmet and placed it on the table next to Marius's notes. It was shiny, with far fewer scuffmarks, denoting the tribune's relative inactivity over the past month.

"Your legion is encamped outside the fort. What brings you here?" Marius asked half-heartedly. He had forgotten just how much he loathed Gallus, who was more politician than soldier.

"I'm on my way to the meet with the prefect. I wanted to speak with you before we went over. I need clarification on a few things," Gallus answered.

"What clarification could you possibly need? He intends on doubling the garrison here and creating two more fortifications between this place and Philae. The rest of the legions will return to Thebes."

"That much I understand," Gallus retorted, stepping in front of Marius. "But what escapes me is why."

"Are you questioning his tactics?"

"Of course not. I just find it strange he is giving them so much ... respect."

Marius took another swig from the canteen. "I don't understand your concern, Decius. A month ago, you thought we weren't cautious enough in our approach to dealing with these people. Now you seem to have reversed yourself."

Gallus shook his head. "I'm not questioning Petronius or his devices. It's just ..."

"Just what?" Marius demanded, his annoyance seeping through.

"I tell you, Cassius, the man has changed. Even Vitelus and the other tribunes that travelled with him have said as much. They said from the moment they left Napata, he engrossed himself in the study of Kushite lore."

"And what's wrong with trying to understand the enemy?"

"Nothing, but he has spent hours in cemeteries roaming in and among Kushite pyramids. Even since they arrived here a couple of weeks ago, he has spent time talking to the priests and scribes in the local villages. It's like he's obsessed with studying the kandace and the Cult of the Queen-Mother."

"He's an astute man," Marius said, "He was probably interrogating the priests to learn more about their customs."

"No, Cassius, he was conversing with them as if they were equals." Gallus paced back and forth. "It's not at all what I expected from a man who spent years on campaign with Julius Caesar fighting barbarians in Gaul."

"These barbarians are different," Marius remarked, recalling his experiences in El-Kurru and Kerma. "They're craftier than those in the north."

"Perhaps, but like I said, Petronius has changed. Had you captured the Queen, he may have simply told you to release her. A gesture, if you will, of his newfound *respect* for their culture."

Marius picked up his galea and put on the headgear, eyeing Gallus apprehensively. "I don't agree with every order Petronius has given me, and I don't need to. He is the prefect of Egypt and the commanding officer of our legions. He can do what he wants. And he alone will be accountable for it."

"You're a good soldier, Cassius," Gallus delivered sarcastically. "I hope he doesn't hold the fact that you were unable to capture that queen against you. It would be a shame if that dishonor sullied your career from this point on."

"Careful, Decius. You should be more thoughtful with your slights," Marius warned. "Here's what I see: Your father foolishly underestimated these Kushites. He took them too lightly in the beginning and paid a heavy political price for doing so, and you will forever be linked to his failure. Your words now are nothing more than your attempt to save face for your family."

"I have no intention of withering my life away in Philae or Alexandria," Gallus asserted. "The Kandace will not dig my grave, and Kush will not be my cemetery. However, if Petronius goes soft and allows her to walk, she may well dig yours."

"Unlike you, I'm a soldier, and I've learned to fight my way out of strategically bad positions. Also, unlike you, I will advance regardless of what happens in this hellhole. Petronius granted you a small mercy and gave you the honor of leading the *Cyrenaica* back from Napata. I suggest that you appreciate that favor as a true soldier would."

"Maybe so. However, be it soldier or politician," Gallus started as he affixed his galea, "at some point, you are going to have to right the wrong concerning the Queen. That's the way Rome works. Trust me, I know from experience."

Chapter 43

The Kushite fort at Qasr Ibrim was a day's march from the village of Kor, but to Amanirenas it felt like a three-day trudge. She made stretches of the journey in the litter that had been fashioned to shuttle Amanishakheto and her children when they traveled with Mshindi. However, she endeavored to complete most of the trek on foot, pressing through the pain that wracked her leg, shoulder, and head.

While she was grateful for the relief offered by the litter, she was more satisfied to know that her sister and two nieces had remained in the relative safety of Kor. There, they would await the outcome of whatever conflict was destined to happen between Kush and the Roman forces.

For the moment, she pushed the empty litter from her mind and focused squarely on taking each step. The forest that had concealed Kor had long since given way to a flat, barren land dominated by small beige rocks and stones, many of which peppered the ancient pathway the party now travelled. Even though a sturdy pair of sandals protected her feet, Amanirenas felt a sharp prod every time she stepped on one of the jagged stones.

Although she tried to maintain a good pace while out of the litter, she was far from the head of the company. She and her contingent of bodyguards came to serve as the dividing line between the forces of Mshindi and those of Amen-Tekah. Thus far, the alliance seemed to be holding steady, with nothing more than a few jeers tossed between the rival militias. Mshindi marched at the head as a Kushite general would—his troops parading behind him in a single column formation designated for travel. Amen-Tekah, on the other hand, did not seem to care, his band of mercenaries eschewing any form of military discipline.

Amanirenas glanced behind to the left and found the man who was serving as her shadow a few paces away. She offered Khai a nod and faint smile to let him know how she was managing. In return, he shook his head pitifully and grinned, jabbing the thick walking stick he carried into the ground several times. Amanirenas looked away and pretended to ignore the playful rebuke issued by her chief bodyguard. Despite the dire circumstances, the soldier constantly provoked a smile from her, and she found her appreciation for his loyalty and protection seemed to grow by the hour. While she tried to treat him no differently than she did Batae, Pedese, Pahor, Akfoor, or any of the others who had joined her in Kawa, she could not deny her affections ran far deeper for Khai. At times, the emotions his voice stirred within her were frightening, and when he drew near, part of her that was long dead came to life in dramatic fashion.

The Queen's portion of the long traversing line slowly completed the curve around a hill and brought the Qasr Ibrim fortress into full view.

"Old and not very impressive," Amen-Tekah piped, walking up to the Queen. "But at least it was built by Egyptians."

"You're wrong on that one, Lord Amen-Tekah," Amanirenas replied. "My father told me it was built by the Kushite king Tantamani."

"Yeah... But he used Egyptian slaves," Amen-Tekah responded with a shrug.

"I take it many of your men were born in Egypt?"

"A majority, yes. Some served in Cleopatra's army, others fought for her brother Ptolemy. But no matter, when the Romans arrived and made war with both sides, many of these men were driven out of Egypt and had nowhere to go."

"I'm impressed with how you've rallied so many of them,"

Amanirenas said as their party cleared the rocky hills and entered the desolate expanse dominated by the fort. The gates to the brick-laden stronghold opened up to receive Mshindi and the group that travelled with him.

"The Egyptians were easy to recruit," Amen-Tekah said. "And the Kushites took even less effort to convince. Piankhi has done much in Nobatia to garner hate. He has confiscated land, increased taxes, allowed Romans to farm slaves. The people were happy when his men went off to war. Even more cheerful when the Romans drove Piankhi from Philae."

"Cheerful?"

"Not that they like Roman occupation," Amen-Tekah added as they approached the weathered ancient stronghold. "However, people appreciate when the enemy doesn't look like themselves."

"Things will change," Amanirenas affirmed, shielding her eye from the sunlight reflecting from the light tan stone walls as they passed through the gates. "I promise."

"Promises are good, but inspiration is better," Amen-Tekah said. "You want to give these men something? Give them inspiration. Give them something to hope for outside of a life of foraging and theft. Hell, even I might change my ways if you can do that!"

☒ ☖

"Pedese is right for once. This place is a deathtrap," Batae said as he and Khai walked along the fort's southern wall. The causeway atop the thick wall ran the fort's perimeter and was wide enough to accommodate just three men walking abreast. "This place wouldn't last long against a siege."

"It really isn't a fort. It's more of a supply outpost," Khai commented. He mentally measured the stronghold's central courtyard, which consisted of a marshalling field and half-dozen one-story structures—all but three of them integrated into the brick walls. He reckoned the complex was designed to house no more than four hundred men—a limit that Piankhi had already exceeded.

Batae looked eastward and watched as the 2,500 men that made up Mshindi's Nobatian regiment formed an orderly encampment a few hundred cubits beyond the fort's eastern gate. Driven by routine, the soldiers broke themselves into units, with each member carrying out a specific duty. It was a sharp contrast to the rabble that had marched under Amen-Tekah's banner. The group was characterized by noise and a general sense of chaos that only their commander could make sense of.

"The Kandace wants to attack the Romans with this? It's going to be a short battle," Batae muttered as the clamor from Amen-Tekah's camp reverberated on the fort's brick ramparts. "I think these guys will run when they see a cohort in formation."

"They didn't do so poorly against the phalanx when we were attacked on the way Kor," Khai countered optimistically. "I've heard a few of them fought against the Romans in Actium."

"Where they're asses were soundly kicked," Batae retorted.

Khai examined the western horizon in the general direction of the Nile. Only a sliver of the mighty river was visible amongst the shimmering heat waves that danced along the vast barren field in between—courtesy of the late afternoon sun. Rocky hills and uneven terrain flanked the expanse.

The Roman fortification at Primis sat on eastern bank of the Nile and was less than one iter to the north. It wouldn't take the Kushites very long to get there.

"It would be very difficult for a legion to approach this fort after clearing that pass," Khai stated, pointing toward the strip of land leading up to the fort. "It's wide enough for maybe three cohorts in maniple formation, but no more."

"At least that means they won't be able to outflank us," Batae said. "We'd have the tools for a defense. But I don't think we'd have the talent." Batae glanced back at the motley crew of fighting men below and shook his head.

"The trick would be getting the Romans to come into this valley. If they did, then we would have a fighting chance."

"Problem is, we're attacking them. They aren't coming here," Batae delivered, leaning against the warm brick palisade. "Speaking of hopeless battles, what's going on between you and the Queen? I noticed it a couple of weeks ago, but it is plain obvious now."

Khai eyed his companion wearily and then focused back on the shimmering horizon. It was the first time anyone had implied what Khai had worked so disparately to hide. Nevertheless, he was grateful that it was Batae rather than Pedese who brought it up.

"There isn't much to say. I've had feelings for her since Kawa."

"You shouldn't feel ashamed. Things like that happen when you spend a lot of time with someone," Batae said, hardly believing he was advising any one about matters of the heart. "The problem is, you can't do a damn thing about it."

Khai stared at Batae as if waiting for an executioner to strike.

"She's a kandace, and you don't have a drop of noble blood—you aren't even a regimental commander. Besides, should we survive the coming battle, Korosko is across the river. You will be able to find female companionship there. I know I will."

"That isn't what I want," Khai said.

"Then what? There isn't anything else..."

"She makes me—feel—and that's something I've never done before."

"Any woman can make you feel good. You just have to put the right effort into and touch her..."

"Not that! I mean she makes me feel alive, as if I have a purpose. I look at her and I am reminded there is more to this life than conflict and death. She makes me feel there's something in this world that should be valued an esteemed."

"Oh. I don't know too much about that," Batae said with a frown. "You know, life would be easier if you didn't think so much, Khai. Men like us, we're just here. We live, we fight, we die, and then people forget about us. But the Kandace is different. People will be writing about her 2,000 years from now. Us, our images, will never be on a pyramid or on the side of a temple."

"It's nice to feel alive though," Khai said quietly. "Even if it's for a little while."

Deep down, Khai knew that Batae's words were true. Amanirenas, Teriteqas, Piankhi, and Mshindi were giants walking through the valley of time, while he was but a mite who would soon be brushed away by the wind of yet another battle. Nevertheless, he would play the role he'd been given with all of his might.

"I won't let the Romans take her, Batae. I'll kill every one of them if I have to."

Chapter 44

Amanirenas dipped her hand into the cool Nile water. The small waves gently lapping the shore beckoned to her to wade into the river, and for a moment, she considered doing so. However, she reluctantly drew herself from the water and promised herself that she would indulge herself at a later date, when circumstances allowed.

She turned and surveyed the barren expanse behind her and tried to envision the plan that Khai had proposed to her as the two of them had ridden from the outpost. The huge brick structure appeared as a miniature toy nestled in a rocky backyard from their current location. Though the loss of her left eye impeded her efforts to estimate distances, the time it took Khai and her to ride from the gate to the river's edge had boosted her confidence in the cavalryman's calculations.

"They would likely land over there and use the shore as a staging area," Khai pointed out, moving past one of the horses drinking from the river.

"It seems large enough for two legions," Amanirenas responded. "And I definitely see the funnel you described. It's wide enough for them to consider making an attempt, but shallow enough to limit the maneuvers they can make."

She walked past Khai and looked down river to the north. The air was still, and there was no traffic on the water. There was no vegetation or trees along that stretch of the river, only a naked shoreline following the river's gentle curve.

"Primis is about half an iter away, so it wouldn't take them very long to get here if they decided to come," Khai said. He stepped by her side and examined the vista himself. "I know it's risky, but getting them to come here would be preferable to making a frontal assault on their fortification."

Amanirenas nodded silently. Khai's bold proposal had won her over almost instantly. Even though it was defensive in posture, it offered the Kushites the opportunity to choose the battleground—something denied to them in over two years of fighting.

"I think it's worth the risk," Amanirenas said. "I just need to convince the others. At this point, no one can agree on a solid plan of attack."

"The harder part will be convincing the Romans to actually come," Khai said. For the first time, a specter of insecurity mingled with his tone. "As Piankhi said, they've known for a year about the soldiers here, and they've never made an offensive move. Why would they come now?"

Amanirenas looked up at him and grinned as a deep frown creased his face. He was always so serious, and she had rarely seen him smile. He glanced down at her and was taken aback by her expression. As beautiful as it was, he found it difficult to focus on her one eye without searching her smooth dark face for the other. Saiesha had masterfully fashioned a colorful stretch of linen into a fanciful fold to cover the Kandace's mangled eye. Even though the cloth accented Amanirenas's dress, the mere presence of it ignited an indignant flame in Khai.

Sensing his discomfort, Amanirenas slowly traced her fingers along the line of his chiseled jaw and watched as his expression gradually relaxed.

"Petronius will come because there's something here he wants very badly," she said softly. "Something he's been unable to seize. Roman integrity requires that they come."

Khai interpreted her words immediately and struggled against the warm, enticing feeling stirred by Amanirenas's calming touch.

Sensing the conflict within him, Amanirenas slowly slid her forefinger over his lips as if to shush the protest brewing within him.

"If a man wants something badly enough, he'll make the effort to obtain it—even if it is unobtainable," she whispered tenderly.

Khai steadily reached up and grasped her finger covering his lips, caressing her hand as he pulled it away. He drew her into a loving embrace and kissed her tenderly. Amanirenas fell into his arms as one would fall into a serene brook and allowed herself to be swept away in the current of his passion.

✠ ଷ

Prefect Gaius Petronius awaited the maelstrom he sensed brewing in the brick-lined chamber. As a commanding general, he esteemed discipline and military order in the strictest sense. However, as the governor of a province, he had long ago learned to temper his dictatorial orientation by allowing his adjutants the opportunity to voice their judgment on a particular course of action, with himself, of course, as the final arbiter of the decision to be made.

At the moment, the eight tribunes and three *pilus priors* occupying the room wordlessly brooded on the prefect's plan. The warm air carried the silence until Petronius had had enough.

"Very well. If there are no questions, then I will expect each of you to make the appropriate mobilization preparations, starting with recommendations on which centuries to leave behind to augment the garrison of this fort," Petronius ordered, clasping his hands. "I want a majority of the soldiers selected to be transferred from the ..."

"Prefect, if I may," Decius Gallus called.

"Tribune," Petronius answered heedfully.

"As usual, your directives are logical and well thought out. But I fail to understand why we are essentially pulling out of the region." Gallus paused, aware that all eyes at the table were focused on Petronius, anxious to see how the prefect would respond to the roundabout questioning of his orders.

"I agree that our expedition has broken the Kushites militarily, but I think the task for our legions is far from over," Gallus added.

Petronius measured the Gallus with steely eyes. Petronius loathed the fact that he now had to contend with the entitled young man, who clearly had his sights set on achieving status in the Roman political system. While he had done an admirable job of leading the *III Legio* from Napata, Petronius knew that there would be very little challenge in the task. Nevertheless, the fact that the tribune was from the equestrian ranks afforded the young man a little latitude—but not much.

"Your point is taken, Tribune Gallus," the prefect answered with a slight nod. "I believe we have accomplished a great deal during our expedition, and I am extremely pleased with how both the *Cyrenaica* and the *Deiotariana* have performed their service to the emperor.

"A great deal of the stolen sacred property has been recovered, and hundreds of Kushites have already been transported to Egypt, bound for the slave markets. I believe you, yourself, stand to profit from this campaign."

"Many of us will prosper, Prefect," Gallus said, "and there is more wealth to be made. The gold in this land is legendary. Instead of pulling our legions out, I think we should petition the emperor to commission the formation of at least two more to occupy this land while its resources are thoroughly assimilated into our economy. Egypt would benefit greatly from such a move."

"That is one option I intend to present to Augustus in due time," Petronius said.

"What other option is there?" Gallus chortled. "Anything else would assume these barbarians are noticeably different than those on Gaul or Britannia."

"I believe they are different, Tribune. In many ways," Petronius responded evenly, raising a thick eyebrow.

"Of course, they're darker. Much darker in some cases," Gallus mocked, his comments drawing chuckles from several fellow officers.

"Very astute, Tribune," Petronius said, his tone instantly driving away the mirth. "Here are a few additional differences you may not have perceived as a commanding officer in a hostile territory. You obviously did not notice them as the sons of the praefactus Aegypti.

"This kingdom is ancient, and they have a sophisticated communication network utilizing a vast series of pathways, of which we've only located a few. According to some of their scribes, they even employ the use of falcons—the fastest of all birds in Africa—to deliver messages.

"Additionally, they have their own written script. I initially assumed they had simply mocked Egyptian writing, but I've learned that they have a distinctive language and calligraphy that we cannot read."

"It's unintelligible scribble," Gallus apprised dismissively.

"Perhaps to you. However, the scribble is written and read in all five Kushite provinces," Petronius retorted as he panned the table, appraising his officers. "They have a common currency based on precious metals. They also have an organized bureaucracy standardized throughout their cities. The system rivals even the Parthia Empire.

"And finally, like Egypt and even Rome, their religious system is based on a pantheon of gods, the foundation of which is rooted in the cult worship of a person."

"Yes, the Queen-Mother," Gallus said, furtively glancing at Marius, whose discomfort was etched upon his face. "Again, Prefect, I fail to see how a strong representation of Roman steel cannot provide a simple remedy to any of these ... obstacles."

"You're as oblivious as your father," Petronius said flatly. "These are not just 'obstacles.' They are five digits that, when brought together, form a fist of solidarity that, if allowed, can resist subjugation for years to come."

"If I may, Prefect," Marius pressed, "if that is the case, then Gallus's assertion of a stronger military presence is a valid one."

"That may well be the case, Marius. In time, we may be able to disrupt any one of those five elements I just described. In doing so, the other four will weaken, and Kushite resistance will wane. This is why I dedicated three cohorts to capturing the Queen, as she is the lynchpin of their religious structure. Our failure to do so will delay our efforts to pacify this region."

Petronius glared at Marius to once again underscore his displeasure with the tribune's inability to apprehend the Kandace and thereby decisively amputate the religious arm of the Kushite threat.

"It was a missed opportunity," Petronius added.

"Enough of her. The dog is probably halfway to the Red Sea by now," Gallus persisted, anxious to focus on a tangible target. "I am more concerned about the thousand or so Kushite soldiers in the outpost fort ten miles to the south. We allowed them to remain last year when we pursued the Queen down the wadi road to their capital. Now I've heard that there are even more of them in there. Please tell me we are at least going to deal with them before we leave."

"I find your lack of foresight most disturbing, Tribune," Petronius said. "Some weeks ago, the regional vizier made an overture to the praefectus castorum and insinuated that he is willing to help facilitate the subjugation of Kush under Roman rule. I was planning on leaving the task of dealing with this man and setting up a vassal to you."

"Prefect ... you do me an honor," Gallus said, dubiously trying to find the prefect's ulterior motive for such a move. As he searched for more words, the door opened, and a legionary entered with a parchment in hand.

"Indeed, I do, Tribune," Petronius said.

The legionary bearing the note approached Petronius and saluted crisply. "Forgive the interruption, Prefect. But a Kushite emissary just arrived bearing this letter. He claims it is from the Queen of Kush."

Petronius received the parchment and perused it carefully. It was not the first time the Kushite ruler had approached him via letter. Written in Greek, the words were sharp and to the point.

At first, the complement of Roman officers conversed amongst themselves as the prefect read the letter. However, Cassius Marius was the first to notice Petronius's face slowly flushing red in anger.

"Well, what did the wench say?" asked an officer sitting next to Gallus.

Petronius's eyes rolled ominously toward the man, who quickly stiffened up.

"Too much," the prefect growled. "Far too much."

Chapter 45

"And why do you believe the Romans will use this strategy against us?" Amen-Tekah demanded derisively, his baritone voice filling the muggy meeting hall.

"Because it is similar to the one we used to capture this outpost from the Romans two years ago," Mshindi answered. He constantly reminded himself that Amen-Tekah possessed very little military experience and had practically no appreciation for the strategic significance of the fort's location.

"This rocky terrain is going to force them to maneuver into this open area," Mshindi explained as he pointed to a group of figurines on the table before them that represented the Roman legion, juxtaposed to a model of the fort. The detailed cache of props had been seized from the enemy when Kushite forces had captured the structure.

"Why would they not divide their forces and attack from the four sides? That's what I would do. And they have more than enough men to pull it off," Amen-Tekah remarked, folding his dark, chubby arms.

"That isn't how a Roman army is designed to maneuver," Amanirenas said. "Their movements are very precise and well-orchestrated. They attack like waves hitting the shoreline, not like water rushing over the falls."

"And just as the waves erode the shoreline, the Roman fighting style eventually wears an opponent down," Mshindi noted.

"Trust me Amen-Tekah, the general's summary is accurate. He has first-hand operational knowledge of Roman tactics. I would have been much wiser had I listened to his advice before," the Kandace said. Mshindi glanced up at Amanirenas, who offered him an understanding and almost apologetic gaze. "We spent all day yesterday studying the area. We believe we can make the terrain work for us."

"So, now that we have an understanding of how they may attack, what next? Even if they have to modify their approach, we can't possibly keep 10,000 men from overrunning this fort," Amen-Tekah said.

"I want one thing understood," Amanirenas started, looking at each of the four men surrounding the table. "We are not defending this structure. Our objective is to attack the Romans. We need only to make them believe that we are defending our position." She turned back to Mshindi, who gestured toward the models on the tabletop.

"We'll line up a central force of 1,000 men directly in front of the fort. We'll have wings of 250 men to the right and left. The Romans will likely attack with no more than two cohorts, each consisting of 600 legionaries."

"1,500 men against 1,200 legionaries? They'll still cut through us like a hot blade through fat," Piankhi declared.

"We will have the advantage," Amanirenas countered.

"Yes," Mshindi confirmed, moving the Kushite figurines across the tabletop. "The two wings will attack the cohorts from the sides. The Romans march in rows. The troops in our wings will funnel into the columns through the rows, not head on. The discipline of the Romans will prevent them from engaging our troops as they filter in."

"The terrain will give our men the advantage because they will be slightly elevated and attack coming downhill," Amanirenas added.

"That may take care of the first two cohorts, but there should be about six more to deal with—and that's if they only bring one legion," Piankhi voiced, shaking his head.

"We believe that Petronius will commit no more than 2,000 men to attacking the fort. The rest will be held in reserve and not even bother to enter the valley," Amanirenas said.

"The Kandace is correct," Mshindi interjected quickly. "It would be a tactical error for him to send the entire legion into a terrain where they can't maneuver and where visibility to the left and right is cut off by the hills. It's doubtful that he will even bring the second legion."

"What of the rest of our forces?" Amen-Tekah asked.

"This is where your troops come in. Four hundred will be concealed in the hills to the left and another four hundred hidden in the hills to the right. When the signal is given, they will storm from cover and attack the Roman formations from the rear—again forcing them to break their ranks," Mshindi answered.

"You should instruct your men to target the centurions," Amanirenas directed. "If they can kill the officers, the centuries will be without guidance and the cohorts thrown into chaos."

Amen-Tekah slowly nodded at the stratagem. "And I suppose the remaining seven hundred of my men are held in reserve?"

"Yes, they will be hidden in the hills behind the fort and attack in waves when signaled," Mshindi answered.

"A complement of 750 soldiers will also be held in reserve inside of the fort. The remaining 1,250 will be stationed just behind the outpost, out of the Romans' sight," the Kandace added.

"Impressive plan," Piankhi confessed sincerely. "But what do we do about the other 3,000 legionaries? Petronius is certain to send them in—maybe even before things start going badly for them."

"I'm not too certain about that," Amanirenas stated, her eye glancing quickly at Mshindi. "This is where we gamble. It may give Petronius pause if we can defeat the first two cohorts. With luck, he will push back and withdraw. If we are really fortunate, he will absorb the losses and march back to Egypt."

The door opened, and a soldier entered. He pulled Amen-Tekah aside and conversed with him for a moment.

Amanirenas gently massaged her left temple through the red linen blind fold covering her damaged eye. The medicine given to her by the healer was starting to wear off; however, she was determined to see the meeting through.

"Even if this works, what's to stop Petronius from coming back in a year with more legions?" Piankhi was asking.

"Nothing," Mshindi stated bluntly. "In fact, that's what he'll probably do. Roman honor will demand it."

"I'll negotiate with him," Amanirenas said abruptly. "If we can defeat a portion of their forces and make them withdraw, I will surrender myself."

Khai tensed up as the other men gasped at the Queen's words. Before anyone could respond, she raised her hand.

"It's the rational thing to do. If we can drive them back and then I surrender, it would seem less like a defeat for the Romans. It would offer Petronius a way out—a way to save face."

"It wouldn't be that simple," Mshindi said.

"But it would buy Kush more time," Amanirenas said. "I've already set it in motion. Yesterday I sent a message to Petronius to provide him with some motivation, and I anticipate a prompt response from him."

Khai thought about the message she had sent to the Roman commander. He was convinced that the letter had provided the Romans with ample incentive to cross the Nile and storm the gates of the Qasr Ibrim outpost. However, he was still opposed to the notion of her surrendering herself and was about to renew his protest when Amen-Tekah cleared his throat.

"I believe you've gotten their response," the warlord announced loudly, "The lookouts at the river report a contingent of the Roman swine have made landfall and are making camp just beyond the mouth of the valley. We shall see the glow of their campfires tonight."

"No doubt they're charting the battlefield to draw up their attack plan," Mshindi said.

"However, all is not lost, and perhaps Montu smiles upon this plan after all," Amen-Tekah spoke before Mshindi could continue his thought. "I've just been informed that close to four hundred men have made their way here to the outpost through the pass. Many of them have horses and claim to have fought in the Battle of Napata."

Amanirenas turned her body completely around in order to make eye contact with Khai, who nodded apprehensively. Although he wanted to rebut the plan she had just disclosed, he yielded to her unspoken request and quickly left the chamber to meet with the new arrivals.

Amanirenas made her way through the warm halls of the fort's dimly lit interior. Like the land it protected, everything about the fort was static and coarse. However, the scores of men negotiating through the structure made sections of the building pulsate with an excitement that only life could bring.

A unit commander hurried toward Amanirenas; however, before he passed her, he paused and bowed reverently, his hands making the slight swopping motion signifying conference of a blessing. She acknowledged the gesture with a graceful nod and appreciative smile. As she turned to resume her progress, she came face-to-face with Mshindi.

"You did well in there," the general complimented, trying not to look at the cloth that replaced her eye. He doubted if he could ever get used to the thought of her bearing such a horrendous scar.

"It isn't difficult to convince men to buy into something if you truly believe in it. Your plan is good," the Kandace replied. "I only hope the Romans cooperate."

"It appears they're arriving in mass; however, Petronius is a prudent man, and he isn't blind. There's no guarantee that he will attack the way we need him to." Mshindi sighed as he thought of the ramifications of the Romans *not* attacking. "They could very well turn around and assault the cities across the river and attempt to draw us out. Make us fight on a field of their choosing."

"They'll attack," Amanirenas said, starting back down the hallway. "I'm certain of it."

"How can you be so sure?" Mshindi questioned as he walked with her.

"Because I appealed to the one vice all men of power have."

"And that is?"

"Vanity. Prepare yourself, general. I have a feeling tomorrow will be a very decisive day."

Mshindi chuckled lightly, more out of disbelief than amusement. "There is a measure of comfort in knowing that the arrogant and obstinate Amanirenas still walks among us."

Amanirenas halted but did not face the general. "I've changed, Mshindi. I've had to. If I could have done so earlier, I would have."

Mshindi placed his hand on her shoulder and gently tugged her around until he was able to see her eye. "Amanishakheto told me about the oath you made her swear..."

Amanirenas dropped her head, but Mshindi tenderly tilted it back up with a forefinger.

"She is honored that you would entrust her to take care of Amanitore. Should the worse happen tomorrow, she will head directly to Meroë and..."

"Mshindi, this is all my fault! I could have prevented this.... I could have prevented the kingdom from being torn asunder."

"No," Mshindi asserted softly. "Like you said, the Romans were going to do what they do—and that is conquer. But what you are doing now, gathering these men to stand up in one voice to say 'no,' is an act of defiance that will be celebrated for a thousand years."

Amanirenas focused intently on Mshindi's molded face and for a moment could see the familial resemblance he shared with Teriteqas. "Sabrakmani said I was jealous of the kingdom, and he was right. I wanted it dead..."

"I know," Mshindi hinted with a nod. "Amanishakheto and I have experienced the same problem, with me constantly being pulled away with the army. It's been very difficult for our relationship. There are times that I wish..."

He shook his head, trying to rattle away memories of the many intense arguments and cold nights he and his wife had shared. "She's a good woman, and she did what was necessary for Kush. Just like you have."

"Tomorrow, Kush will need a good warrior queen more than it will need a good woman," Amanirenas confessed with a stern but unsure visage.

"Amanirenas, there's no reason you can't be both. Make no

mistake; you are exactly what Kush needs at this moment. I know there were times you felt the kingdom competed with you like a lover for Teriteqas's heart.

"But he never saw Kush as a mistress. He saw it as a child—and you—he always saw you as its mother. A confident, persevering, and immovable Queen-Mother. And I am honored to fight under the banner of the mother of Kush."

Amanirenas grasped his hand and squeezed it affectionately. At that moment, her entire five-week ordeal came into focus, and she somehow knew that he needed her to endure just as much as she needed him to culminate it.

She slowly started back down the hall, reflecting on her brother-in-law's words.

"Do you need anything? I can have your meal brought to you," Mshindi offered respectfully.

"No. I'll be eating among the men tonight."

☿ ♃

Word of the late-afternoon Roman arrival spread through the Kushite encampment like a sandstorm. In every corner of the camp, men were preparing themselves for the looming conflict. Most passed the early evening sharpening their weapons and reinforcing their leather shields with additional material.

Khai made his way to the stables housing the dozens of horses brought by the late arrivals to the army. Though he recognized a few of the men, he was disappointed that none of them were from his unit. For weeks, he had held on to the possibility that he was not the sole survivor of the cavalry unit that had charged into action with the prince. Nonetheless, he was inspired by their account of the battle and was proud to know that many Kushites had heroically fought their way through the Roman maelstrom and managed to withdraw to safer regions. He was even more moved to hear that they had never lost faith in the dream that the Romans would be ejected from their land and was ecstatic when they heard rumor of the Kandace rallying a force to again take up arms against the invaders.

He found a speckled horse that resembled the steed he had ridden for many years. He stroked the animal's long brown mane and admired the muscles that rippled along the horse's neck.

"Fine animal."

Khai looked up and suddenly found the sturdy frame of Pelmes Mshindi on the opposite side of the animal.

"Yes, sir. I rode one just like him in Napata," Khai replied.

"I was never one for the cavalry. I spent some time as a charioteer, but that's about as close as I got to the horses," Mshindi said with a slight smile.

The soft sound of drums cascaded into the stables, followed by the boisterous clamor of dozens of men singing.

"Sounds like they've started the war chant," Khai noted, imagining Pedese in the midst of the ritualistic spectacle that many soldiers from the Kerman province engaged in to stimulate themselves for battle. Others used it as a means of preparing themselves spiritually while entreating Apedemack and Montu for the strength to confront the enemy.

"Are you going to head out there?" Mshindi asked.

"No, I've never been one to pray much. I think it's better to spend the time thinking about your plan, your enemy, and yourself."

"You're just as she described you," Mshindi mused lightly.

"My lord?"

"I asked Saiesha about you. I wanted to know more about the man who had managed to guide the Queen to the Semna region after Sabrakmani was captured," Mshindi replied. "Saiesha may have been out of her element while travelling through the back country. However, when it comes to the Kandace, she is very perceptive and notices every detail."

"She served her mistress well," Khai said, undoing a knot in the horse's mane.

"She told me about the way you comforted the Kandace when Sabrakmani was lost," Mshindi said, with a distant look in his eyes.

"How she embraced you and didn't push away. That she's comfortable enough with you to do that says a great deal."

"I was just there.... I didn't mean anything by it," Khai uttered, his heart starting to pound.

"Perhaps you didn't, but it meant something to the Queen. There are certain things I didn't need Saiesha to tell me because I was able to see them for myself. For instance, the way Amanirenas looks at you."

"My lord, I honor the Kandace and would never disrespect her," Khai said. For the first time, he looked Mshindi in the eye—utterly surprised by what he saw: a fountain of sympathy meshed with a modicum of envy. "I give you my word that I am focused only upon my assigned task."

Mshindi nodded, reflecting on the Kushite song flowing through the night air. "I believe you'll find you've been assigned a task that only one other man has been able to perform. You conducted Amanirenas to bodily safety; now you have to do it for her heart—whatever form that takes."

"How do I do that?" Khai questioned, gazing out the stable door, still unwilling to confess his feelings to the general.

"I've found that women of the Amani-aa'ila appreciate truth and forthrightness. And despite of their revered position in the Cult of Isis, they want to be loved and cherished just as any woman," Mshindi said as he turned to leave. "I've known Amanirenas long enough to know that there are times she wants and needs to be treated not like a warrior queen to be obeyed, but like a woman to be treasured."

"But she's more than a woman," Khai said. "How do you love someone who is the mother of her nation? Protecting her is one thing, but loving her is another."

Mshindi stopped and pondered his words. "Do you have a family, Khai?"

"No," Khai responded contritely.

"I do. My wife has given me two daughters, and both are as strong-willed as their mother," Mshindi said with a smile. "I've been a military man all my life, and I've always found myself in the midst of iron-willed officers and stubborn administrators. I swore I'd never marry a strong woman. The last thing I wanted was to be debated before eating or making love."

"Yet you married one."

"Yes, I did, and Amanishakheto is much like her sister," Mshindi said with a shrug. "We've had more than our share of fights. A strong woman can be intimidating to a man—especially if he is insecure. But I've learned through my relationship with my wife that just because a woman is strong does not mean that she is inflexible. And often times, her strength helps me to move mountains—or at the very least to believe that I can."

"Relationships require vulnerability. I don't know if I can be what she needs," Khai said, thinking about his fear of making emotional attachments that could be ripped away.

"You're right, it is a matter of trust. But we never know unless we take a chance."

The words resonated in Khai like a bell as Mshindi quietly left the stable.

Chapter 46

Amanirenas entered the room serving as her personal chamber and headed straight for bed. She unfastened her sandals and tried to massage the stiffness from her feet. Though her efforts were successful, other parts of her body quickly reminded her of just how sore she was, given the past five weeks.

Nevertheless, despite the acute pain in her leg and the constant throbbing from her defunct left eye, she reveled in the evening she had just spent with the bravest men in Kush. She had eaten and sung with them until her body had demanded a pause, and then she had done it some more. The food was burnt, the water was foul, and the men were rank, but she knew that she would remember it as one of the greatest evenings in her life.

She laughed as she envisioned Pedese, singing the Kerman war chant, wearing a Roman helmet taken from a dead centurion. Her heart pounded as she recalled the harrowing stories that Batae shared about fighting three legionaries at once. She dropped her head and laughed even harder as she replayed how she had stood in front of the fire before fifty or so men and testified about how she had skewered a Roman commander with a spear. The cheer that arose had rattled the stars in the sky.

She closed her eye, inhaled, and wondered what her mood would be like at that time tomorrow evening. She somehow knew that even if they defied the odds and managed to steal a victory, it was unlikely that she would feel as good as she did at the moment. Thus, she wanted to enjoy it.

She removed the fanciful blue and gold shawl she used as an outer garment and was about to undo the linen cloth folded about her head when there was a knock at the door.

"Enter," Amanirenas answered. She looked up, expecting to see Saiesha, but was taken aback when she saw Khai standing before her with a bowl of fruit. "Khai, is there something wrong?"

"No, I just wanted to stop and say good evening. I've brought the food the healer wants you to eat." He placed the bowl on the table. "I enjoyed your story tonight."

"I still can't believe I did that," Amanirenas smiled, shaking her head.

"You told it well. You made it sound like the Roman was a giant."

"He was to me."

The Queen plucked one of the purple berries from the assortment Khai had brought in and slowly bit into it, relishing the sweet juices it released. "Thank you for bringing this. In fact, I appreciate everything you've done. I don't know how things will go tomorrow, but I'm grateful for what you and the others have done to help bring us to this point. I think the men are..."

"You're a very beautiful woman," Khai said, pushing away the discomfort gnawing at his nerves. Amanirenas glanced at him.

"You know I can have you impaled," she said with a tired smile. "Not for addressing me out of your place, but for lying to me."

"It's no lie," Khai said, moving closer. "You're very beautiful and you've always been."

Amanirenas backed away and turned her head in disdain. "You deceive yourself. There's nothing beautiful about me any longer. I've killed men," she said, looking at the Roman gladius on a nearby table.

Khai slowly picked up the shawl from the bed and covered the sword with the decorative garment.

Amanirenas' gaze fell on the mirror suspended on the wall. "I don't even look like a woman anymore," she murmured, shaking her head. "I'm so thin and gaunt."

Khai drew near and tenderly ran his hands along the curves of her hips. Amanirenas observed in disbelief as he drew her into an embrace, his hands affectionately caressing every part of her body.

Amanirenas breathed deeply, her feelings wavering between jubilance and despair, confidence and insecurity. Her body quivered in his arms as she struggled against the images racing through her own mind.

"If you only knew what I look like. What I've become, you'd know how untouchable I am."

Khai reached up and unfastened the knot of the cloth covering her left eye.

"No," Amanirenas whispered, reaching to stop him.

He paused for a moment and waited for her minimal resistance to abate. He placed the cloth on the table and slowly turned her around to face him.

"This is what I look like. This is what I am."

Khai ran his forefinger over the contour of her face. A long vertical wound slashed through her eyebrow and down to the top of her cheekbone. Still in the process of becoming a permanent scar, the abrasion was inflamed and secreted a hazy fluid. An ashen eyelid, sealed shut, could be seen in place of a gorgeous brown eye.

"I am a soldier," Amanirenas muttered to herself.

Khai ran his fingers through her curly hair and gently drew her closer. He kissed her forehead, and then her cheek. He drew back, gazed lovingly into her right eye, and then lightly pressed his lips on the injury that disfigured her face.

Amanirenas moaned at his touch. She tried to pull away, but quickly found herself drawing him closer as their lips locked into a deeply passionate kiss.

Chapter 47

The late morning sun hung menacingly over the eastern horizon and bathed the Roman army in a shower of golden light. There were 1,440 legionaries standing at the ready, awaiting the order to advance into the expansive barren basin that contained the outpost housing the final Kushite army. Petronius sat atop his horse in the rear observation post and studied the Kushite defenses, the main body of which stood in front of the outpost, waiting patiently for the Romans to make the first move.

Satisfied with how efficiently his legionaries fell into the three lined manipular formations he had devised the previous day, Petronius prepared to issue the order to advance. Though the terrain was somewhat condensed, he determined that they still had enough space to execute his battle plan. While he was confident that the three primary cohorts were more than capable of eliminating the enemy, he held five more in reserve, in addition to a covert maneuver waiting in the wings.

"The fourth and fifth cohorts are in place, Prefect," Septimus reported, pulling his horse alongside Petronius. "We estimate the number of visible Kushite defenders at 1,500. As you noted last night, they likely have at least a thousand more concealed in the hills and the fort."

Petronius glared at the fort in the distance, heat waves literally causing it to shimmer, with the black soldiers in front of it appearing as hellish apparitions. He harbored little doubt that the Kushites were attempting to bait him into a full-frontal attack while a majority of their forces were concealed. The insolent message he had received from the Queen two days earlier was proof positive of their desire for the Romans to attack.

Try as he could, Petronius was unable to shake the sensation of being manipulated by the faceless Queen. Her scathing rebuke in her audacious letter was aimed squarely at Roman pride and contested every aspect of Roman domination over the region. Although Amanirenas directly challenged Caesar's authority, she did so in such an eloquent fashion that Petronius was actually eager to make her acquaintance. For months, he had envisioned her being no more than a brutish woman who likely manipulated her subjects via some form of cryptic Kushite witchcraft. However, the words she used to argue for Kushite independence gave him pause, particularly with his deeper understanding of how the Kushite Queen-Mother concept was interwoven with spirituality, hope, and loyalty.

Over the past year, the Kushites had been driven from their strongholds in the north and soundly defeated deep within their own kingdom, while their army was obliterated in the process. Nevertheless, a little more than a month later, here they were again, following a woman who had been nearly captured at least twice within the last couple of weeks alone. Her tenacity and determination rivaled that of any foe Petronius had faced within the past three decades, and it was a fortitude he could ill afford to let fester beyond today's sunrise.

The Amani-aa'ila would end today.

"Give the signal," Petronius ordered.

ɸ ƌ

Mshindi stood on top of the fort's western facing wall and watched as the large wooden gates swung open to allow Amanirenas and her bodyguard troop to leave the fortification. The Queen's chariot slowly wove through the formation of Kushite solders, most of whom bowed reverently as she passed. For the first time since the battle of Napata, she wore her gold tiara studded with turquoise and rubies.

Just as she had done with the contingent of troopers inside of the fort, she addressed the men and implored them to fight not for her, but for their families and the thousands of Kushites who did not have the power to fight for themselves and resist the tyranny the Romans would surely visit upon future generations.

Though Mshindi could not hear it, the Kandace must have said something funny, as a roar of laughter arose from the throng of armed black men as Amanirenas unsheathed the Roman gladius she captured weeks earlier. Although he had objected, she had insisted on leading the initial charge. He took one last look at her and quietly prayed for her protection. Her husband Teriteqas and her son Jaelen were both struck down leading charges against Roman infantry, and Mshindi could not help but wonder if she secretly desired to depart this life in a similar fashion.

The sweat rolled into Mshindi's eyes as he peered into the distance. A cloud of dust mingled with the shimmering heat waves, signifying that the Romans' advance was now underway.

ℵ ℵ

The moments before going into battle were always the same to Khai. His senses were focused, and he felt more aware of everything surrounding him. Though elevated, his heart pounded at a steady pace, as if waiting for the rest of his body to get into sync. The familiar feeling of a horse underneath him was a welcome one, and part of him longed to urge the beast into a full gallop so he could feel the warm air blow past his face.

Batae and Pedese rode next to him; however, neither one of them looked very comfortable on a horse. Batae even petitioned to run alongside the Queen's chariot but was overruled. Ten other bodyguards rode with the Kandace, and Khai was satisfied that they would be able to provide her with ample protection as long as she didn't breech the Roman skirmish line and become surrounded. Although she had agreed to maintain a prudent distance from the enemy, Khai was suspect of her motives for leading the assault and knew how easy it was to be swept up in the chaos of combat.

In an effort to relieve some of the mounting tension, Khai glanced at Pedese, who had decided to wear the Roman helmet he had acquired when they were ambushed back near Semna. The shiny headgear contrasted sharply against his dark skin and gave him the appearance of a black phantom. Without fail, Khai cracked a smile at the ridiculous yet intimidating sight.

Amanirenas stopped to address another section of troops. While she did so, Khai rallied the dozen guardsmen to his side. He looked each one of them in the eye and noted the staunch resolve the men carried like a spear.

"Weeks ago, we were given a charge in Kawa," Khai started, noting the Romans skirmish line methodically moving their way. "Each one of you has honored the commitment you made with the courage and fortitude only a man of Kush can possess. I am proud to command this unit."

Khai turned toward the man holding the tall staff bearing the blue and gold banner of the Amani-aa'ila. "Rhonde, keep that standard flying at all cost. I want every Roman legionary to know that this army fights under the banner of the Kandace of Kush."

"Yes, sir!" Rhonde responded crisply.

"The soldiers in the regiment may fight for their families," Khai continued, his eyes falling on Amanirenas, "but we fight for the Queen! *Respect* and *protect!*"

ᛟ ᛣ

Amanirenas steadied herself as Akfoor guided the two-horse chariot along the Kushite frontline. She sheathed the Roman sword and brandished a long Kushite spear armed with a flat iron head. She wanted the weapon launched from her hand to be unmistakably Kushite.

The dull rumble emanating from the Romans' approach grew

louder, and soon it was apparent that the clamor was the sound of the legionaries clanging their spears against their shields.

"Let them come!" Amanirenas urged at the top of her lungs. "Let the murderous thieves come to their judgment!" She jabbed her spear into the air and urged Akfoor forward.

As the Queen's chariot bolted ahead, Khai signaled the bodyguard into a formation around the vehicle. The body of Kushite forces sprinted forward as well, their thunderous war cry echoing through the expanse.

Khai knew the timing had to be perfect and counted on the Kandace to slow her advance at the appropriate distance from the Romans. Just as Mshindi had predicted, the legionaries stopped abruptly, set their shields, and prepared to launch their javelins, waiting for the Kushites to run themselves into range.

Akfoor slowed the Queen's chariot almost to a complete stop. As he did, a hail of arrows streaked overhead from the rear and pelted the Romans before they could throw their spears. Amanirenas arced her spear into the air into the Roman formation. Like most of the arrows, the spear skimmed off the hard surface of a Roman shield with a harsh thud.

Another volley of Kushite arrows soared over the Kandace and into the Romans, this time striking dozens of legionaries in the act of throwing their javelins.

The Kushite regiment rushed past the Queen while a third stream of arrows streaked into the Roman skirmish line. Amanirenas heard the centurion order the Romans to launch their missiles; however, the Kushites had already closed the gap and hurdled themselves into the shielded line, deliberately attacking the creases where the shields met.

"Now!" Amanirenas shouted. Her order echoed throughout the ranks, and hundreds of Kushite soldiers flung their spears into the Romans' defenses.

Within moments, the skirmish line was broken, and the Roman infantry swiftly retreated behind the second maniple and quickly formed a new deadly arm of the larger formation.

Chapter 48

Pahor could feel the droplets of sweat gathering in the balls of his fists as he struggled to keep track of the Queen's standard on the battlefield. Everything within him wanted to mount a horse and fight alongside the bodyguard contingent his father had commissioned to protect Kandace Amanirenas. However, his wounds testified against him and relegated him to the command post behind General Mshindi.

"The maneuver worked," said one of the general's adjutants. "They retreated before they could throw their javelins."

"But they're already back in formation," Mshindi observed. Hours of study had helped Mshindi to anticipate their enemies' tactics, but he was still amazed at how quickly the Romans could recover from a setback and deliver a counterblow.

The Roman manipular lines maintained their checkered formation and advanced to a steady cadence. Then, like a swarm of ants, the Roman front formations broke from their rectangular shapes and formed a single line that had to be at least three soldiers deep.

The sudden maneuver was executed so sharply that Pahor actually questioned what he saw. The scheme clearly gave the Romans an advantage, as one line would fight for a while and would then be replaced by the next. The mechanical nature of the Roman advance reminded Pahor of a waterwheel driven by a steady current. Although the Kushites fought fiercely, it was almost impossible for them to stop or even slow down the enemy's encroachment.

"Send the signal to the right wing now," Mshindi ordered calmly.

Pahor scanned the dusty field for the Queen's standard as a messenger quickly relayed the general's order. Though it took him a while, he found it surrounded by a swirl of dust, making it impossible to see what was happening beneath it.

✍ ✑

Khai somehow managed to keep the bodyguard troop between Amanirenas and the advancing Roman front line. Thus far, the invaders had held to their traditional disciplined attack method and maintained strict shoulder-to-shoulder ranks. Their approach simplified the task of protecting the Queen, but Khai knew that the respite would not last much longer.

"Attack the edges!" Amanirenas shouted to the Kushite soldiers pressing toward the Romans. "Hit between the shields! Make them split!"

Batae watched with pure joy as scores of his compatriots used his maneuver to break into the Roman lines—if for just a moment. The brief confusion it caused bought a few Kushites the time needed to get through the third Roman line and attack them from the rear.

"Here they come!" Khai yelled, pointing to a swarm of Kushite soldiers cascading into the Roman formation from the side. As the two hundred plus men rushed in, the Romans almost immediately broke their ranks to form a defensive front. However, before they could complete the effort, the Kushite assault overran them.

Amanirenas's chariot lurched forward into the shattered Roman line and nearly disappeared from Khai's sight before he could follow her.

Rhonde hoisted the standard high and charged after the Queen into the thick haze of dust and death.

✍ ✑

"Clever maneuver," Septimus noted to Petronius as they watched the once-rigid Roman line melt away like wax. "Not nearly enough, though."

"It was a logical move," Petronius assessed, eyeing the second wing of Kushites. "Those others are no doubt waiting for the next maniple to advance."

"Their strategy might work because the terrain will limit our approach. However, they're still suffering heavy losses." Septimus glanced at the prefect with confidence. "No matter what, we have the numerical advantage."

Petronius gritted his teeth as a sour feeling started to roll through in his stomach. True, the Kushites were losing many men, but they had managed to smash the first Roman maniple very quickly and were positioned to repeat the feat at least two more times. Keeping in mind the goal of exterminating the last Kushite army, Petronius decided to raise the stakes and press on with the assault.

"We're committed, Septimus," Petronius said stoically. "Let's test their mettle. Advance the next cohort and bring it into formation."

☙ ❧

Akfoor tussled with the horses to keep the chariot facing northward. His effort insured that Amanirenas could engage the Romans from her right and limit the enemy from approaching her via her blind side. Khai was attempting to insulate the Queen with the bodyguard troop, but the chaotic nature of the conflict soon multiplied tenfold. With their offensive line dissolved, the Romans scattered across the battlefield and engaged the Kushites one-on-one. Batae, Pedese, and at least several other bodyguards abandoned their horses and fought the enemy at ground level.

Fighting from her chariot, Amanirenas appropriated a long Kushite spear and pierced any Roman that came within her range. The golden tiara restrained her curly black hair from falling across her face, but it could not prevent sweat and dust from obstructing her sight. She paused to wipe the grimy sweat from her face and was nearly decapitated by a Roman rushing in from her left. Akfoor quickly jerked the chariot forward, causing the attacker to stumble. Although the man recovered, Pedese immediately hacked him down permanently.

Khai had seen enough and approached Akfoor to order him to pull her out of the widening battle zone. However, before he could garner his attention, Amanirenas commanded the young driver to rush through a wide crease in the fighting. The chariot trucked through the opening, hammering several Romans in the process. Somehow, Rhonde managed to stay behind the Kandace, the brilliant blue-gold banner of the Amani-aa'ila waving defiantly against the gray haze created by the battle.

Khai dashed after the Queen, promptly followed by his men. They broke through the fighting rather quickly and entered an unexpected zone of calm. Khai quickly realized that they were face-to-face with the next Roman maniple, aligned in the familiar pristine battle formation a mere three hundred cubits away from them.

Amanirenas ordered her chariot stopped and looked back. Most of her bodyguard troop had caught up with her, but she was only interested in seeing the standard-bearer. She acknowledged Rhonde with a curt nod and turned until Khai came into view. Her eye met his, and he knew exactly what she was thinking. Before he could utter a word in protest, she ripped away the drenched bandage covering the dreadful scar residing in place of her left eye. The sight captured Khai's thoughts as his heart was flooded with feelings of bitterness and malice, mixed with the warm passion he shared with the only woman he had allowed himself to love.

A corner of Amanirenas' lip curled up ever so slightly as she afforded her heart a moment to recall every gentle touch from Khai's hand, every night she had slept under the shadow of the protection he had willingly offered, every word that had passed between them, every time he had kissed her passionately, every time he had made her feel like a woman. She realized how much she truly loved him and cherished what he had helped her to reclaim. She exhaled slowly and enjoyed the rapture of the moment, not just savoring the love of a man, but the renewed ability to love. It was a capacity she had feared lost long ago and had never found again.

She turned toward the approaching legionaries, her countenance hardening like a sculpted piece of granite. She turned toward the left just as the Kushite wing started its furious charge into the Roman flank. Like before, the infusion of black soldiers into their ranks incited a hasty collapse of Roman discipline that rippled like a wave from one side to the other. Before long, chaos reigned supreme.

"Keep the standard high," she commanded Rhonde.

"Yes, my kandace," Rhonde replied, gripping the pole firmly.

The Queen and the bodyguard troop waded into the fray, followed by hundreds of hungry Kushite soldiers, ready to dine on another confused Roman maniple.

ᛟ ᛈ

Tribune Marius could scarcely believe his eyes as the Kushites managed to route another manipular formation—this time doing so even more efficiently and losing fewer soldiers in the process. His cohort was the next to draw up a formation against the dark-skinned barbarians.

Legionaries who had survived the attack rushed back to the relative safety of the approaching cohort. While their retreat was an orderly one, it was far too hasty for Marius's taste, and he vowed to remind them of it in harsh fashion after the battle.

Although it was an unorthodox practice, the tribune served as first spear centurion for the lead century of his cohort—a necessity born of the fact that the Kushites had killed the commanding centurion during their last engagement. He surveyed the hills to the right and noted yet another two hundred or so Kushites preparing to stream down into his advancing formation. As if struck by a lightning bolt from Olympus, the tribune broke from his position and demanded the attention of the signifier.

"Form the wedge!" Marius commanded. The signifier offered a perplexed glare, but only for an instant. He quickly issued the signal, to which the leading three centuries responded by coalescing into living wedge of 240 legionaries.

☙ ❧

Mshindi managed to conceal the awestruck horror he felt as he watched the Roman front line morph into an arrowhead pointed directly at the fort. Remarkably, the invaders maintained the pace of their advance even as they shifted into the deadly formation.

With the lines gone, the Kushite soldiers from the hills had no lanes to invade and thus were either mowed down by the wedge or skirted along its edges until they came face-to-face with the third cohort. Groans arose from the contingent of lieutenants behind him as the drama played out, but Mshindi remained silent. He had anticipated that the Romans would make this adjustment, but not this early in the battle. Kushite losses were mounting, and he had to make a play.

"Signal in the cavalry. First wave only," Mshindi commanded an adjutant.

"Yes, my lord," the young man replied.

Within moments, two hundred cavalrymen streamed from the side of the fort, aiming directly for the right side of the Roman wedge.

The ground shook under the Romans' feet as the horses approached. Marius knew immediately that they were doomed if the horses reached the formation. There were more than enough of the animals to trample them, and there would be nowhere for them to run, due to the tightly packed formation.

"Ready javelins," the tribune commanded.

Scores of iron-tipped Roman spears were elevated in nervous anticipation, waiting for the horses to come into optimal range.

"Fire!"

☙ ❧

Akfoor lost control of the chariot as two to three javelins struck one of their horses, sending the beast crashing to the ground. The harness pulled the second horse down as well, forcing the chariot to flip violently, crushing Akfoor and hurdling Amanirenas thirty cubits through the air. She bounced along the rocky ground, her makeshift leather armor taking the brunt of the friction.

She tried to push herself up but lost her ability to focus as the entire world appeared to spin in circles. The one thing she could make out was a crowd of men coming at her—their swords were drawn, and their skin was white.

Chapter 49

Petronius tapped his finger on the hilt of his sword as he considered the melee playing out before him. He assumed it was Tribune Marius who had deviated from the original battle plan and ordered the cohort into the wedge configuration. The bold maneuver was successful until the Kushites countered with an unexpected cavalry charge that quickly reduced the battlefield into a mangled mess. Petronius could see centurions straining to restore formation, but the fight was rapidly degenerating into a hand-to-hand brawl—a format that still favored the Romans—for the moment.

"Septimus confirmed the order to proceed in the manipular formation," Petronius stated. "I want the third cohort to carry out the original orders."

"Yes, Prefect. Shall I have the fourth cohort move into position?"

"Not yet," Petronius answered, his gaze fixed on the hills behind the outpost. "Have them ready, though. The Kushites should be receiving their gift right about now. This battle ends soon."

ॐ ॐ

Tribune Marius offered a prayer of gratitude to Mars for the gift the god of war bestowed upon him. There, on her knees before him, was a woman who fit the description of the Queen of Kush. The tiara suggested that she was of royal blood, but the scar over her left eye socket testified the loudest against her.

"Petronius can have your body," Marius declared, moving over her as she tried in vain to focus on the menacing voice she heard. "But I'm going to take your head."

Marius raised his gladius over the Queen's neck and took aim. As he brought it down, a sudden flash of steel sliced through his forearm, sending his hand and weapon flying away. The tribune shrieked in pain and spun around to see a Kushite wearing a Roman helmet rearing back, with his sword aimed for the Roman's torso. Marius's armor was not enough to deter the blade, which slid through his gut and protruded from his back.

Pedese extracted his sword from the gasping tribune and paused to examine the man's headgear. "Oh, I like this helmet much better," he remarked as he unfastened Marius's decorative galea and placed it on his own head.

He turned to see Khai with the Queen in his arms, stroking her face tenderly. Her breathing was light, and she grasped incoherently at the air.

"You better get her back to the fort," Pedese said.

"She wanted to stay here," Khai muttered, not really thinking about his words.

"Take her back; we'll stay here with the banner," Batae said placing his hand on Khai's shoulder.

Pedese searched the area for Rhonde. He found the dead bodyguard a few cubits away, still clutching the Queen's banner. Pedese retrieved the standard and called to Khai as he mounted a horse with Amanirenas.

"We'll be right here, the Kushite raisins in the Roman dough."

Khai nodded and rode off, holding the Kandace to his chest.

Batae looked at Pedese and shook his head. "You look stupid."

"The Roman I took it from looks worse. What now?" Pedese asked as four other bodyguards formed up around Batae.

"We need to push through their cohort," Batae said, surveying the field of Roman soldiers. "Let's get the banner to their rear. That's what she would have wanted."

"Is that all? I thought you were going to ask for something more difficult," Pedese sassed as the group pressed forward.

∅ ᛞ

Pahor and two healers met Khai and the Queen as they rode into the fort. The hundreds of Kushite soldiers waiting in reserve gasped as they saw the disoriented Kandace gently dismounted from the horse. Some swore curses upon the Romans while others simmered in silent anger as they contemplated how best to exact revenge on the fair-skinned invaders who had dared to assault the Queen-Mother in such a ruthless fashion.

"Mshindi is going to release them in a few moments," Pahor said to Khai as the healers tended to Amanirenas, who could barely keep her head up.

"Already? What about the rest of Amen-Tekah's men in the hills and the 1,250 men behind the fort? They should have been moved into position by now," Khai stated, breathing heavily.

"They won't be coming," Pahor said despondently. "The Romans sent over half the *Cyrenaica* legion behind us during the night, and they're now attacking us from the rear. Mshindi had to send Amen-Tekah to defend against them. It's hopeless."

Khai knelt down before Amanirenas, who scarcely clung to consciousness. He placed his hand tenderly on her cheek, and for a moment, her eye came to bear squarely upon him. She tried to utter something and prompted Khai to lean in close. He drew back slowly and traced his finger along her scarred face. He grasped her hand and kissed it lightly, sharing an intimate smile with her as he stood up.

"We should probably get her out of here while we can," Pahor suggested.

"No, this is where she wants to be. This is where she needs to be," Khai responded, moving back toward his horse.

"Where are you going?" Pahor asked, hurrying behind him.

"I'm a cavalryman, and my men need me." Khai nodded at the young man. "You served well, Pahor. Your brother is very proud of you."

Khai prodded the horse toward the massive gate, which was open just wide enough for him to gallop through.

ɸ ʠ

Petronius was impressed with how hard the Kushites fought and noted their determination to resist their inevitable defeat. Their well-crafted rouse attempting to bait him into relying upon a singular frontal offensive was a ploy worthy of the Parthians. However, Petronius was a seasoned commander and knew better than to rely upon attacking a stronghold from just one angle.

He estimated that the *III Legio* was finishing off the reserved Kushite troops in the hills and behind the fort. Keeping in mind that the rough terrain had probably hampered the attack to some degree, he still projected that the legion would march victoriously around the fort at any moment.

"Septimus, have the fifth and sixth cohorts prepare to lay siege to the fort," Petronius commanded. He had initially hoped that the Kushites would simply surrender once their forces outside were routed, but their resolve to fight meant that their intentions would likely be otherwise. Originally, the task of laying siege was to fall upon the third cohort; however, the Kushites' battle scheme had all but shredded the third cohort, and the unit was clearly in disarray.

"Septimus," Petronius called, turning to look for his aide, who was uncharacteristically silent. Petronius found him, receiving a report from a centurion. Septimus briskly approached his commander, trepidation etched upon his face.

"Prefect, our southern lookouts report scores of boats carrying Kushite soldiers heading downriver. Many of them are empty, suggesting that a large number of the soldiers have already disembarked."

Petronius blinked at Septimus indifferently. "Have they estimated the number of Kushite warriors?"

"They believe that over a thousand have already landed behind us to the south," Septimus answered ruefully.

"*Behind us*," Petronius seethed. He surveyed the landscape to the rear. There was a rocky hill and then the river, but no enemy as of yet. After assessing his options, he turned to Septimus. "Redeploy the fourth and fifth cohorts to defend the southern flank."

"Shall I send for the remainder of the *XXII* at Primis?"

"No. We need to know what we're dealing with first."

Chapter 50

Agentle breeze pushed Amanirenas' sailboat along with the current. She dipped her hand in the cool river water, enjoying the slight chill it sent along her arm. It was a lovely day—much like those she had spent with her father sailing north from the Isle of Meroë.

She closed her eyes and recalled such day when she was a teenager.

The river was smooth, and it felt as if they were gliding through the air. Their luxurious barge must have looked like an enormous treasure chest to the people along the shore. She recalled admiring the greatest gem on the vessel—her father. He was a man who had stood out from others not for his appearance, but for his wisdom and uncanny ability to mesmerize his subjects with only a few words.

To a teenage girl, he was essentially a god dwelling among mortals, and the world was simply unworthy of his presence. Indeed, there was something enchanting about him. Every word he uttered to her had bolstered her confidence. Every touch of his hand had gently affirmed love and self-assurance within her, along with a conviction that everything was possible. She loved her father and dreamt of having a man just like him.

As she opened her eyes, she saw another boat plodding past her, going upriver, bearing five passengers. She squinted and grinned, as she was able to make out the people waving at her as they passed. Sabrakmani, her sons Khararpkhael, Akinid, and Jaelen, and finally, her husband Teriteqas each acknowledged her with a bow as they silently continued up the river.

Amanirenas thought it odd for them to keep going without her, but she somehow knew it was only temporary, and she would she them again.

When she dipped her hand back into the glassy river, she noticed yet another craft coming her way. It was larger and contained some thirty men. Like before, each one nodded at her politely as they drifted by. She knew them all, but three stood out above the rest, for they were the three who had believed when no one else would. The three that chose to see life instead of death, hope instead of dismay, and beauty instead of ashes.

She locked eyes with Khai and mouthed a simple phrase.

Thank you.

He smiled appreciatively and then faced forward as their boat followed a gentle bend in the river and floated out of sight.

Amanirenas opened her eye and drew a deep breath to counter the fierce pain gripping her left shoulder. She pulled herself up, wondering just how much of her immediate memory was the product of a dream. She recognized her room, as well as the fact that her armor was stacked neatly in a corner.

She slowly stood and waited for the lightheadedness to pass. The only pain that was noticeable was her shoulder, which she rubbed firmly.

The door opened, and Saiesha peered in to check on her mistress.

"My kandace, thank the gods!" the young woman said, coming in and embracing the Queen.

"Saiesha, what has happened? How did I get back here?" Amanirenas asked.

"You don't remember anything?"

"Just ... shadows. I remember charging the Romans and then... How... How long have I been here?"

"Khai ... said you took a very bad fall. You were unconscious for a little more than a day." Saiesha poured the Queen a cup of water. "You woke up a few times, but you always passed out again. The healers ultimately thought that you were simply exhausted."

Amanirenas drank the water and then reached for the bowl of fruit on the desk. "Saiesha, what has happened? Where are the Romans? Where are Khai and Batae…"

"I'll be back," Saiesha responded abruptly. "General Mshindi wanted to know when you were awake."

No sooner had the door closed then did someone knock, begging entrance.

"Come in," Amanirenas said as she laced up her sandals. A young man slipped into the room and bowed.

"Pahor. It's good to see you."

"I'm not supposed to be in here, but I had to make sure you were all right."

"I'm sure Khai won't mind. He's strict but forgiving," she replied with a smile that quickly faded as she observed the young man's reaction. "What has happened, Pahor?"

Pahor looked at her fighting to maintain his composure. Amanirenas walked over to him, but he would not look her in the eye.

"What has happened?" she asked softly.

"They're all dead. Khai, Batae, my brother. All of them," he said as tears spilled down his dark cheeks. He fell into Amanirenas's waiting embrace and sobbed.

"I know," she whispered reflectively. "I know."

☙ ☙

Mshindi and Amen-Tekah were stunned when the Kandace entered the meeting chamber. Young Pahor escorted the Queen, who was not wearing a blindfold to cover her scarred eye.

"Kandace Amanirenas, you didn't have to come here. We were about to come to you," Amen-Tekah said with a bow.

"It's all right. I want to know what is happening now."

Mshindi nodded and referred to the figurines on the table as he had a couple days earlier. "In short, my kandace, we've had a miracle. The Romans flanked us just before you were brought in. The *Legio Cyrenaica* attacked us from the rear—something I was not expecting."

"How could they fight on that rocky terrain?" Amanirenas asked.

"They funneled through the paths and just kept coming," Amen-Tekah said. "Once they were able to get into formation, my men had a difficult time with them."

Mshindi shuffled Roman figurines around the model of the fort. "When they showed up, they prevented us from supporting your charge as we had planned. But then, more Kushite soldiers appeared from the southern pass. Over a thousand of them."

"So many?" Amanirenas questioned. While not very surprised that men in the region had arrived to render assistance, she was shocked at the number. "Where were they from? Kerma, Nobatia?"

"Most of them, yes," Mshindi answered. "That's how they knew to take the pass. But another force landed on the river behind the Romans that changed everything. It was the regiment from Meroë."

"What?" Amanirenas blurted.

"Yes, they were led here by Qar Amanitore and the remaining members of the war council," Mshindi continued. "If you recall, Amanishakheto dispatched runners to the south to inform the viziers and peshtes that you planned to make a stand in Qasr Ibrim. As it were, Amanitore left Meroë with the regiment several weeks ago. Fortunately, she received word from a runner and knew where to come."

"Where is she?" Amanirenas asked, her maternal instincts rising to the fore.

Mshindi referred back to the map. "She's still with her regiment, and they are encamped just south of the Romans. I advised her to stay where she is."

"And the Romans? How has Petronius responded?"

"Once our soldiers started pouring through the pass, the *Cyrenaica* retreated back to Primis," Mshindi reported. "They had no idea how many men they were going to have to face, and given the terrain, retreat was their best option."

"Men are still showing up from everywhere," Amen-Tekah added. "An outfit of Medjay warriors arrived this morning. The Romans are basically outnumbered."

"Yes, but that didn't stop Petronius before. What's his position?" Amanirenas asked.

"They went directly across the river and have held their station there," Mshindi replied.

"He's waiting to see how many more Kushites appear and from which region." Mshindi folded his arms contemplatively. "Moreover, he's probably waiting to see what we do next."

Amanirenas quietly absorbed the information. As she considered the various scenarios, it slowly dawned on her this was the first time since she had taken over the campaign that Petronius had actually made a defensive move. She was curious if she could force him to make another.

"General, if we moved our forces from the outpost to the banks of the Nile, what do you suppose Petronius would do?" she asked.

Mshindi studied the map, his eyes darting between the Roman figurines and their stronghold in Primis. "There's nowhere that a legion can skirmish along the Nile. The logical thing for him to do would be to retreat to Primis and try to do to us what we just did to him."

"Bait us into attacking a fortress with terrain favorable to him," Amanirenas mused.

"We could try to cut him off from Primis," Amen-Tekah suggested. "Cut him off and kill him."

"Hmm," Amanirenas sighed as she turned away. "Let me think about it."

⌀ ꙮ

Amanirenas walked through the wide central courtyard of the outpost. Pahor quietly accompanied her, speaking only to prevent soldiers from breaking her contemplative mood. She did not want to seem unapproachable, but she was so consumed by her thoughts that she hardly noticed the few soldiers who were in the courtyard to begin with.

Many of the men were on burial detail, performing the undesirable yet sacred task of gathering their dead comrades. Ironically enough, the Romans were doing the same, mutually agreeing to postpone the fighting while the dead were honored.

Amanirenas came across her standard, propped up in a lonely corner. The banner was frayed and dirty, yet it still maintained the unmistakable crest of the royal family that for centuries had adorned the standards of Kushite monarchs. The last time she had seen it, in the hand of Rhonde, the courageous young man from Kawa had followed her into the broken jaw of a Roman cohort.

"Pahor, how did they die?" the Kandace asked quietly.

Pahor was instantly by her side and recounted what he knew of the bodyguards' final act of valor. How the men had picked up the banner and fought their way through the third Roman cohort as if fighting alongside the gods themselves.

How one by one, they had been killed, but not before inflicting substantial losses upon the Romans. Down they went, with Batae being the last one to go, using the standard as a spear. While some witnesses testified that Khai was the last one standing, Pahor knew for certain that it had to have been Batae.

"They died well," the young man said quietly.

"They didn't have to do that," Amanirenas said sadly.

"We were glad they did," Pahor offered humbly. "When the general saw your banner being waved that far behind the Roman line, he ordered in the second cavalry wave. The fourth Roman cohort actually stopped their advance once they saw how our men had butchered their legionaries. I'll never forget that as long as I live.

"Our regiments kept going until they got to that banner. They all kept yelling, 'Respect and protect! Respect and protect!' They did it for you, my queen."

"There have been so many sacrifices," Amanirenas reflected in a hushed voice. "Perhaps it's time for me to make one."

Instantly, Pahor thought of the Kandace's plan to turn herself over to the Romans if it would spare her people further suffering. He searched for the words to offer to avert her thoughts, but fear and something else begged him to remain silent.

A rare afternoon breeze danced through the courtyard and prompted Amanirenas to think of the men in the boat from her dream. She vividly recalled how they were peacefully headed upstream without cares or worries. The more she thought of it, the more she realized that each one that had passed her had made a lasting impression upon her life, no matter how long or fleeting the association. Moreover, each one had made a substantial personal sacrifice so that she would not have to.

Amanirenas reverently removed her tiara and wiped away the tear from her eye. She started to withdraw from Pahor but then turned to face him.

"Pahor, please have Mshindi, Piankhi, and Amen-Tekah meet me in my room. It's time to send the Romans another message."

Chapter 51

The Roman encampment was quiet and subdued. The late afternoon sun sank into the western horizon and promised the Romans yet another evening of uncertainty. Smoke from the Kushite campfires across the Nile bellowed into the sky like a distant storm cloud.

All throughout the camp, men busied themselves with the tasks of repairing armor and sharpening weapons, all silently anticipating the orders few of them wanted to hear, but none would dare question. The prospect of crossing the Nile and reengaging with a scrappy Kushite force reinvigorated by a steady stream of reenforcements was undesirable, to say the least. Nonetheless, every legionary dutifully prepared himself to follow any dictate issued from Prefect Petronius's command tent.

Petronius stood in the mist of his tent surrounded by his officers. After the dust had settled from the previous day's conflict, the prefect had lost three of his six tribunes, including Quintus Publius and Cassius Marius. Two of the three cohorts sent in to attack the Kushite stronghold had lost at least a third of their company—the first cohort was nearly obliterated, with only a handful of legionaries surviving the battle.

Petronius worried most about the mental wounds inflicted on the remainder of the *Legio XXII*. The battle had ended in more of a stalemate, with the Kushites' losses outnumbering their own, but the

Romans were the ones that scampered across the Nile like bilge rats. As methodical and orderly as the retreat was, it was still a retreat—a first for any Roman legion pitted against a Kushite army.

The prefect listened as Tribune Ventidius finished presenting the latest reconnaissance report—information Petronius did not find helpful.

"So, what is the latest estimation of the barbarian force, tribune?" Gamal Abasi inquired, standing in the stead of Tribune Marius.

"Adding the figures from yesterday to those who arrived several hours ago, their force is likely between 5,000 and 6,000. Possibly more," Ventidius answered. "We simply have no way of knowing how many men they have in or behind the fort at this point."

"You'd think we would have gotten a better idea when they allowed us to go and collect our dead this morning," another officer grunted.

"And Gallus has been no help whatsoever," another man asserted spitefully, referring to the tribune who had presided over the *III Legio's* hasty withdrawal from its prime position behind the fortification. "Where is he, anyway?"

"I've ordered him to remain at Primis," Petronius stated, wanting to steer away from the subject of Decius Gallus. If the tribune had been there, Petronius would likely have killed the man himself for having pulled the legion away from the battle so quickly. His decision to do so curtailed the Romans' best chance to capture the outpost. "He serves me better out of my sight."

"Prefect, given this situation, how do you wish to deal with these barbarians?" Ventidius asked.

"We should call up the *Cyrenaica* and attack!" an officer shouted. "They're just barbarians!"

"These are not barbarians!" Petronius exclaimed, slamming his fist on the table before him. "How many times must you men be taught the lesson? These people have an ancient culture. They think critically and reason not with their emotions, but with a sensibility that rivals the Greek philosophers who taught you how to read.

"They entreated us to collect our war dead under the flag of truce.

Such is an act of a civilized people—not barbarians. I'm surprised you men are so blind to the truth."

"What are you saying, Prefect?" Ventidius questioned. "Do you believe that they are stronger than we are and actually have the ability to drive us from this land?"

The other officers glared at Ventidius cautiously, but they were grateful that someone had the fortitude to pose the obvious question.

"They will never have the capability to dispel Rome," Petronius said, clasping his hands behind his back. He pondered the defiant letter from the Kandace and cursed himself for not having seen the harsh reality a year earlier. A reality his personal hubris and Roman honor had worked vigorously to veil from his view. A reality from which he had no apparent means of escape.

"However, they will always have the ability to resist Rome," Petronius said, noting the legionary who entered his tent and offered a salute. "And such a disposition will lead to generations of rebellion and carnage."

"Prefect, a communiqué, from the Queen of Kush," the soldier said, handing Petronius the parchment.

Petronius read the note and scowled. "The Queen requests a meeting tomorrow at noon. She wishes to discuss her terms."

"For her surrender?" Ventidius asked skeptically.

"No, for our withdrawal from Kush."

At least half the men in the room erupted with laughter.

"And she means for us to take this seriously?" Ventidius questioned with contempt.

Petronius rubbed his eyes. He was weary of the conflict and the ignorance that fueled it. He searched for the right combination of words to help his officers see the true gravity of their situation. "All things as they are, we may not have a choice in the matter, Tribune."

Chapter 52

If not for the black stripes, the large gray tent set up by the Kushites would have completely blended in with the barren background. Petronius found it ironic that the pavilion was erected not far from spot where his army had been encamped just two days earlier.

The Roman prefect surveyed the battlefield in the distance as he approached the Kushite delegation. Dark blotches of dry blood pock-marked the landscape, but there were no corpses in sight.

A dozen Kushite armed soldiers stood next to the tent, one of which held a tattered yet defiant standard bearing what Petronius had come to know as the insignia for the Queen-Mother's family. Four men and a woman occupied the tent itself. One of the men appeared to be somewhat young and sat at a table with a stylus and papyrus.

The twelve legionaries who had accompanied Petronius across the river remained outside the tent as the prefect entered with Septimus and Abasi. As the Romans stepped out of the noon sun into the modest shade offered by the shelter, Petronius finally came face-to-face with the woman who had caused Rome much embarrassment and stubbornly refused to cooperate with his efforts to end her reign.

She was taller than he had envisioned and was thin, despite having a large frame for a woman. She wore a dark dress trimmed with gold that accentuated her distinctive womanly shape. While she was definitely feminine, she possessed a markedly hardened aura that was apparent when one read her face, which bore the physical signature of combat in the form of a missing eye and a jagged scar.

Other than that—she was a charmingly exotic beauty.

The man standing next to the Queen stepped forward. He was dressed in a blue and yellow ephod testifying some level of rank.

"Prefect Petronius, welcome," the man greeted him in the Greek tongue. "I am Piahnki, vizier of the Kushite province of Nobatia. May I present Pelmes Mshindi, Lord Amen-Tekah, and this is Kandace Amanirenas, the queen of Kush."

Petronius offered a curt head nod to the delegation. "This is Tribune Septimus and Evocatus Abasi. He is fluent in your language. Where did you learn Greek?"

After translating the Roman's question to the Queen, Piankhi turned toward Petronius. "I spent part of my youth in Thebes, where I was educated among the Egyptian nobility."

"Very well," Petronius said, focusing on the Queen. "Your defense of the Qasr Ibrim outpost was commendable; however, your continued resistance is unwise. You may outnumber us now, but we have already proven that our superior tactics easily nullify your numerical advantage. Surrender is your only sound course of action."

Piankhi translated the Roman's words and awaited Amanirenas' response. The Queen's icy glare spoke volumes before she even said a word. "Prefect, I, too, must offer a compliment. Although misguided, your efforts to subjugate Kush were courageous. To trek so far into enemy territory to make a point of your superiority simply because you can is admirable. However, you must realize by now that your goal to subdue our land is unattainable. I assure you, we will continue to fight."

"Rome will not tolerate rebellion," Petronius stated evenly. "Caesar is now your king, and he will do with the land of Kush what he pleases, just as he has done in Egypt."

"Kush has existed for a thousand years and has fought off invaders before," Amanirenas retorted, her visage hardening even more. "We will not be a Roman colony or vassal state. As for Egypt, I knew Cleopatra, and I do not believe for a moment that she wanted Egypt annexed into the Roman world. It was something that Octavian forced upon her, but he will not do the same to me."

"Cleopatra's options were limited due to the company she kept. Your options are not much better," Petronius noted.

"She was encumbered by emotional attachments," Amanirenas countered, raising the jagged eyebrow over her scarred eye socket. "I am not in love with any Roman men, and I have no problem with killing every last one if it will protect my people."

"Perhaps you do not fully understand. There are benefits to being subjects of Rome. Education, rule of law…"

"Roman law," Amanirenas interjected. "In addition to slavery, exploitation, the pillaging of our resources."

"You assume too much," Petronius said.

"No, it is Octavian Caesar who has assumed too much. To believe that Rome could continue to expand southward into our territory freely was a mistake. To demand that we pay him tribute was a mistake. And to conduct this war without even attempting a diplomatic resolution was nothing more than an insult."

Petronius held the woman's hard gaze while he scrutinized her choice of words. He had realized long that ago the Kushite society was multifaceted, making any problem associated with it just as complex by default. It was a realization that Caesar had not been exposed to and had no way to appreciate.

In addition, the Queen's words had merit. An extended military campaign would result only in more bloodshed, and he had no desire to spend the rest of his governorship over Egypt fighting an obstinate foe that possessed the resources and manpower to resist Rome for decades to come.

"As the prefect of Egypt, I speak with the voice of Caesar. However, he has made it clear that he wishes to be involved in intricate negotiations with sovereign kingdoms. I believe he would be interested . in discussing the unique situation that surrounds Kush."

"You're saying that we should address our grievances directly with Rome's ruler?" Piahnki inquired.

"Indeed. Caesar commissioned me to quell a rebellion and pacify a region for Roman occupation. However, what I have found and what you have proven is that you are a sovereign kingdom built on the foundation of an ancient history. I believe you should be given the opportunity to express that to Caesar yourself."

Amen-Tekah and Mshindi exchanged looks as Piankhi finished translating the Roman's statement—a declaration that had been inconceivable a few hours earlier.

"We would like to present our issues to the emperor of the Roman Empire as soon as possible, to prevent any further misunderstandings," Amanirenas said, maintaining her gaze on the prefect. She refused to let her guard down and give way to the emotions brewing within her like a cauldron.

Petronius raised an eyebrow at the Queen's use of the term "emperor," as it was her first conciliatory gesture in the conversation. "Understandable. The emperor will be headquartered on the island of Samos for the next six months. I can provide an escort for your delegation whenever you are ready to dispatch one."

"Your offer is very generous, Prefect," Amanirenas said. In the same breath, she exhaled a great deal of the tension that had been strapped to her psyche for the better part of four years.

Petronius noted the relief that washed across her face and admired her effort to hide it. He, too, felt a reprieve of sorts and relished the sensation gifted by the moment. However, he sensed that there was one additional gesture he could make to allay her concerns completely.

"It is obvious that this region is a source of dispute between our kingdoms and will no doubt be a subject of your negotiations with Caesar. Until those issues are resolved diplomatically, I will order the withdrawal of all Roman forces to Aswan. You may consider the hostilities between Rome and Kush suspended."

"Thank you, Prefect," Amanirenas said, stunning everyone in the tent by using the Greek language.

"The Greeks say that the hallmark of a civilized people is their ability to talk and resolve their differences through dialogue instead of the sword. It is unfortunate that I was unable to see that sooner," Petronius said.

"Your sentiment is appreciated, Prefect. However, I carry my share of the blame. It is a burden of guilt I will bear for the remainder of my days," Amanirenas said, silently admitting that she would forever be haunted by her initial vindictive response to her husband's death.

Petronius nodded in understanding, somehow cognizant of the painful prison in which she forever would be trapped. He stepped back and bowed his head respectfully, then left the tent in a whisk, his red cloak swirling behind him.

Chapter 53

Mother and daughter walked arm-in-arm along a secluded bank of the Nile. By some miracle, they managed to find a greenbelt that stretched along the eastern shore of the river not far from where the regiment from Meroë was encamped. The two walked for what seemed like hours, as they talked, laughed, and cried together. All the while, Amanirenas refused to lose physical contact with her daughter—the last member of the family that she nurtured and cherished for nearly twenty-five years of her life.

Amanitore was speechless as her mother described her harrowing exodus from Gebel Barkal and the Napata region. To think that the Queen could have fled to the relative safety of Meroë but had refused to do so in part to protect her daughter moved Amanitore to tears several times. However, her mother's disclosure of her five-week love affair with a cavalryman from Kerma touched her the most. While the setting of their relationship could hardly be termed romantic, Amanirenas described a connection laced with intimacy, devotion, and self-sacrifice, with the sole night of physical passion they shared being enough to sustain her for a lifetime.

"I'm sorry I'll never get to meet him. It sounds like he meant a lot to you," Amanitore said.

"He did. He saved my life when he could have walked away,"

Amanirenas said, offering her daughter a loving smile. "But I'd like to believe I meant just as much to him."

"How so?"

"I opened my heart to him and made myself available. When I did so, it offered him an opportunity to fall in love. I believe it saved both of us."

Amanirenas stopped and faced her daughter, the smile on her face melting into a somber thin line.

"Tore, no matter what happens in your life, no matter the losses or even the successes, never close your heart to love, for if you do, something else will surely consume you. Hatred nearly caused me to lose the kingdom. There was no room in my heart for anything other than vengeance until this man forced his way in with one selfless act of kindness after the other. That's what love is: giving at the expense of self. It isn't a feeling; it is a choice."

"I'll remember that, mother," Amanitore said, falling into her mother's embrace. "I'll remember it always."

⌀ ꙗ

The city of Korosko, which once shuddered under the shadow of the Roman occupation, was now the epicenter of the celebration that traditionally followed the formal funerary ceremony for the soldiers killed during the Battle of Qasr Ibrim.

Red, yellow, and green incense burned continuously from the temple complex while the jubilant population danced euphorically in the outer courtyard. Officials from throughout the region descended up Korosko to exalt the end of the war and to heap praise upon the Queen-Mother, who had united Kush and miraculously staved off the mighty legions of Rome.

Fatigued by the constant flow of attention, Amanirenas dismissed herself from the celebration and headed north toward the cemetery. While most of the soldiers who had fallen during battle were buried across the river near the fort itself, a handful had been chosen to be interred in the cemetery outside of Korosko.

Kushite law prevented their interment amongst the nobility, but Amanirenas suspended the edict for the men who had intrepidly guided her to Nobatia.

A large temple constructed by a monarch some five hundred years earlier sat in the midst of the graveyard. Days earlier, Amanirenas gave orders to adorn it with the same mural she had planned to use to decorate her own funerary pyramid in Meroë. The painting depicted her riding into battle in her chariot surrounded by three men, with beams of golden sunlight shooting from the sun above. The artist was fast and extremely skilled, for the completed colorful image now breathed life into the sun-worn cemetery.

Not far from the temple were the graves of Pedese, Batae, and Khai. She made it a point to bury them side-by-side as a testament to the bond they had shared in life and now in death.

A familiar man stood over Pedese's grave. At first, Amanirenas was going to leave him alone, but she felt compelled to share a moment of grief with him.

"You should be very proud of him, Ethaan," Amanirenas said. "I want you to know, he saved my life on the battlefield. I wouldn't be here without him."

The dignified Kushite nodded, his eyes moistening. Amanirenas placed her hand upon his shoulder as if to absorb some of his heartache. As she did, she recalled an earlier desire during the celebration to have a word with him in private.

"Pahor is a remarkable young man, and I have need of him in Meroë. I apologize for taking him from your household."

"We are here to serve you, my kandace," Ethaan said somberly.

"One other thing," Amanirenas started, a subtle smile gracing her face, "I need a new vizier in Kerma, someone to rebuild the city. Someone I can trust to undo the corruption authored by Shabakar."

"Viziers are usually selected from blood relatives of the Amani-aa'ila. We have no familial connection of which I am aware," Ethaan said.

"No, we do share a connection," Amanirenas said, glancing down at Pedese's gravestone. "And it will be there for the rest of my life."

"I am here to serve you," Ethaan affirmed with a reverent bow. "You are a complete kandace. The epitome of a Queen-Mother."

"Khai told me what you said to them in your stable, that day in Kawa. How you commissioned them to respect and protect the Queen of Kush. I want you to know, Ethaan, the sacrifices made by those men made me more than a complete kandace, they made me a complete woman."

Chapter 54

Rahman recognized the woman standing at his door instantly. The turquoise blindfold draped over her left eye did little to conceal her identity, though he was quite certain it was not the garment's central purpose.

"My kandace! Please come in!" Rahman exclaimed. He ushered the Queen and her two companions into the modest home and begged them to sit down.

"Rahman, you remember my servant, Saiesha," Amanirenas said as the two young people smiled warmly, as if they were old friends. "And this is Pahor. He is the brother of Pedese."

"Welcome to my home," Rahman said. "Please allow me to offer you a drink of water."

"Thank you," the Queen answered as Rahman started the process of pouring them water from a nearby vessel.

"I heard about your victory. The runners brought word over a week ago," Rahman said enthusiastically as he offered each visitor a cup. "Everyone is so glad the Romans are gone. No one thought it was possible. However, the way you spoke the night you were here convinced me that you would find a way. I have to hear every detail."

"And I will tell you," the Queen responded.

"Besides, no Roman could possibly beat Batae.... Where is he? On guard duty outside?"

"No, Rahman. He died in battle at Qasr Ibrim," Amanirenas said slowly.

"Oh," Rahman responded, sitting down next to the Queen. He rubbed his hands against his thighs uneasily, not certain how much emotion to demonstrate before the Queen-Mother of the kingdom.

"I'm so sorry, Rahman," Amanirenas said, reaching for one of his hands and squeezing it compassionately. "He was an outstanding soldier, loyal, brave, and faithful until the end. I wanted to tell you and your father face-to-face that he died a hero, preserving this kingdom and saving my life. Where is Malae?"

"My father died a week after your party left for Kawa," Rahman said, wiping the tears away from his brown eyes.

"I'm sorry," Amanirenas whispered, rubbing his shoulder.

"Don't be. He was so proud of my brother. He could not stop talking about how the Queen of Kush had slept under his roof. He bragged about it for days in the marketplace and didn't care what the peshte had to say."

Amanirenas smiled as she recalled the vibrant old man and inwardly rejoiced that the final memory of his son was one rife with pride and adulation.

"Thank you coming to tell me personally. It will always mean a great deal to me that you made such an effort," Rahman said, composing himself.

"I have a few of Batae's things I wanted give to you. Pahor will see that you receive them." Amanirenas glanced around the humble home and looked back appreciatively on the cheerful evening that they had within these four walls; it seemed like a lifetime ago. It also reminded her of a silent vow that she made that night.

"Rahman, there is another reason why I came. I would like you to come with me to Meroë to train as an administrator. Batae said that you were good with numbers, and I am going to need assistance in the treasury as we rebuild."

Rahman's eyes went wide. "I've never been to Meroë or even worked in a dufufa. I won't know what to do."

"Pahor will help you learn the necessary protocols," Amanirenas said.

"I have no noble blood, but ... but I am honored you've chosen me. I will do the best I can."

"Nobility is character trait to be demonstrated, not an inheritance to be given," Amanirenas mused aloud. "That's something your brother taught me."

Amanirenas stood up and surveyed the home once more, its shear simplicity conjuring a tear in her eye. The unpretentious home had sheltered and nurtured the very foundation of the Kushite kingdom—a simple family knitted together in love and unity.

She watched as Pahor and Saiesha showered Rahman with attention, welcoming him into their distinctive family, crafted and bound by crisis and purpose.

Family.

It was all Amanirenas had ever wanted, and it was all she had ever asked for.

Epilogue

In 21 B.C., a Kushite delegation was conducted to the Greek island of Samos, where Augustus Caesar was temporarily headquartered while touring the eastern Roman provinces. The Kushite embassy marked the first recorded instance in the history of Africa in which diplomats on behalf of a black African leader independent of Egypt journeyed to Europe to effect a diplomatic resolution. Kandace Amanirenas sent a quiver of golden arrows to Augustus, stating they could be received as tokens of friendship or as symbols of war.

The Kushites and Romans negotiated and signed a peace treaty that not only remitted any tax liability to Rome, but that also established a buffer zone that served to demarcate the southern Roman border.

To gain the favor of the people of Kush, Augustus directed his administrators to collaborate with the priesthoods of the region and erect a temple at Dendur, which, among other things, served as a war memorial.

Gaius Petronius served two separate terms as the Praefactus Aegyptus. Petronius's understanding of the Kushite culture laid the foundation for nearly eight decades of amicable relations between the two empires. The next armed, albeit brief, conflict between Meroë and Rome would not occur until 68 A.D. and was precipitated by the Roman Emperor Nero's violation of the Treaty of Samos.

Amanirenas never remarried. After the Roman War, she embraced the role of Queen-Mother and dedicated herself to rebuilding the kingdom and making life better for her people. As a result, she was revered among her people and became an inspiration and symbol of hope for generations.

Upon her death, the right of rulership and title of Queen-Mother was passed to Amanishakheto, who ruled until 1 B.C. The title was then passed to Amanitore, who is mentioned in Acts 8:27 of the Holy Bible.

Along with her husband Natakamani, Amanitore fulfilled her mother's dream and instituted building and cultural programs that took the Kushite Empire to its heights. Together, they built reservoirs, temples, and scores of pyramids. Amanitore died peacefully in 35 A.D.

Amanirenas died in 10 B.C. Her pyramid is located next to that of her husband Teriteqas in the royal cemetery outside of Napata, near Gebel Barkal.

Glossary

Alondia – Southeastern province of the kingdom of Meroë

Amani'aa'lia – dynastic title that refers to a royal family in the mid to late Meroitic period of the Kushite Empire.

Amun – Other names: Amen, Amon-Ra. Chief of all gods in the Nubian religion. Was believed to be the god of Creation, the father of all the gods, and the god of the sun.

Apedemack – Nubian deity of warfare. Resembled a man with the head of a lion. Often depicted holding a bow or spear.

Apis – Egyptian deity that resembled a bull with a solar disk between its horns

Booza – A pasteurized beer originally developed by the ancient Egyptians

Cataract – A great waterfall. There were six such waterfalls along the Nile that often served as landmarks and boundaries.

Centurion – Officer rank, generally one per 80 soldiers, in charge of a centuria.

Century (centuria) – denotes Roman military units consisting of 100 men.

Cohort – A division of a Roman legion that consisted of 500 to 600 soldiers.

Cubit – An ancient unit of measurement used in Egypt and Kush. While it varies, it is generally the length from the elbow to the tips of the fingers

Dufufa – Large, complex structures that served as the administrative and religious centers for Egyptian and Nubian cities and settlements. Dufufas were often fortified and used as military outposts.

Evocatus – A soldier in the Roman army who had served out his time and obtained a discharge but had voluntarily enlisted again at the invitation of the commander.

Galea – A Roman soldier's helmet. Some of the helmets used by legionaries had a crest holder. The crests were usually made of plumes or horse hair.

Gebel – Nubian/Kushite term used to describe a mountain or large land mass

Gladius – A short sword used by Roman legionaries.

Henel – the Meroitic afterword and the peaceful abode of the deceased.

Horus – Egyptian royal god represented by a falcon. Denoted as the sky-god, he was regarded as the son of Isis and considered the ruler of the day.

Isis – Egyptian / Meroëtic deity regarded as queen of all gods, goddesses, and women. In addition to Africa, she was worshiped heavily in the Roman empire.

Iter – An ancient Kushite and Egyptian unit of measure for length. One iter is equivalent to 20,000 cubits or 10.5 kilometers

Kandace – Official title for the queen of Meroë

Kha – Meroitic term for the abstract personality or translucent spirit soul that could exist outside the body.

Khentekhtaya – The Egyptian deity represented by the Nile crocodile

Kerma – Western province of the kingdom of Meroë

Kizra – A flat tortilla-like bread made by the Kushites and Egyptians

Kush – Terminology used in antiquity to describe the lands south of Egypt and the Great Desert. People originating from those lands were termed as "Kushites" or "Nubians"

Legio Cyrenaica ("Cyrenean Third Legion") – A legion of the Roman army stationed primarily in Egypt. It is believed the legion was probably founded by Mark Antony around 36 BC, when he was governor of Cyrenaica.

Legio Deiotariana ("Deiotarus Twenty-Second Legion") – A legion of the Roman army, stationed near Alexandria in Egypt with the Legio Cyrenaica. The two legions had the role of garrisoning the Egyptian province from threats.

Legionary – A professional heavy infantryman of the Roman army

Legion – The principal unit of the Roman army comprising 5000 to 6000 foot soldiers with cavalry

Makoria – North eastern province of Meroë

Maniple – A Roman regiment of roughly 200 fighting men (two centuries).

Mechir – sixth month of the Kushite calendar

Montu – A falcon-god of war in ancient Egyptian religion

Necropolis – A large, designed cemetery with elaborate tomb monuments.

Nobatia – Northern most province of Meroë. Borders Roman-Egypt

Nubia – "Land of Gold" and the term used to describe the land south of Egypt

Optio – Second-in-command of a Roman century

Osiris – Egyptian deity regarded as the dead king that watches over the netherworld. He serves as the symbol of eternal life.

Paqar – Administrative title given to a prominent court official, usually a royal prince. Paqars were generally placed over provinces.

Pelmes – Title for the commanding officer of a Kushite army. The pelmes reported to the vizier or paqar of a province.

Pelmes-adab – General of the land. Administrative position in a Nubian province responsible for ensuring that the trade routes was secure. Generally reported to the peshte.

Pelmes-ate – General of the water. Title of the administrative officer responsible conducting commerce and communications along the Nile River. Generally reported to the peshte.

Peshte – Leading officer in charge of administration; usually reported to the vizier of the city/region

Pilus Prior – Senior centurion of a cohort.

Porta Praetorian – principle entrance into a Roman military camp.

Posca – a popular everyday drink among Roman soldiers made by mixing sour wine or vinegar with water and flavoring herbs.

Pugio – a dagger used by Roman soldiers as a sidearm.

Praefactus Aegypti – Official title of the prefect or chief magistrate of the Roman province of Egypt.

Praefectus Castrorum – 3rd in command of a Roman legion. Also responsible for maintaining the camp, equipment, and supplies.

Praetor – A Roman magistrate elected annually. Major area of concern was law. At the end of his year in office, a praetor could govern a province or command an army.

Prefect (praefectus) – A magisterial title which basically refers to the leader of an administrative area.

Prinicipes – Latin word meaning the first, chief, the most eminent, distinguished, or noble. It is primarily associated with the Roman emperors as an unofficial title first adopted by Augustus in 23 BC.

Qar – Feminine version of the term "paqar." The title given to a princess of the royal court

Qeren – Official title for the king of Meroë

Scutum – a large, often times rectangular and semi-cylindrical shield used by Roman soldiers. Generally made from three sheets of wood glued together and covered with canvas and leather.

Seth – Egyptian deity regarded as the god of the desert and foreign lands

Siafu – Large army ants found primarily in central and east Africa.

Tribune (Tribunus Laticlavius) – 2nd in command of a Roman legion and usually a young man serving his apprenticeship before getting his own legion to command

Vizier – Official title given to magistrates and administrators in ancient Kush. The Grand Vizier held the highest rank and often ruled as the governor over a province or state. Though the term is Egyptian in origin, it was often utilized by Nubian officials.

Wadis – Dry path of a river. Wadis were often formed during the dry seasons and channeled water to the Nile during the wet seasons.